MILLICENT

ALSO BY VERONICA ROSS

MILLICENT

A MYSTERY

Veronica Ross

Midnight Originals / THE MERCURY PRESS

ACKNOWLEDGEMENTS
The author wishes to thank the Canada Council for a short term grant, which assisted in the early development of this novel.
  Excerpts from the diaries of MacKenzie King, The National Archives of Canada and The Dana Porter Library, University of Waterloo, Manuscript Group 26 J13, National Archives.

The publisher gratefully acknowledges the financial assistance of the Canada Council and the Ontario Arts Council, as well as that of the Government of Ontario through the Ontario Publishing Centre.

Edited by Beverley Daurio
Cover design by Gordon Robertson
Composition and page design by TASK

Printed and bound in Canada by Metropole Litho
Printed on acid-free paper
First Edition
1 2 3 4 5 98 97 96 95 94

Canadian Cataloguing in Publication Data

Ross, Veronica
    Millicent
ISBN 1-55128-016-7
I. Title
PS8585.O842M5 1994   C813'.54   C94-932113-3
PR9199.3.R67M5 1994

Represented in Canada by the Literary Press Group
Distributed by General Distribution Services

The Mercury Press
137 Birmingham Street
Stratford, Ontario
Canada   N5A 2T1

To Kristen

PROLOGUE

The story of Millicent Mulvey, a Canadian woman who not only claimed to have married Edward VIII, Duke of Windsor, in the twenties when he toured Canada as the Prince of Wales, but had this fact inscribed on her tombstone, began for me as a kind of Cinderella story.

There was Edward, whose smiling face filled the newspapers of the twenties and thirties. He was the most eligible bachelor of his time. He danced and charmed his way through Canada, Australia, India, Africa, and the United States. Women of all ages dreamed about him. Society writers speculated about his choice of bride.

And there was Millicent, a Scottish-Canadian teacher from a small town in Ontario, a woman no one had heard about, who insisted she had been married to Edward.

Everyone knows the story of Mrs. Simpson, "the woman I love"; Edward abdicated to marry her, and she became the Duchess of Windsor.

I found the possibility that Edward had made an earlier, secret marriage to an unknown Canadian woman exciting and romantic.

Millicent Mulvey was my friend. After her death in 1985, I broke into her house hoping to find a box of letters reporters had mentioned.

There was no box, but I discovered photographs, leaving no doubt in my mind that the marriage had taken place.

These photos were stolen from my house, but I went on to research Millicent's story, so I could tell it to the world.

I had no idea what was to follow. Mysterious people tailed me. Conversations were wire-tapped.

People were killed.

Reading about royalty is seductive in a reassuring way. One writer says creamed chicken is served in the palace nursery, and ten writers cite him. Queen Mary poured tea for her husband, George V, out of an ordinary brown teapot.

Queen Victoria covered the furniture at Balmoral in tartans. Charles and Diana drank tea out of mugs in the kitchen at Highgrove.

The mind does not boggle; it is lulled to sleep with familiar lines from nursery rhymes. Kings and Queens become everyone's ancestors and remind us of characters from fairy tales.

Recently, these cosy tales have been replaced by Chuck and Di, Randy Andy and Fergie, Squidgy and Camillagate. Windsor Castle has burned, and even the Queen has not been exempt from rumours in the tabloids.

I had decided not to tell Millicent's story. Over the years, it assumed the remote and untouchable cosiness of old sepia photographs. Her story became my secret, and the secret of the few people who shared my research.

But *annus horribilis* changed my mind. The door to the king's hut has been yanked open. Daylight has revealed a prince wanting to become a tampon and a duchess having her toes sucked.

The light can now shine on Millicent and her more honourable story.

CHAPTER
ONE

Death at ninety-five is not a tragedy unless you consider all death tragic.

When I was a child in Maine I liked to wander down our country lane to the old fenced-in graveyard. It was a small cemetery elevated above the ground, at the side of the road. Only eight people were buried there. One stone made me feel incredibly sad: Mathilda Brenner, Beloved Wife and Mother. Her monument had the most beautiful carving of an angel on it, like an angel you see on a Christmas tree. Mathilda was twenty-one when she died in 1857. Who was she? Who were her "people"? My grandmother knew most of the stories of that graveyard— who had started out as a pauper and grown rich, which family had never been any good— but she could tell me nothing about the Brenners.

I imagined that Mathilda's husband had moved to the west, following the sunset in a covered wagon. I was a fanciful child and believed that he remained true to her. Sometimes I cast myself as the new love who would finally touch him; sometimes I was Mathilda, come back to life: not drowned as it was thought, but appearing suddenly (stepping out of a coach) in a western town...

But this story isn't about Mathilda Brenner or about my own childhood. It is about a woman called Millicent Mulvey, who was ninety-five when she died in 1985.

I have wondered where to begin this story and it seems to me that I had better begin with her death.

Millicent A.M.M.M. Mulvey
1890 - 1985
Wife of
Edward VIII
Duke of Windsor
1894 - 1972

9

What will they make of this inscription a hundred years from now? They will realize who Edward VIII was from the history books, in the way that we know that Henry VIII chopped his wife's head off and that Queen Victoria was not amused. But they won't know one single thing about Millicent, unless they're interested enough to look at old newspaper clippings at the library. Then they'll discover an eccentric old lady, a retired school teacher who kept cats and who had a portrait of the Duke of Windsor hanging in her house in Starleigh, a village near Guelph, Ontario, "The Royal City"; a woman who said she had been married to the Duke of Windsor in the nineteen-twenties, when he was Prince of Wales and touring Canada. Millicent would not give details, yet hinted the marriage had been dissolved by the British parliament. She was a woman whose house was broken into shortly after her death; a woman who was said to have a box under her bed containing letters from the Duke.

"No one believes me but it's the truth," Millicent told a reporter. "The truth will come out after my death."

Millicent was my friend.

And I am the person who broke into her house.

Thanksgiving weekend, 1985— the Canadian Thanksgiving that is, in the second week of October. My husband, Peter Hall, and I had spent the afternoon touring the countryside around Kitchener looking for pumpkin fields so he could take photos for the cover of my latest cookbook, *Harvest Ovens*. We had eaten turkey at The Stone Crock, a cosy Mennonite restaurant near Kitchener, Ontario. It was an ordinary weekend afternoon for us, poking around in art galleries and antique shops, eating out somewhere. Peter, as usual, gravitated to piles of second-hand books and found a first edition of *George Leatrim* by Susanna Moodie. I bought a cup and saucer with a pine cone pattern on it, advertised as being a reproduction of china used in a local hotel at the turn of the century.

Millicent's recent death— combined with the fields, nippy air and what I have called "country charm" in my cookbooks— farmhouses, fields, the gingham curtains in the restaurant— had brought up the old mystery of Millicent's story, and made me restless. I imagined the story in sepia: a

Canadian teacher, cloche hats, girls in pinafores, the Duke with his smiling boy's face, old photos of Queen Mary with her fringe and pearls and that ramrod straight back...

Was it really possible that Millicent and the Duke of Windsor had once been married? In truth, her story hadn't played a big part in our friendship, although the mystery of it had initially attracted me when I came to Guelph in the early seventies with my draft-dodger first husband. I was writing restaurant reviews for *The Clarion*, a fly-by-night weekly that soon closed down. Millicent wrote a letter to the editor about my reviews. She said I showed good grammar and style, but did we really have to concern ourselves about shrimp in garlic butter when there was so much hunger in the world? The editor of *The Clarion* told me about Millicent, and I dropped in to see her.

"The Duke gave me these pearls," she would say, modestly touching a strand of what could have been dime-store pearls; she had sent the Duke— "Ted" as she sometimes called him— a birthday card... Sometimes I think now she wanted me to ask questions, but at the time I thought doing so would have meant I distrusted her few revelations.

Besides, she stopped giving interviews after the two or three she allowed after the Duke's death (when the papers felt they could write about her claim without fear of libel) and I was a journalist when I met her. By the time we became friends, she was simply Millicent, "Miss Mulvey" as most people called her, a giver of advice, an upright Presbyterian Scot, witty, insightful, opinionated. A writer of letters to the editor. When I was with her I believed, I had to believe, and yet, her story was so incredible, so unbelievable, that doubts always followed.

Now she was dead and I had decided to break into her house to see if I could find the box of letters she was supposed to have kept under her bed.

"I wonder who that man was who said he was Millicent's half-brother?" I mused to Peter as we drove home.

That was another mystery. A nurse at the hospital had told me this tidbit. This elderly "English guy with the most fantastic accent" had stepped into Millicent's room, where she lay comatose, saying he was her half-brother from England.

"Prince Charles, maybe."

Peter didn't believe one word of Millicent's story. An old lady with a fantasy, he said; a senile woman living in a world of make-believe, although he met her just before she was moved into the nursing home.

"I keep thinking the English guy was some kind of reporter," I said.

"Wanting a deathbed confession, or should I say scoop?"

"You never know. Still, it's strange."

"Nothing strange about it," Peter said. "Another wing-ding who thinks there's something to that story. You really want to go to Starleigh tonight? You're not going to see a thing. It'll be dark when we get there."

It was almost dark then. Driving through the outskirts of Kitchener, all strip malls and Texaco dealers, I was impatient to reach "Bellevue Cottage," as Millicent had called her little house.

"It's all the better in the dark," I said. "Those nosey neighbours won't be poking their heads out of the windows."

"What're you going to do, break into the place?"

"Don't be silly," I lied. "I'm just going to walk by. You don't even have to come along. You could go home."

"I'd better make sure that a reporter or a royal spy doesn't nab you. But don't worry. I won't tag along. I know you want your privacy."

Easy-to-get-along-with Peter. I'd met him five years before when I went to his store, The Bookworm, to autograph some cookbooks. My first impression of him was no impression. He's really rather bland-looking, with a thin face, short blonde hair and glasses. Even nerdy. He wears a tie and old-man cardigans to the store. I might never have seen him again if I hadn't, to my embarrassment, signed a book by another author by mistake. That book is in Peter's safe, in reserve for when I become famous and it becomes a collector's item. He laughed at my goof and said, "This may be my retirement fund, Miss Archer."

Miss Archer? There was a hint of an English accent in his voice. I had just dumped an unemployed film-maker who'd camped out at my place for six months and I wasn't looking for a man, but Peter interested me. He reminded me of men in old English novels, someone out of Thomas Hardy perhaps. Our first date was for tea and he didn't even kiss me. He had never been married, although he'd lived with someone. I guess we had what could be called a romance. He even bought me an engagement ring.

With his British background I expected him to take an interest in Millicent's story, but that didn't happen. For one thing, Millicent was in decline when he met her— her arteries were hardening— and soon after that she went into a nursing home, a place Peter wasn't exactly in love with.

And he didn't care about royalty. He simply didn't believe that a snobby British prince would find a provincial, country school teacher interesting. The English, he said, thought they were better than other people and English royalty thought the rest of humanity simply didn't exist. It was inconceivable to him that as a young man, the Duke of Windsor would have even noticed the likes of one Millicent Mulvey. And where would they have met, anyway?

But Millicent adored Peter. She hadn't thought much of my first husband, Charlie Trott, although she held her tongue until Charlie and I split up. She hated the film-maker, whom she met one day in Guelph. He was wearing my raincoat (a second-hand man's trench coat which she called "a most unsuitable garment and not at all ladylike"). The film-maker was "a free-loader" and the separated realtor I saw for a while was "immoral."

"I wouldn't tell him about the others," she whispered to me when I introduced Peter to her at Christmas. She even had me buy whiskey. Peter was "a gentleman" and "cultured." A book-lover— she used to write children's stories herself. The only thing she had against Peter was that he wasn't Scottish, but then the Duke of Windsor hadn't been Scottish either.

"When we get there you can park at the bottom of the hill and wait for me," I said as we took the cut-off leading to Starleigh. "I won't be long."

I knew Peter wouldn't like the idea of me breaking into Millicent's house. His father, Hugh, is chief-of-police in the small northern town of Meredith, and Peter detests any hint of low-life.

If I didn't find anything I wouldn't have to tell him of my dirty deed. And if I did find something, I'd have the proof to change his mind.

Anyway, those were my thoughts then.

It was after eight by the time we reached Starleigh. It's a pretty, leafy village, with the Speed River flowing through it and a population of about a thousand, but on Sunday evening it was deserted and dark. Peter parked at the bottom of the hill, near the bridge.

"Better take a flashlight," he said. "There's a small one in the glove compartment. And don't go up the front steps. They were already rotten years ago."

"Yes sir!"

"Just don't let any royal spies get you," Peter said, patting my back.

Five minutes later I was walking up the hill to Bellevue Cottage.

As my feet crunched the autumn leaves— why wasn't Peter following in the car? I wondered perversely— I thought of the "English half-brother." What if he were waiting beneath one of the large maples? What if he had followed us to St. Jacobs and now here to Starleigh? What if he had returned to the hospital and someone had told him about Millicent's "granddaughter," as I had claimed to be so I could see her in intensive care?

I've always been a scaredy-cat. Once I invited Millicent to my apartment for supper. It was growing dark, and Millicent was beginning to worry about getting home to feed her cats when some punks entered the lobby and began tinkering with mailboxes. We could hear them laughing and speculating about which apartment to break into. I called the police. No one came (a large traffic accident and a murder-suicide had kept them busy elsewhere, I learned the next day). Millicent wanted to leave, but I wouldn't even take the chain off the door. "You little mouse!" Millicent snorted and threw open the door. "Off with you, you young criminals!" The boys fled.

Governor's Lane was dark, except for glimmers of living room lights coming through the trees. It was starting to rain, a light drizzle, which added to the spooky atmosphere, and my feeling that someone was watching.

I almost turned back at Millicent's house. Everything dark, empty, no soft TV light flickering here, just overgrown bushes and black windows. It's a small house, built around 1920 when Millicent arrived with her mother in Starleigh to teach. Today her house has been repainted and repaired, but that night the rotten boards of the front steps creaked under my feet. One board was loose, half-eaten away. My heel caught in a hole.

I shone the light on the front door. So *closed*. So mysterious: what did it hide? My last cookbook, *Country Ovens*, has our front door on the cover (blue door, willow wreath, box of firewood at the side). The editor hadn't been crazy about the idea. Looking at Millicent's door, I understood his reluctance: who knows what is behind any door?

I clinked the flashlight experimentally against the pane, and the noise sounded very loud to my ears. I tried the doorknob, but of course it didn't turn.

A car drove by, beaming its headlights in my direction before speeding off. I shut the flashlight off and crept to the side of the house where years ago Millicent's mother had grown petunias and dahlias, but it was all rocks and weeds now. I had to cling to the side of house to keep from stumbling over the boards and garbage someone had dumped there.

The back porch was even worse than the front, and higher off the ground. Before Millicent went into the nursing home, her neighbours had been afraid that she would fall through the boards, and suggested she tear the back steps down, to her great fuming anger.

The railing creaked and the steps swayed as I gingerly felt my way up to the back door. If I ever reached the back door I knew I'd have to get inside right away, because the porch wouldn't hold my weight for long.

But at least no one would see me back there, I told myself. The porch floor moved. I gripped the flimsy railing and shone the light against the back window pane. Nothing. I rattled the doorknob.

My instinct was to run but I closed my eyes and swung the flashlight against the pane. Glass splintered. I had to grip the light in my teeth to find the leather gloves in my purse so I wouldn't cut my hands reaching inside to unlatch the door.

The door creaked open. Something furry rushed by my feet. I screamed and bolted for the inside, to a terrible smell, to the sound of a thousand little feet scampering with a rustling, whistling noise.

Squirrels. The beam of the light caught their tails as they dashed away. Something— droppings— crunched underfoot.

I was in Millicent's kitchen, a dreary room with open shelves— her "larder"— where a single can of Campbell's tomato soup sat above the sink along with the remnants of her chipped dishes and dented pots. Clothes—

after laundering– had gone to Millicent in the home after firemen cleared out her cats. Much of the flea-ridden furniture had been discarded. Millicent didn't know this. In her mind, her little house– "my wee cottage"– had stayed intact, awaiting her return. The key remained with her.

Now the smell was awful, a dank heavy odour, a zoo smell of urine and mould, a feral mustiness. What was worse was the sound of animals moving in the walls and overhead.

A car drove up and stopped. I shut the flashlight off and the squirrels became still, too.

Someone rattled the front doorknob. My feet propelled me, sending me blindly forward, feeling my way to Millicent's front room, where the street light, filtered through the autumn trees, cast a ghostly light. I could just make out the Duke's portrait, half-mouldered away now, buckled in the middle, but still in its gilt frame. I crept along the walls to the corner of the room where Millicent's knick-knack shelf had been.

A bright light shone into the room.

A face appeared at the window, at the front. A thin face, ghostly white in the beam of the light, with blond hair sticking out. Glasses. An open mouth.

Peter.

"What are you doing in here?"

"I wanted to see if Millicent left anything."

We were both whispering. He turned the flashlight on. He'd brought the big one, from the back of the car, which we keep for road emergencies.

"Shut it off, someone will see."

"I can't believe you actually broke in here." He shone the light around the room, showing up the old green sofa, half-eaten away now, the empty desk where Millicent had kept copies of her letters to the editor and newspaper clippings about the foibles of the government.

I couldn't make out Peter's face but I knew he was angry. "Lots of documents," Peter said. "All kinds of goodies. Take a good look. We might as well do the tour of Buckingham Palace."

"I'm sorry I lied to you," I said.

Peter ignored me and turned to the room off the living room. Millicent's bedroom. The mattress was half off the bed and the wardrobe stood open, revealing a green dress hanging limply from a hanger. Peter lifted the mattress, ran his hand under it, pushed it back with his foot.

He opened the night table drawer. "Here's a document for you," he said, and shone the light on a Presbyterian church magazine. "Might as well keep it. Maybe she wrote in it in invisible ink. You can send it to Scotland Yard for forensic tests."

"I just about had a heart attack when I saw your face."

He threw the church magazine on the bed and returned to the front room, where he focused the beam on the Duke's face. It was a portrait of Edward as a young man and painted, Millicent had told me, at Balmoral Castle in the Scottish Highlands. Edward stood against a background window and he wore that wistful, remote look which had always seemed more appropriate to me than "the smiling Prince" in old newspaper photos. "He wanted to present me to Queen Mary at Balmoral," Millicent said once.

Peter snapped the light off.

"When you didn't come back I thought maybe you'd fallen or something. I never expected this. What if someone saw you?"

He turned the light on again and opened the door to the second bedroom, where Millicent's mother had slept a million years ago. It was empty, except for a chamber pot in the corner, a remnant of Millicent's fight with the water company. Peter lifted the lid, replaced it. "One empty chamber pot with nothing in it."

I returned to the living room and peered behind the Duke's portrait. Nothing.

"Let's get out of here," I said.

"How'd you get in, anyway?"

"I broke the back window. There was just a simple hook."

"Break and enter," Peter said.

"We haven't taken anything."

"Nothing to take," Peter said.

"There was supposed to be a box with letters and things."

"I guess Scotland Yard got that."

"Let's get out of here."

Peter walked into the kitchen where Millicent had kept his whiskey that Christmas.

"Campbell's soup," he said. "Canada's finest."

Beneath the sink was the rusty kettle which Millicent gave me to have mended by "a tinker." I waited a week and bought her a new one, but she'd apparently kept the old one. Couldn't be mended, I said, and listened to a speech on "waste not, want not." "My wee kettle," she said. "You would think an honest workman would be interested in repairing it, but such does not seem to be the case."

As I reached for the kettle, squirrels scampered overhead. Peter jumped. "Squirrels," I said and lifted the lid.

Inside— a brown envelope. A warm feeling came over me.

"Shine the light," I told Peter.

The envelope was stiff and thick, bent almost in half. Peter didn't say anything as I opened it and pulled out photographs.

The top one showed the Duke of Windsor as a young man, and beside him, Millicent, wearing a nineteen-twenties cloche hat.

CHAPTER
TWO

There were four photos.

Millicent wearing the cloche hat and a long, closely-fitting coat over a longer, flared skirt. Beside her, the Duke, in a tweed jacket and plus-fours. They are standing near a fence, in a field— rocks, a bush, a tree in the distance. The Duke has a cigarette in his hand. It seems like a cloudy day, a fall day, without any sun in their eyes. Millicent's face is soft, but unsmiling. The Duke— Prince of Wales then— caught off-guard. His mouth is open, as if he's been interrupted in the middle of a conversation. Face unformed, not "the smiling Prince," but a young man totally wrapped up in the slightly older woman beside him.

Millicent and Edward, in the same clothes, in the doorway of what appears to be a barn. Edward sitting, legs wide apart, Millicent standing behind him, hands in her pockets. An older man holding a pipe sits beside Edward.

A group photo on a country lawn, beneath trees. Millicent's head is bare, unlike the other women, who wear large hats with ornamental feathers, flowers. Millicent is leaning forward, turning away from the woman beside her (a heavy-set matron, big strain of bosom) to greet the camera. Edward lolls a little to the side, behind Millicent, talking to a heavy-set man. A table holding crockery has been set up. Some of the guests sit in wooden lawn chairs placed in a circle. Only Millicent is aware that her photo is being taken.

These were amateur photos, perhaps taken by a guest, or maybe Millicent handed her own camera to someone. They weren't sepia, but coloured with age, yellowed, the corners bent from handling. There were no notations on the back, but spots of glue on some of the corners indicated the pictures had been in an album once.

The fourth photo was larger, professional, on thicker paper, posed in front of a drape. Millicent, dressed in a *white dress*, ankle-length, with tight sleeves, sits in a wing chair. Edward, in a tail coat and striped trousers, stands behind her. Neither is smiling. Millicent looks serene, untroubled. Her hair is swept smoothly back in what I think of as a chignon, and if it weren't for her strong jaw, she would be beautiful. What she has is dignity. There's something in these younger images of her that reminds me of the Duchess of Windsor, although Millicent isn't frivolous or arch, but dignified.

Edward's face is blank, impossible to read.

Millicent holds a small nosegay. She wears pearls.

The pictures lay on my kitchen table.

We'd drawn the curtains, turned off the lights in the front of the house and settled in the back, in the kitchen. We live in what is called an "Ontario Cottage." Picture a child's drawing of a house, a door between two windows, and that's our house. They're everywhere in Guelph, built of limestone or grey brick, originally workers' cottages. Today they're chic, part of the rather artsy inner-city of downtown Guelph, and adorned with shutters, stained glass, wrought iron railings.

Our large kitchen, with a cathedral ceiling and office alcove for me, was a recent addition to the back of the house and invisible from the street. For all anyone walking or driving by could tell, we'd gone to bed.

The photos didn't convince Peter.

"All they prove is that she met him," Peter said.

"Lots of people met him," he went on. He looked tired, shrunken. The rain had made his hair stick to his head. "Lots of women. Even going to bed together is unbelievable. She wasn't a beauty, she wasn't rich, she was just a straight-laced Canadian teacher. Society women threw themselves at him. What would he have wanted with Millicent?"

"But what about the studio picture? It's like a wedding photo."

"There could be lots of explanations. They were guests together at some function. People took turns having their pictures taken with the prince. I don't know. But it's something different than a wedding. They didn't get married. If there'd been anything in it, we would have heard about it."

"But we did, from Millicent."

"You can have anything put on a tombstone."

"Sure. I'll go tomorrow and order a stone saying I'm married to Prince Charles."

"They'd put it on if you paid for it."

"Of course they wouldn't. Don't forget the papers wouldn't write of it while the Duke was still alive."

"They wouldn't write about it because they knew it wasn't true. It wasn't true, therefore the Duke would sue. She also said she was a Princess of Stuart. Another fantasy."

"You don't know that."

"Come on. And what about that cup and saucer business? She said she'd painted a cup or some damn thing which she showed to the Duke."

"She made that up. She admitted that. It was the only lie she ever told, but she said it to get the reporters off her back. Just a spur of the moment thing. I don't know what you're so worried about anyway. We only took some old photos."

"If there was anything to them, Millicent would have given them to the press. But she didn't do it."

"She said she was told not to say anything. She said the truth would come out after she was dead."

"Right. Buckingham Palace is going to issue a press release saying that Her Royal Highness Millicent Mulvey, the true wife of the late Duke of Windsor, has passed away. Don't hold your breath. The big question is, what are you going to do with them?"

"Do with them?"

"You didn't take them just to hide them away."

"I haven't decided what to do with them. No one's going to be able to prove I stole them, for one thing. I could say Millicent gave them to me. I could always send them to a newspaper anonymously."

Peter sighed, heaved himself up, and went to the window. He lifted the curtain.

"No one can prove a thing," I said, referring to the break-in.

"That's right. Photos or not, no one can prove anything," Peter said, meaning Millicent. "I think you should leave the thing alone. It would be just a wild goose chase. You'd look like a fool, like those people who say Elvis is alive."

He turned from the window.

"Anyone out there?" I asked. "Any spies?"

He didn't answer, but poured himself a cup of tea and grimaced when he took a sip. The stuff was cold. He dumped it in the sink, plugged in the kettle, and made more tea.

"I don't even understand how she could have met him. She wouldn't have been invited to balls or anything like that," Peter said.

"Someone said out west when she was teaching school out there," I said. Peter sat down with his tea. He hadn't poured me any.

"But she never said, did she?"

"She used to talk about going to 'the farm' out west when she was younger.

I bet that's where the pictures were taken, on that ranch he owned in Alberta. They could have met there."

"Yes, at a Saturday night potluck supper. Edward just moseyed on over and there was Millicent dishing out the baked beans."

"But they met! The photos prove it! They show there was some intimacy between them, that they knew one another very well."

"The most I'd say is that they went to bed together. Maybe he was attracted to bossy older women."

"He was! Some people say Wallis was older than he was. And he had this long-time mistress in England who was older. They say it's because his mother never showed him any affection. Queen Mary was supposed to be very cold. Some writers have claimed he looked for a nanny in every woman he met."

I rattled on like this while Peter drank his tea and looked bored. I never read a book about royalty until I met Millicent, but her story drew me to "those boring damn things" as Peter called them. "She wouldn't have been like the society women he knew. She wouldn't have been like anyone else he'd ever met. She wouldn't have been fawning— she believed the Stuarts had a better claim to the English throne than Edward's House of Hanover did— and she would have spoken her mind."

"But he wouldn't have married her," Peter said. "I refuse to believe it."

I got up to pour myself a cup of tea.

"There'd be trouble if you did anything with those pictures," Peter said. "My advice to you is to forget about them."

"Trouble? What kind of trouble?"

"Trouble from the bloody Royals. They're not going to like any kind of scandal. They'd have ways to keep you from doing anything."

"They didn't make trouble when the inscription went on up on the stone, did they?"

"They probably didn't even know about it. Or if they knew, do you think they'd pay any attention? The Royals would assume people would just think it was a made-up story. They wouldn't lower themselves to notice, the bastards."

"They'd have to notice the photos," I said.

"Just another of Edward's women. Why should they notice?"

"I thought you said they'd cause trouble if I did anything about the photos? And Wallis would care. The woman Edward gave up the throne for," I added, in case Peter didn't remember. I'd watched the TV special, *The Woman I Love*, but Peter hadn't bothered. "She's still alive."

"Another reason why they wouldn't want any publicity about this thing."

"But they hate her. King George wouldn't allow her to use the title 'Your Royal Highness.' They always blamed her for the abdication."

"Royal Highness, royal nothing. It's all nonsense. It's all nuts as far as I'm concerned. Why don't you just hide the pictures and forget about them? Aren't you driving to Toronto tomorrow?"

I had to deliver corrected book proofs to my publisher. I wanted to take the pumpkin pictures along, too.

"Throw the pictures out in Toronto," Peter suggested.

"Not a chance. I'm going to stick them in the blanket box."

Peter frowned and studied the pictures. "Not much to look at, is he? If Edward hadn't been who he was, he would have been a bank clerk or a waiter. That's what he looks like. They're all supposed to be inbred, aren't they?"

"His parents were cousins."

"He definitely looks backward. That old British class system's for the dogs." Peter always said his father got to be chief-of-police because of his English accent, but in England he would have remained a mere constable because he didn't have the right background. "I don't know why anyone would want to put it on a tombstone even if it was true. It's nothing to brag about."

I arranged the pictures in a neat pile. The studio shot was on top.

"Married," I said, tapping the picture.

"Let's go to bed," Peter said. "You have to drive to Toronto tomorrow. We don't have to make any decisions about the pictures tonight. Let's sleep on it."

He watched while I stowed the package of photos in the bottom of the pine blanket box in the guest bedroom.

In bed, his arm crept around me as it always did, but I could feel his tension and disapproval. I'm usually the one to instigate the arguments we do have, and the feeling that Peter was angry at me was unusual. I didn't like it one bit.

Now I think he had a prescience for what would follow. It wasn't just the break-in. I'm sure he knew I had embarked on something which would create a rift between us.

And there was the mystery. Despite what he claimed, he had to be interested and mystified, I thought. He might pooh-pooh royalty but he had grown up singing "God Save the Queen" in school and he had grown up with those famous royal faces, bland and horsey and therefore all the more intriguing— what was in the king's hut that ordinary mortals were not allowed to see?— for their very ordinariness. His mother, Marion, was somewhat of a royal watcher in an amused sort of way, and Hugh, Peter's father, talked about "the King's English" (which the clodhoppers in the bush did not speak).

But as I lay there awake, Peter's doubts spread to me. One big question had always gnawed at me: How had they met? Edward had been to Canada in 1919, 1923, 1924, and 1927, but except for the 1923 visit, he had been strictly supervised, surrounded by his suite, Canadian security, and the press. Reporters speculated that he could have met Millicent in 1919 when school children sang for him in Guelph and Galt. At the same time, newspapers had been filled with rumours that the prince had a Canadian sweetheart. Millicent would never say where they met, although she claimed it hadn't been in Guelph or Galt.

Where, then? And how?

What if it was all a fantasy on her part? What if the pictures were, as Peter claimed, casual photos? The studio shot could have had other explanations...

Peter was still awake when I crept out of bed and went to the blanket box.

In my study, I turned the writing lamp on, spread the pictures out on my desk and shivered.

This will sound crazy, but as I looked at Millicent and Edward under the strong beam of the overhead light, I heard Millicent's voice saying, "Carolyn!"

She sounded exactly as she'd always done when I did something to please her— when I'd given her a brooch or book on her birthday, or brought her a little Christmas tree, for instance: surprised, joyful, glad, touched. It was a cultured voice with a faint Scottish ring to it.

"Don't you know I'm royal? You can't treat me that way!" senile Millicent had cried at the nursing home, according to a nurse.

I took the magnifying glass I use to decipher old handwritten recipes out of the top desk drawer and began to scrutinize the pictures. Blown up, Millicent's face was entirely open, forthright, relaxed: Here I am, a married woman. I have nothing to hide. It reminded me of the time I drove her to the cemetery after the engravers added the Duke's year of death to her gravestone.

Reporters rushed to her door after the Duke died (and that was when she told the ludicrous teacup lie) and finally she shut herself away, refusing further interviews, but by the time Edward's death date had been added, she was herself again.

She was satisfied that day, serene in her knowledge that she had done what was right by *her husband*. A *widow* who had done right by her husband.

Never mind that the Duchess of Windsor had flown in the Queen's Flight to stay at Buckingham Palace for the funeral. Never mind that the Duchess was the "the woman I love" who had made a king relinquish his throne.

The photos before me spoke of a more simple love, younger and more dignified. More private. It was easy to imagine the Millicent before me, resting by a fence, tramping through the highlands at Balmoral Castle, joining the other royal ladies to meet "the guns" for luncheon.

Is that what Edward had thought, too, that Millicent would fit in? A Canadian school teacher, yes, but of good background, a royal Stuart background...

And then? And then?

"They" would not allow it, Millicent had said.

Less pushy than Wallis, more sensible, Millicent had agreed to keep her secret until she was old... Edward, more jaded, more cynical, more experienced, older, got tangled up with Mrs. Wallis Simpson... who bewitched him. Maybe the reason King George did not let Wallis use the title "Her Royal Highness" had to do with the fact that Edward had another wife...

I held the lens over the studio shot.

On Millicent's ring finger I saw a slender, simple wedding band.

CHAPTER
THREE

Hendricks Publishing is not a big firm. They deal mainly in Canadiana, large glossy coffee table books on history, gardening, wildlife. Cookbooks like mine. These volumes subsidize the very occasional book of fiction or poetry they bring out. Their biggest seller is a travel atlas, updated yearly.

The office is on Greenfield, one of the older streets in the Toronto city core. Originally, the three-storey granite house belonged to a lumber baron, which is a nice touch since one of Hendricks' most successful editions is a colourful, richly illustrated book of old woodsmen's songs and lore, ghost stories and anecdotes.

Hendricks suits me to a "t," and as always, when on Tuesday afternoon I stepped into the reception room with its faded Axminster carpets, squashy leather sofas and chairs, walls of books, and Group of Seven reproductions (including two originals by A.Y. Jackson) hanging beside blow-ups of book covers, I was at home. The cover of *Country Ovens* was there, the one Jake Hendricks had been so hesitant about at first— the front door of our house— but which, he agreed, had after all drawn the would-be hopeful nesters to my book, as the sales had proven.

Not that Jake Hendricks is all that interested in the contents of my cookbooks. Irish stew and potato cakes and tales of children helping to store vegetables in the root cellar are hardly his thing. The Hendricks are an old Canadian family, grown more wealthy during Prohibition. Jake and his brother, Henry, were educated in England. The Canadiana stuff is what sells books. Henry is more interested in book design, and Jake is, wants to be, a poet. The firm keeps his one slim volume in print, but I find his poetry stiff and awkward. At the same time, he espouses contempt for the literati, and in recent years has talked of the firm publishing mysteries under another imprint.

It was raining and I placed my umbrella in the umbrella stand. My umbrella was the third one— Henry's was there, and Molly's, the secretary's, but Jake, who affects the bohemian workman, wouldn't be caught dead with an umbrella.

Molly took my coat. Plump and small with sixties wire glasses sliding down her nose and frizzy greying hair, wearing a long wool skirt, she reminded me of the Vicar's eccentric wife in English novels. The title "secretary" was an insult. She practically ran the bread-and-butter end of the firm, swore like a sailor, and shared a house in the Beaches with three young men. Hendricks had recently published a book of short stories by one of her guys— we'd attended the book launch— and I had a hunch that a little arm-bending had taken place.

"Jesus," she told me, "Jake isn't back yet, but I reminded him you'd be in at one-thirty. Sit thyself down— " she motioned to the leather sofa— "or come keep me company in my goddamn den. I don't know why the hell Jake can't come back when he's supposed to. If he tells you he took an author out to lunch, he's lying. He just went down to the corner for a corned beef."

I followed her down the narrow hallway framed with more book covers. The walls of Molly's office are papered with Grateful Dead and Rolling Stones posters— no Group of Seven here, thank you very much. She swept a pile of unopened manuscript submissions off a chair. "He's supposed to bring me back something too, the bastard."

"Do you want me to run out and pick something up for you?"

"Nah, it'll be an excuse for me to go out when he comes back. Did you bring the proofs?"

"Why else would I be in Toronto?" Molly and I always spar like this.

"To get mugged, maybe?" She grinned as I handed her the proofs. "Henry's been waiting for them. The same old panic."

"I was sidetracked. Something came up." What would Molly make of Millicent's story? I wondered. I couldn't imagine Molly being remotely interested in royalty.

But I wanted to talk about Millicent.

"A friend died, actually. A good friend."

"Oh, I'm sorry. Anyone I know?" She peeked into the envelope.

"I brought along photos of pumpkin fields too. Don't lose them. The negatives are in there too. There won't be another pumpkin harvest until next year."

"Pumpkins, eh?"

"Pumpkins. *Harvest Ovens*, you know. No, you wouldn't have known her. An old school teacher I befriended years ago when I first came to Guelph. I had to rush around to one of those shopping mall developing places to get the film processed this morning. Everything got behind after Millicent died."

"Millicent. That sounds like an old school marm."

"She was a real character. She was ninety-five when she died."

"Holy fuck. I hope I don't last that long." Molly closed the envelope. "Ninety-five," she said.

"She was an interesting person," I said and then I was telling her about what Millicent had had engraved on the stone. I liked Molly. If it hadn't been for her I might never have started publishing cookbooks. It was Molly who dug my first manuscript, *Summer Gardens*, out of the slush pile and brought it to Jake's attention, but her brashness and glibness always made me a bit flighty. I thought Molly saw me as a goody-goody. The down-home cooking lady. Once, she drove to Guelph to rush me some final book proofs. Usually people say something like, "Oh, there's the platter that was in the photograph in the book," but not Molly, who politely refrained from comment. Around her, I tended to drop the occasional "fuck," or prattle away.

"Holy fuck," Molly said.

"Well, she had it on her stone."

"I'm not big on royalty. Nothing but a bunch of brood mares and clotheshorses. Who did you say she was married to?"

"Edward VIII, the Duke of Windsor. The one who married Mrs. Simpson. You know, the abdication and all that."

"Oh, yeah."

"I don't know if it's true. But she had it on her stone."

"She must have been crazy." Molly shook her head and was about to say something more, but then Jake came in.

Jake, with his windbreakers and flannel shirts, and always-needing-a-hair-cut hair, made me feel as if we were in a conspiracy: the cookbooks were silly, but good business. Beneath this lay a common but undiscussed passion for poetry. Right after my first husband Charlie and I split up, Jake and I got drunk together at a tavern in Guelph, and spent the evening quoting Matthew Arnold and Robert Frost to each other. He looked like a chunkier version of Leonard Bernstein.

Jake peered at the pumpkin photos and said he didn't know what Henry would think. I didn't see Henry often. He usually remained in his studio office, and with his three-piece English suits resembled a banker. But unlike Jake, he took Hendricks' books seriously. A tract on forgotten railway stations was Shakespeare to him. Henry didn't write poetry.

"We'll get this off to the illustrator right away," Jake said. "Get it out for the Christmas sales. Too bad it's not called *Christmas Ovens*."

"Next year," I said.

"So what else are you doing these days?"

"Still thinking about writing the mystery, if that's what you mean," I said.

"Just thinking? That's what I do, think, and look where it gets me."

This was the time when I might have mentioned Millicent and her story to Jake, but I let it go. Not because Jake would sneer. Beneath his worker's image was a kind and gentlemanly soul. But Millicent and the pictures seemed, then, important but in a secret way. Silly, too. I felt silly. *She must have been crazy* had been Molly's reaction, and I had a feeling Jake would feel the same way. I didn't need to hear any more doubts.

I felt depressed driving home on the 401. It was pouring; I could hardly see. The windshield wipers slish-sloshed without stop and I felt trapped in the car.

What if Peter was right?

What if Millicent had taught school out west, in Alberta, and been invited to the ranch? Teachers would have been respected in the wild west. A woman with education might know a reeve, a warden, and receive an invitation to a social gathering at the ranch. I seemed to remember reading that Edward had hosted a large party for his neighbours... Edward could have noticed her. Like Wallis, she would have spoken her mind. There was Wallis' well-known statement upon meeting Edward— he had mentioned the lack of central heating in Britain, and Wallis had told him that she expected something more original from the Prince of Wales. Millicent could have come up with something as startling, as lacking in protocol.

Perhaps they went to bed together, I thought, although that was hard to imagine considering that Millicent had regularly chastised me about my "friendships" before Peter came along.

"You'll be sorry one day, my girl," she said, "for all this flitting about. No good will come of it, no good at all."

I couldn't imagine Millicent having an affair. And marriage was sacred to her. She didn't criticize Charlie until we split up and I came running to her, perversely weeping and wailing (I'd been desperately unhappy with him, but it was different when he left me for someone else).

If she had gone to bed with the prince— *if*— could she have twisted this affair, this liaison, into a marriage? To placate her, Edward could have posed for that studio portrait...

A truck driver beeped, sending a splash of water against the windshield, but not before I had seen his ugly face, the raised finger: I was driving too slowly. After finishing the proofs, I have always felt cheerful and carefree, relieved: there, that's done! Now I can relax! But that afternoon I was ready to chase the trucker down the highway and give him a piece of my mind. I told myself I would have copies made of the photos the next day and hide the secret second set somewhere.

The Bookworm is small and crowded with bulging shelves. Wooden chairs and stools are placed throughout so "bookworms" can browse to their hearts' content. The little available empty wall space belongs to portraits of Dickens, Virginia Woolf, Dylan on tour in America, and for colour, scenes from *Alice in Wonderland* and the Beatrix Potter books. I usually found all this cheering and comforting, a cosy refuge, but with the rain outside, the store felt suffocating.

Peter was brooding nervously at the front desk. There were no customers.

"Look at this. Take a look."

He spread a newspaper over the counter.

"I knew it would be discovered," he said. "Now what? On page three. At the bottom of the page. I just hope no one saw us."

Millicent's house had been broken into. Undisclosed items had been removed. The Ontario Provincial Police were investigating. Millicent's claim was briefly summarized from newspaper accounts published in 1972. The reporter speculated whether letters and documents mentioned back then had been the reason for the break-in.

"Tomorrow morning I want you to drive up to Meredith with the pictures," he said. "The sooner we get them out of the house, the better."

I agreed. But I would have copies made first, I told myself.

"Let's just go home," I said. "I'm sure no one saw us in Starleigh."

"Closing early, how will that look?"

"There aren't any customers anyway," I said, "with the rain. Why shouldn't we close early? Anyway, even if they do suspect us, what does closing a bit early on a slow afternoon have to do with that? Let's just go home. No one's going to connect us to the break-in."

But what if someone had seen us or our car and told the police?

"Don't forget they know you in Starleigh. Me too. Maybe you should leave for Meredith tonight," Peter said gloomily.

The bell dinged as the door opened, and not one but two customers walked in. Peter sighed and busied himself at the counter, checking invoices. I straightened the special rack by the door that held my cookbooks. *Summer Gardens* was mixed in with *Ontario Ovens*, and several mystery paperbacks were stuck on the bottom rack.

A small man wearing a beret inspected the travel books. A young woman in a business suit looked at the fiction. "Can I help? Is there anything you're looking for?" The man waved me away, the woman asked if we had the new Danielle Steele. More sighs from Peter. I returned the mysteries to their proper place and started on the magazine rack. Peter disappeared into the back.

Both customers stayed for ten minutes and left without buying anything. We drove home.

Peter went right to the drink shelf in the Dutch cupboard. I changed into jeans.

"Carolyn? Look at this."

Peter pointed to the shelf over the bar. I kept old cookbooks there, rare editions I used for research and reference. At one end of this shelf were notebooks of handwritten recipes in a papier-mâché box. Several of the notebooks were piled on top of the bound books.

"I don't remember moving the notebooks," I said, "but maybe I did. I could have."

But I hadn't touched them. I was careful with the notebooks, having misplaced one years ago which I never found and which, I finally concluded, had been swept out with the newspapers.

"Nothing else has been moved. I haven't noticed anything."

Together we went to the spare bedroom and opened the blanket box. Ugly green placemats lay on the top, over the Hudson Bay blanket. They'd been on the bottom before.

"I don't believe this. I'm sure the placemats were underneath."

Peter rummaged through the box, throwing the blanket on the floor, tossing flannelette sheets on the bed.

"Goddamn it, goddamn it, goddamn it!"

Millicent's photos were gone.

We had been burglarized. They— he— she— had gone through the deep freeze, mixing up the meat parcels with containers of chicken stock and tomato paste. Our suitcases had been opened, and in my study the desk diary lay on the chair, not by the telephone where I always kept it. Small things, all of them, things we might never have noticed had Peter not seen the notebooks out of place.

Peter poured us each a large Scotch.

"We can't even call the police," he said gloomily.

CHAPTER
FOUR

Peter's brilliant idea was to run away. "A holiday to commemorate another completed book!"

We fled two days later to Niagara-on-the-Lake, that graceful old town that's home to the Shaw Festival. In October it was peaceful and devoid of tourists. We stayed in an elegant bed and breakfast, drove to Niagara Falls, crossed to the American side and indulged in an orgy of shopping. I bought winter boots, a plaid-lined green Melton cloth cape, a flannelette nightie with ducks on it and half a dozen five-hundred page notebooks— hard to find in Canada— for future writing projects. Peter, who likes to wear his clothes until they're frayed and comfortable, bought outdoor trousers with secret pockets on the inside. I found thick blue wine glasses, a brick red ceramic juice pitcher, novelty plastic-handled cutlery. We spent a fortune and lied conspiratorially on the customs' declaration. Back on the Canadian side, we ate at the revolving restaurant at the Falls and told a couple in the elevator we were on our honeymoon.

The next days in Niagara-on-the-Lake we browsed in the boutiques and tried a different restaurant each night. I bought a sweater imported from Ireland and a candy cookbook. Peter cased the bookstore.

We didn't discuss Millicent very much, although I thought about her story constantly. In a way, losing the photos freed us. Now there were no decisions to be made about them; there would be no arguments.

Walking by the stately houses in the old town, I pictured Millicent waiting in the upper room of an inn, looking out of the window for a certain automobile to arrive at dusk, watching for the sight of a familiar and beloved face.

Would she have waited in Toronto? Ottawa? Quebec City? Certainly in Alberta. She had once spoken about dancing with Edward— "It was like fairyland, Carolyn!"— but I did not think she would have attended official banquets and dances. I knew from my research into the cookbooks that in the twenties there had been titled Canadians, Lords and Ladies, and these would have been invited to Rideau Hall, where dowager mothers and their hopeful daughters whirled over the dance floor with Edward.

And— Millicent in an upstairs bedroom, waiting...

My doubts had disappeared with the photos. The very fact that they were stolen had to mean something.

And it was easy to think of Millicent in this graceful town. I have always loved old things and places, perhaps because I grew up in my grandmother's hundred-and-fifty-year-old home in Maine. This longing for the past, for simpler ways, led to my cookbooks (and to my downfall as a serious writer, Jake maintained) which are filled with anecdotes and trivia about rural Canada fifty years ago. It was a sentiment Millicent shared. Up to a point. People had manners then, were more neighbourly, considered the feelings of others, found their own amusements, but women also died in childbirth, she said, and toiled from dawn to dusk unless they had servants. There was no penicillin and children died of pneumonia.

But in Niagara-on-the-Lake I forgot the "up to a point" business and Millicent's story with its secrets and mysteries returned with all the romance it had once held for me. *I had seen the photos. Someone had thought them important enough to steal.*

She did marry Edward, I thought. She married him secretly and then the King and parliament would not allow the marriage to stand.

"They would not allow it," Millicent said.

They had stolen the pictures.

Royal minions. Royal spies.

The phoney half-brother in the hospital, I told myself, hugging the possibilities. I said nothing to Peter.

We arrived home on Sunday evening. There were several frantic, garbled messages from Cass MacDonald, Peter's assistant, that The Bookworm had been broken into. Constable Quincy of the Guelph City Police wanted Peter to call. And Jake Hendricks' voice asked me to phone a.s.a.p.

Cass came over to our house right away.

"It's been a terrible week, just awful!" she cried, wiping her eyes. "I just couldn't believe it when I unlocked the door on Friday and everything was all over the place! And I didn't know where to reach you, you didn't say where you were going!"

Cass was a big-boned, slightly overweight young woman of twenty-four with a broad country face. If there was a protest march around, Cass was in it, and she took the fate of whales and baby beavers very much to heart. You wouldn't think she was high-strung and delicate, but she had had to drop out of a Master's program in American Literature at Iowa State when her father died. She worried constantly that she would make a mistake on the cash register and when she first came to work for Peter, it was on the condition that she wouldn't have to operate that complicated machine unless it was absolutely necessary.

But in other ways, she was perfect for The Bookworm (she had grown used to the cash register). No one knew more about books than Cass. Name a poet, and Cass had read a review, if not the poems, in obscure literary journals. She organized poetry readings in Guelph, remembered customers' names and suggested titles they might like, which was wonderful for sales, and would have held Kiddy Story Hour on Saturdays if Peter hadn't put thumbs down on this (who wanted to browse to Mother Goose?). Sometimes this ardour was annoying and led to mistakes, as when she had a local author autograph all ten copies of his poetry book, which meant that Peter couldn't return the unsold ones to the publisher, but she was hard-working, sincere, responsible and honest, and Peter would have been lost without her.

"I just didn't know what to do," Cass said. She bit her thumbnail. "First I had to wait for the police to come and make an inspection and I couldn't reach Peter and then I couldn't even open up on Saturday because the place was such a mess."

"But that's not your fault," I said.

Peter returned from my study where he'd been talking to Constable Quincy. His face was white as he sat on the couch next to Cass.

"There's been a rash of these break-ins lately," he said. "Just like ours. A big mess, money taken. We're lucky they didn't defecate on the floor— that's what they've been doing. And breaking beer bottles, that type of thing."

"And then I had my purse stolen on Saturday," Cass went on. "At the Bookshelf." She blushed. The Bookshelf Café, a splendid bookstore-cum-restaurant, was Peter's main competitor.

"I shouldn't have gone but I needed a break. I just couldn't look at the mess another minute."

"You had your purse stolen?" I asked. Peter frowned.

"My knapsack, you know the big green one. On top of everything else I had to call the police about that and phone Visa and Mastercard. I had to cancel all my cards and it's a good thing they know me at the Bookshelf because I couldn't even pay for my lunch. First the police said I should have my locks changed because my apartment keys were in the knapsack along with my driver's license which of course has my address on it, but my keys and everything were still there. They only took the money, eighteen dollars. But then the janitor at the sports complex found my bag that night. I had to call the credit card people back because I had my cards returned but they had already listed my numbers as stolen."

"That's awful," I said.

"Nothing like this has ever happened to me in my whole life. I'm always so careful with my purse, but in the Bookshelf I set it on the empty seat beside mine without thinking and just read the New York Times Book Review."

"Did you notice anyone?"

"The police asked me that, too." She shook her head. "But I was reading this article about a new biography of Virginia Woolf and I didn't see anyone. I had the crazy thought that having my purse stolen was connected to the break-in at the store, but I guess that's crazy."

"Did you tell the police that?" Peter asked.

"No, should I have? I can still tell them. The strange thing at the Bookshelf was that there was this ten dollar bill lying on the next table. Just lying there. Someone's big tip. I know because I was going to sit there but the table wasn't cleared and I saw the money still there when my purse was missing. And then these two people, a man and woman, were arguing."

"Maybe they took your purse," I said.

"No, they left before me. And my bag was still there then. I know because I took a pen out to write a note to myself on the review of the Virginia Woolf book. Should I tell the police that I wonder if the two are connected, my bag and the break-in at the store?"

"There's no connection," Peter said. "It's a crazy idea."

"Well, I don't want to bother them. I don't like the police much, as you know, but they were pretty nice about the whole thing. They said they'd never find who took my purse. Happens all the time, they said. Anyway, whoever took my bag sure went through it. I had a marker in *Literary Women* and the bookmark was just put back any old place. I keep thinking they were looking for something, but I guess I'm imagining things."

"I'd feel just like you if I had my purse stolen," I told Cass.

"I'll come in on Monday, tomorrow, even if it is my day off. I didn't get half the books put back. All I can think now is what if they'd come into the store to rob it when I was there alone?"

"They came at night, though," Peter said, flexing his fingers the way he does when he's nervous. "That's the pattern with the other stores."

"Still," Cass said. "I don't know how I'm going to stand being alone in the store for the next while. Just thinking about it gives me the creeps."

"I'm through with my latest literary project," I said. "I'll come in if Peter has to be away from the store."

This was against our principles. We'd agreed that I wouldn't get in the habit of being in the store. I had my own work and Peter thought if I started "helping out," before long I'd be spending half my time there. I've only "helped out" a few times when Peter had the flu and once, for a whole week, when he had his wisdom teeth out while Cass was attending a conference.

"I don't mind coming in a bit in the next little while," I assured Cass.

"No one's robbing stores in broad daylight," Peter reminded us.

"But if Cass is nervous," I said.

"You'd be a wreck too if you had your purse stolen on top of everything else," Cass told Peter.

But was it a coincidence? I wondered. Cass, many cups of herbal tea (Cass drinks nothing caffeinated) later, had finally gone home. Our holiday might never have happened, and as I finally dragged all of our purchases into the bedroom, playing hookey seemed a silly indulgence, a flight from reality.

Fact: our house had been broken into, Millicent's photos had been stolen; fact: the store had been robbed at night; fact: Cass, the one employee, had had her purse stolen and the contents inspected.

"But other stores have been broken into as well," Peter said as we drove to The Bookworm. "We have to remember that. The Bookworm wasn't the only place. And they did steal money."

"Of course it's connected. They took Cass' money but they apparently went through her purse as well. You know how Cass remembers exactly what she's read. If anyone would know where a bookmark was, it would be her."

"The bookmark could have just fallen out and they stuck it back any old place."

"In the book? Why didn't they just toss it in the purse then, or in the garbage? It seems to me whoever took her bag didn't want her to think they were after anything but the cash. It would have worked if Cass wasn't such a book-conscious person. Of course it's connected! Cass didn't have anything to do with Millicent, but she works at your store. They probably thought we'd discussed the photos with her. Maybe they think we found other things, like those letters Millicent was supposed to keep under her bed."

"The letters we never found," Peter said.

"But they wouldn't know that, would they? Don't you see? There has to be something to Millicent's story or someone wouldn't go to all this trouble."

"I think someone working for the Royals is behind all this," I added when Peter didn't respond.

"You're talking like a John LeCarré novel," Peter said. "Give me a break."

"You're the John LeCarré fan."

"The kind of character you're talking about would use more discretion," Peter said. "He wouldn't rob other stores along the way. He'd do it so no one would know. All this is the work of thugs."

"What better cover than to act like a thug?"

"Don't be ridiculous."

"Then who stole the photos, tell me that? Not thugs."

"Some tabloid journalist," Peter said. "Some idiot. But nothing else is connected. Believe me. Anyway, don't you think the royal spy would have removed the photos long before this? Do you think if there was anything in Millicent's story— and there's not— do you think they would have left those pictures lying around in a rusty old kettle, which, frankly, wasn't the best hiding place in the world? I mean, we found the pictures there, right off the bat."

Cass had managed to replace the children's books, but everything else was still piled in stacks on the floor. The poster of Virginia Woolf lay across a chairback and Ernest Hemingway dangled from a thumbtack. Magazines were heaped on the floor near the cash register. Someone had ripped the store apart, torn the books from the shelves, as if they wanted to see what lay behind.

And why disturb the posters— unless someone believed there was something hidden behind them?

"Thugs," Peter said. "It wasn't enough getting the money. They had to trash the place as well."

I examined the safe. The rare books were still in their protective envelopes, but the flaps were open. Financial statements had simply been tossed helter-skelter back into the safe. The old cash box had been forced. You could see marks around the keyhole.

"They were looking for something specific," I said.

"More money," Peter said. "Illiterate bums. They didn't even know enough to take the first edition of *Roughing It in the Bush*."

"I still think the same people are behind the theft of the pictures and this, here."

"They didn't trash our home," Peter said.

"It's all connected."

Peter turned the lights off and went to stand by the front window. I peered over his shoulder. A Volkswagen van was parked across the street. The old-fashioned kind, not a customized van. It looked dirty orange in the streetlight. It hadn't been there before.

This time at home I fixed our drinks. As I was getting the ice out of the fridge, I heard Peter go to the bedroom and bang open the blanket box.

"You think there's a connection but you won't admit it," I said when he joined me in the living room.

"No way."

"Then why were you looking in the blanket box just now? I heard you in there."

"I don't know. I don't know why I did that. I'm just tired."

"I think you were hoping to find the photos miraculously replaced so you could prove to me there's nothing to Millicent's story."

He shook his head and sighed.

"It's just all been so stressful, coming home and finding the store robbed and trashed. I'm not acting logically," Peter said.

"I really think—"

"It's just nuts, that's what it is. There's nothing to Millicent's story. It couldn't have happened. They would have watched him too closely. He had people with him all the time, people who would have reported back to the king."

"The king who ruled the marriage was illegal. And who got parliament to secretly annul it."

"So there wouldn't have been a marriage then," Peter said. "An annulled marriage is no marriage."

"But she had it on her stone. Even an annulled marriage happened. And the only reason they would have had to annul it was that she wasn't royalty. She wasn't divorced. And she wasn't Roman Catholic."

"Roman Catholic?"

"It's the law that no heir to the throne can marry a Roman Catholic," I said. "Remember Henry VIII?"

I went on some more about British history and kings and queens. Peter kept his eyes closed.

I took a big sip of Scotch and suddenly remembered Jake's message. I had forgotten to call him. *Harvest Ovens* seemed irrelevant now. Jake could panic in a most unbusinesslike way sometimes. He might have found a page missing in the middle of the night and called me more out of impatience than anything, in the spirit of "Let's get this business over with as soon as possible." His call had been sandwiched between Cass' calls from Saturday and today's, but Jake hadn't left a time. He hates answering machines and his own message says, "You've reached the home of someone who hates answering machines and telephones."

Jake answered on the first ring.

"Carolyn? Where on earth have you been? I left a message yesterday and I've been trying this evening."

"You didn't leave any more messages."

"Damn machines."

"We were on a short holiday. To Niagara Falls. We just got back."

"Niagara Falls, the honeymoon capital," I started to add, but Jake cut me off.

"Your photos are gone," he said.

"Probably Henry threw them out so he could use his own design," I said.

"Nope. Stolen. We had a break-in. And not only your photos. They took the original manuscript too. They made quite a mess of the place. Luckily I had your proofs home with me."

I asked if only my manuscript had been stolen.

"Far as we know, but we're still checking. They went into the safe where we keep original manuscripts. We'll know more tomorrow. Henry just about had a nervous breakdown. Of course you'll have a copy of your manuscript in the computer, but if you want pumpkins on the cover, you'd better get Peter out there taking more pictures. And we wouldn't mind having another print-out, just for the record."

I told Jake I'd get another print-out to him as soon as possible, that I didn't know about more pumpkin photos, and downed the rest of the Scotch.

CHAPTER
FIVE

Cass didn't come in on Monday after all. Her doctor had prescribed rest; she was going to spend the day in bed.

Peter put a "Closed for Inventory" sign on the door and by two o'clock we had most of the books back on the shelves in a semblance of order, or at least with enough order that Peter could open up the next day. I set aside a box of books on royalty: *Edward VIII* by Frances Donaldson, *A King's Story*, Edward's autobiography, several books about Queen Elizabeth, and one about the Duchess of Windsor.

Peter frowned.

"What are those for?"

"Just to refresh my memory."

"Refresh your memory for what?"

"Some background information. I've read them before but I think I'd like to read them again. I might find something I missed before."

"You're not really going to do anything about this whole Millicent business, are you?"

"I don't know yet. After seeing the photos— "

"But they're gone."

"Stolen. That has to mean something."

"It means we'll see them in *The National Enquirer*. Let someone else get egg on their face. Why should it be you?"

"But I knew Millicent."

"And she told you her life's tale. I really hope you won't pursue this, Carolyn."

I stowed the box beneath the front counter and we went for lunch at The Bookshelf Café. We ordered quiche. The plan was that I would go home and crank out another copy of *Harvest Ovens* while Peter finished at the store, but I decided to check the historical file on Millicent at the Guelph Public Library first. I asked Peter to bring the royalty books home with him. He shook his head but agreed.

"I wish you'd forget the whole thing," he said.

"I'm just going to read the books."

"And I know where that will lead."

"Where will it lead?"

"Trouble. All kinds of trouble."

"Trouble from whom?"

"You think the royal family will like having all this old garbage raked up?"

"Why should they care, if there's nothing to it? If they do cause trouble it'll only mean there is something to the story."

"So you are going to do something about it."

"I don't know yet."

He shook his head.

"You're the one who said the store break-in had nothing to do with Millicent," I reminded him.

"You'd be glad if it was connected, wouldn't you?" Peter asked. "You want it to be some thugs working for the Royals, don't you?"

"It would prove Millicent told the truth anyway. You know, you don't make sense. First you say there's nothing to it and that I'll get egg on my face and then you say there could be royal agents who'd do anything to stop me."

"*Us*," Peter said. "I'm involved in this too. I was there in Starleigh. They took the photos from *our* house. I can't stop you, but I wish you'd think twice."

"Charlie always wanted me to milk Millicent for information," I said. "He wanted me to get a bestseller out of her."

"Bestseller, sure. That asshole."

"Now I wish I had asked her questions."

"Maybe you should have listened to Mr. Know-it-all," Peter said sarcastically.

I felt my face grow hot. We hadn't discussed Charlie for years. It was on the tip of my tongue to retort, "Maybe I should have," but Peter was apologetic right away.

"Just think about what you're doing," he said. "I don't have a good feeling about this. Ever since we took those damn photos there's been nothing but trouble. Just think twice, that's all I ask."

"I don't like us arguing like this," I said.

"I don't like it either."

"And being sarcastic and awful, that's not like you."

"I hate to think of you getting involved in this crazy story. Just think about it. Please."

The library did have a historical file on Millicent Mulvey. The librarian didn't glance at me twice as she handed it over, but murmured that quite a few people had been asking to see it.

There weren't many clippings, however. The latest, the one announcing her death and the one about the break-in, had been added to the few I remembered from years ago when Millicent gave her few interviews.

But there was one clipping I hadn't seen before, published by a newspaper from Hamilton. Millicent hadn't mentioned the interview to me, which focused on her ninetieth birthday and her long teaching career. Perhaps she'd forgotten all about it. She never agreed to another interview when her mind was still sound.

There was also a picture of Millicent looking old and lined and surprisingly like photos of the aging Duchess of Windsor.

The stone was mentioned merely in passing and Millicent also talked about someone called "Daddy" who had straightened out an electricity bill.

The article said that Miss Mulvey had a long and varied teaching career. She began teaching at an early age at West Montrose, where her annual salary was $350 a year. She went to teacher's college in Toronto, taught at schools in Starleigh, and later went on to teach in Etobicoke, Malton, and Meredith, northern Ontario, where she remained for a few years.

Meredith. She'd mentioned northern Ontario to me once or twice, but I was sure she'd named another place.

I made photocopies of all the clippings, but shoved the original clipping from the Hamilton paper into my purse.

It was, alas, Thursday before I was able to drive to Toronto to deliver another print-out to Jake. Cass took Tuesday and Wednesday off as well. She still had a fever, and her doctor insisted on more rest. Peter didn't protest my presence in the store and my postponing the trip to Toronto, as if by keeping me with him he could change my mind about looking into Millicent's story, and also about going to Meredith on the weekend. He'd never been too keen on visiting Meredith and going there because of Millicent didn't make him too happy. Yes, he would come along, and yes, he would call an old teacher, but he didn't like the idea very much at all.

At night and during quiet moments in the store I read the royalty books. Frances Donaldson said nothing about Edward's 1923 Canadian visit. Edward wasn't exactly forthcoming about the visits to Canada, but after the 1924 visit— a very brief one, he'd spent weeks on Long Island watching polo and only spent a few days at his ranch— he wrote that he hadn't been lucky enough to find a bride at that point in his life and that he would only marry for love. Frances Donaldson stressed the royal family's dislike of Wallis.

I watched customers carefully, but no one unusual came in. I recognized most of them and the new ones— a young woman looking for anything by Bobbie Ann Mason, a teenaged *Star Trek* fan, a middle-aged woman seeking books on astrology— were run-of-the-mill.

I had placed threads in the blanket box and arranged papers in and on my desk in a certain order, but nothing was disturbed.

No one phoned and the only message on the machine was from Henry— the first time he had ever called, I think— to say that the pumpkin photos had been lost and had Jake contacted me? He sounded less than friendly when I got back to him, but Henry was always reserved. I assured him I'd bring in a new manuscript in a day or so, and tried to stall on the photos.

Finally, on Thursday, Cass returned to work and I had no more excuse to avoid going to Toronto. I knew I'd have to confide in Jake.

Molly was not her usual cheerful salty self when she informed me that as far as anyone knew only my manuscript and the accompanying pumpkin photos had been taken, although they had made a helluva mess.

"I suppose you've brought another print-out of the manuscript," she said. She had her glasses perched on her nose and was opening a stack of manilla envelopes. She sounded as if a new copy of my manuscript was the last thing she wanted to see.

I put the manuscript on her desk. "Where's Jake, anyway?"

"He went out around eleven. Haven't seen him since. Didn't say where he was going."

She frowned at the contents of an envelope and added it to a growing pile on the floor.

"Nothing much there, I guess," I said.

"If they'd only query first," Molly said. She sighed.

"Maybe I'll walk to Yonge Street and look for Jake. He's probably taken a long lunch. At that deli he always goes to."

Molly shrugged. "Long lunch is right," she said.

I located Jake at once. He was in the deli, as I'd thought, and doing the crossword puzzle in the *Toronto Sun*. The *Sun* is Toronto's daily tabloid, a paper filled with ads for stereos and used cars, and gaudy photographs. No one I knew bought the *Sun*. It's the kind of paper you read in doughnut shops.

Unlike Molly, Jake was friendly. Maybe he'd left the office to get away from Molly's rotten mood.

"I have to talk to you," I said.

"There are no more pumpkins," he ventured. "Peter won't be able to get more photos as they've all been harvested. Henry was going to call you again. He's suddenly gung-ho about re-titling the book *Winter Ovens*. More appropriate for the Christmas sales he says. And of course he wants a winter scene for the cover. I'm beginning to think Henry engineered the theft of the pumpkin photos so he'd have an excuse to go with something else. Never was crazy about the pumpkin idea. Has it all worked out. But it's up to you. We won't do it unless you agree. If you brought more pumpkin photos he'll be very upset."

I didn't hesitate. *Winter Ovens* was fine, I said and I knew the last thing Peter wanted to do now was to run around the countryside hoping to find pumpkins.

The waitress came over. I ordered coffee.

"The cookbook's the last thing on my mind," I said. "We've had some troubles."

Jake shoved the *Sun* away.

"It's about the break-in at Hendricks. I have to talk to you about it."

Jake shrugged.

"That was garbage," he said. "The break-in. I'm sorry I pressed the panic button when I called, but remember Igor? Igor who lived with Molly? We think he did it, although we can't prove it, of course. Igor at that book launch? Julian's cousin? Maybe you weren't introduced."

Julian Amberly was one of the men who lived at Molly's. The short story writer. But I didn't remember meeting Igor.

"They took him in, he'd just gotten out of the hospital." Jake tapped his head. "He's had a personality disorder for years. One of those old acid cases. Molly took your manuscript home to check it over a while back and— you won't believe this— one of the guys copied a recipe and when he made it, Igor came down with cramps. What a story. Igor spent the night at Emergency and some days after that boozing it up and wandering the streets. The cops found him passed out at the Eaton Centre the day after he robbed us. He kept jabbering to the cops about pumpkin and it was pumpkin soup he ate. So put it together. But we didn't tell the police this lovely little story."

"That explains Molly's bad mood."

"Julian wants to take Igor in for two weeks until they can find a place for him. Molly won't have Igor in the house again. Absolutely not, she says. Julian's upset, he feels he should help. Promised the guy's mother or something. I don't know why Molly doesn't kick Julian out too. All of them, as far as I'm concerned. Idiots. She ends up doing everything. All their laundry, the cooking."

"Except the pumpkin soup." With curry, I remembered, and a touch of grated orange rind. Not a dish any pioneer would have cooked. "But I don't think this Igor did it."

"Makes sense to me. Henry, of course, thinks we should throw the book at him. Of course Igor did it. It's just crazy enough to make sense. They didn't even put Igor in the hospital. Just kept him in lock-up overnight. The streets are filled with these crazies."

"But I know Igor didn't do it."

"Of course he did. You didn't meet him that night? The guy in a three-piece herring-bone, carnation in his lapel. Suit came from Goodwill. He stuck out like a sore thumb."

"Don't remember him. I guess he just faded into the background with the lawyer types." "Patrons of the arts" always turned up at Hendricks launches. Most of them went to Upper Canada College with Jake and Henry. "But I very much doubt it was Igor."

If it had been Igor, then the incident wasn't at all connected to our two break-ins.

But only my manuscript and photos had been taken. Would not an Igor have done more damage?

"So what's your hunch on this?" Jake asked. "Anything's possible in this crazy world."

"Our house was broken into. The Bookworm too. And we broke into a house, Peter and I, and took something."

Jake signalled for more coffee.

He didn't say a word while I told him the story about Millicent and the photos we had taken. I described Millicent, my friendship with her, the stone in the cemetery, the photographs, and the rest.

"No one has ever believed her around Guelph," I said. "They saw her story as a fantasy an old lonely woman created. Peter doesn't want to get involved and he doesn't like the idea of me pursuing this."

"He doesn't, does he?"

"But he's not going to stop me. Peter isn't like that. He just doesn't like it very much. And this weekend we're going up north to Meredith. That's where Peter grew up and I've found out Millicent taught there for a while. The thing is, I think whoever stole the photos from our house broke into Hendricks."

"Anyway, it all makes sense to me," I said when Jake didn't respond. "More sense than the story about that Igor guy."

"I don't know what to say," Jake said.

"I thought you should know. I didn't tell Peter I was going to tell you."

"It's an incredible story."

"I suppose you don't know very much about royalty. Or care."

"Did you know I used to collect plates and mugs with the Queen's picture on them?"

"What?"

"It was camp. 'There's Lizzie,' I used to say. I finally sold the whole bunch to a second-hand dealer. It was just one of the weird things I did after I came back from Jolly Olde England. Don't ask me why. It was more snubbing the establishment than anything else, I guess. Very much in the spirit of 'Spitting Image.' Plus my girlfriend of the day was a flea market addict. The royalty junk gave me something to look for when I followed her around."

"I mentioned Millicent to Molly when I brought the proofs in. Just that a friend died and what Millicent had carved on the stone. I didn't tell her about stealing the photos. You're the only one who knows about that, except for Peter and me."

He raised a palm: your secret is safe with me.

"Don't tell Henry."

"Not a word. But I don't think our break-in had anything to do with your old friend. I think Igor the Nutcase did it all right. It's an incredible story though, about your friend and the Duke of Windsor. You've never lived over there, in England. It's very much the upper crust against the plebs. WE against the scum. The tabloids over there—" he tapped the *Sun* "— are filled with scandals and scoops on royalty but the Royals are above it all, don't concern themselves with that kind of garbage. They wouldn't bother with some long-ago scandal involving the Duke of Windsor and a Canadian woman. I wouldn't worry about any royal agents. That's pretty far-fetched if you ask me."

"Peter's always said that a royal prince wouldn't have bothered with a small town Canadian woman except maybe for a roll in the hay."

"That's quaint. 'Roll in the hay.' I haven't heard that since I was a kid."

"I don't know if he used those exact words, but that's what he meant. I wish you could have seen the photos."

"Write a novel," Jake said, picking up the check and fishing in his pocket for change for a tip. He rolled up the *Sun* and stuck it under his arm. "That shouldn't disturb Peter too much and maybe it'd satisfy your curiosity."

"But I want to know the truth."

"Trouble ahead," Jake said. "Not from royal spies, but from Peter."

"Don't be a chauvinist. He might be unhappy about the whole thing, but he's going to Meredith with me."

Jake raised an eyebrow.

"So what would you do if you'd been the one who had the photos?" I asked Jake on the street. "One of the reasons I came to Toronto— other than to tell you about Millicent and the photos, was to see if you had any ideas."

"Ideas?"

"What to do now. I can't just forget about the photos. Millicent was a good friend, an old friend. I don't know what to do."

"I'd wait and see what happens next," Jake said. "Do a little investigating, talk to people, see if there's any corroboration. I'd say that having the photos stolen means something."

"That's what I think too. I'm not going to drop it. Do you think I should drop it?"

"Not if you have a passion for it."

"I do."

We paused for the lights. Yonge Street was busy with the usual sidewalk hawkers of jewellery and t-shirts, winos and panhandlers, as well as businesspeople with their attaché cases.

Jake took my hand.

"You're worried, and I don't think it's just about Peter. It's the break-ins that have you so worked up," he said. "I wasn't the basket case Henry was when Igor broke into the office, but I had a strange, violated feeling until we figured it out. Years ago, someone broke into my apartment and stole my TV and that was worse because the cops never caught the guy. I always had this feeling the fellow would return. But once you know who did it, that goes away. Maybe if you check around, things will fall into place. Maybe the break-in at Peter's store was just a regular business break-in. For the cash. No self-respecting thief would steal books."

"Let me know if you come up with any ideas," I said.

He held my hand until we crossed the street.

"What do you think about Millicent's claim?" I asked him.

"Not impossible," he said. "You never know. The press boys practically fell at royalty's feet in those years. They had a gentleman's agreement not to publish anything about Mrs. Simpson before the abdication. I doubt if you'll find any record in an archive either."

Back at Hendricks, he walked me to the Volvo in the carpark and kissed me good-bye on the cheek.

"Let me know what happens," he said. "It's a fascinating story."

A dusty orange Volkswagen van was parked in the next space. Just like the VW we had seen outside The Bookworm Sunday night.

But the vehicle was empty. Would someone following me use the next parking space?

Jake waved as I drove off.

CHAPTER
SIX

Meredith's Main Street has to be one of the ugliest main streets in small town Canada. The usual stores are there— IGA, Metropolitan, a hardware store, hairdresser, a ladies' wear with fifties manikins in the window— but you won't find a charming little boutique displaying antique dolls, or a café with ruffled curtains selling quiche.

Meredith is too far north for that. There are no trees on Main. A fire destroyed most of the "downtown" in the thirties, and the buildings still have that hastily erected look. Once there was a gold mine, but today most people work at a small lumber mill or at logging. Makeshift bungalows with added sections and sagging roofs line the narrow side streets, except at the north end where the "elite" live in brick houses.

Why on earth had Millicent come here in the forties? It was dreary enough now; I could only imagine what it had been like then. It would have required organization to get away. Unpaved roads, snow and more snow, the school-house filled with noisy and stubborn boys. The hockey rink the only entertainment in the winter. Black flies in the summer.

And if Millicent had taught in the countryside, not in Meredith proper, as I suspected, it would have been worse.

I remembered Millicent saying that life in the north had been difficult; that people had to work hard there. She had told me this back in the dark ages, when I was married to Charlie. He was going to school and working part time at Canadian Tire and complaining about his boss. Millicent said, "Bah! Be glad you are able to work in a comfortable store. If you had to work in the bush like the men up north, then you might have something to complain about! Why, it was so cold in the winter, I'd have to break the ice in the water pail in the morning."

(*In the late forties* the Duke and Duchess of Windsor had left the Bahamas, where Churchill had dumped Edward as Governor-General for the duration of the war because of his Nazi sympathies, with its provincial matrons and the scandal of the murder of Sir Harry Oakes, and were back in Paris. The Duchess searched for a house, decorated, bought antiques, got the china and silver out of storage. The Duke visited Queen Mary at Marlborough House in England. In 1946 the couple stayed with friends in England and the Duchess had her jewel case stolen; she wanted the servants searched. Edward and Wallis sailed to New York, to Palm Beach; dined with Winston Churchill, entertained Society. The Palace wouldn't give the Duke a job and they would still not receive Wallis, but there were compensations...)

And Millicent, *the rightful wife*, in Meredith with the snow, the bush. Her secrets— *the secret*— would not have seemed like a secret at all, but a reason for discontent, for sleepless nights. No one knew. She couldn't speak of it, not only because she had been told not to, but because no one would have believed her.

The one good thing about Meredith is Peter's mother. I cheered up as soon as she kissed my cheek.

"Carolyn! How lovely to see you!"

Many women have mother-in-law troubles, but I adore Marion. My own mother, Shirley, parked me with Gran for a "year or two" after her divorce. The year or two stretched to forever. Charlie's mother was frosty and polite; she blamed me for Charlie's defection to Canada. I was ready for a mother when I met Marion.

Marion is a knitter of sweaters, a collector of china teacups, and is gentle in her fine English manner, unlike her husband, hearty Hugh, the Old Colonial Boy. On the surface, there is nothing interesting about Marion's life. She stays home and isn't employed (and where could she, realistically, work in Meredith, except in a store?). Hugh holds forth daily at the Ritz Café on Main Street. Hugh's in Rotary and Hugh chairs committees on building a new skating rink or a drop-in centre for teens, but Marion does none of these things.

Marion is saved from stagnation by her inquiring mind and intelligence. She's an astute reader, takes out a dozen books a week from the Meredith library, belongs to book clubs, and says that the decision not to partake of the daily life of Meredith is conscious: why should she? Let Hugh involve himself in small town gossip and shenanigans. She's having none of it.

Marion often visits us in Guelph. We go to the Royal Ontario Museum, spend a day shopping in Toronto, see a play in Stratford. She knits and reads and goes for walks if I have work to do. Sometimes she helps out at The Bookworm. I love listening to her English accent as she speaks about her youth in England, the church bazaars, the local characters of the village where she grew up. She makes it sound like a cosy English novel, the kind of book you curl up with when you have the flu.

I had never told her about Millicent and her claim because I thought she would sneer at the story. Unlike Peter, Marion takes an interest in "The Royals"— an amused interest in their foibles, the money that is spent on them, the petty scandals— but an interest that I imagine is a very English one.

I had come up with a plausible cover-up for my interest in Millicent in

Meredith: I was writing a book about school teachers long ago and dedicating it to my good friend Millicent Mulvey, an old school teacher herself. I could even say Millicent had given me the idea for this book. Naturally, I would want information about her life for the introduction, which would explain my interest in teaching in the days of the little country schools.

"At least it's better than telling the truth," Peter said.

But he still didn't like it.

"A book about teachers," Marion mused. "It'll be a change from the cookbooks."

"A welcome change," I said. "Sometimes I get so tired of recipes. I finally got the last masterpiece off to the publishers. They want to call it *Winter Ovens*. Maybe *Last Ovens* would have been a better title. The last of a line."

We were alone. Hugh had nabbed Peter as soon as we arrived to accompany him to an estate recently bought by German businessmen who were turning it into a hunting camp for overseas visitors. The property was out of Meredith proper and under the jurisdiction of the Ontario Provincial Police, but Hugh knew everyone and some German fellow had asked him to drop by.

"You should write a mystery," Marion said. She was knitting a Mickey Mouse sweater for her youngest grandchild, Allison's little two-year-old, Matthew. Allison, a chunky young wife and mother, married to huntin' and fishin' Joe, was a baby when they arrived in Meredith and lives and breathes the small town.

"Half the mysteries I take home from the library are hardly worth reading. I wonder how they ever get published? I read a chapter or two and can't be bothered with the rest. Your mystery would be wonderful, I'm sure."

"My publisher's suggested the same thing," I said. "Maybe this book about teachers will mean a break from the cookbooks. Maybe after I do the teachers' book I'll feel brave enough to tackle a mystery."

"Not that your cookbooks aren't fine, but you could set a mystery in the pioneer days, with your knowledge of the subject. Was your teacher friend very interesting?"

"Just an eccentric old lady, but I liked her a lot. I met her ages ago when

I first came to Guelph. She used to write letters to the editor complaining about my restaurant column."

"Quite the beginning to a friendship."

"She said with all the starving millions, people were selfish to think about eating snails, that kind of thing. Not that I disagreed with her. She was ninety-five when she died a few weeks ago."

Later I hoped to visit Miss Henderson, the principal, now retired, of Peter's elementary school. Peter'd agreed to come along but only if I stuck to the teachers' book idea. I was sure Peter hoped his father would keep him away until all hours.

"I don't think you ever mentioned her."

"She was probably already in the nursing home when you and I met," I lied.

"I hope Miss Henderson remembers her. And that she doesn't talk your ear off. Imagine your friend having taught up here in Meredith. Poor duck."

"We only learned about Meredith from— the obituary. Millicent once told me she'd taught in northern Ontario, but I didn't think it was in Meredith. Maybe it was around here somewhere. But it did say Meredith in the obituary."

"Quite the coincidence."

"Yes, I know."

I was dying to tell her the truth. I was sure, now, she would have a new perspective on Millicent's story and I really wanted to hear what she thought of it. She knew how to keep a secret too.

"I can picture what Meredith was like in those days," Marion sighed. "I don't think the highway was even paved then. It was bad enough when we first arrived. And if she taught in one of the country schools, life would have been grim for her. Rather primitive I should think."

She shook her head and bent over the wool. Marion is a small, fine-boned woman, and until you really look, quite ordinary in appearance. She hasn't gone in for the dye jobs, the bright clothes. But her features are fine, her lightly greying hair curls charmingly over a smooth forehead. She was wearing a Fair Isle sweater she'd knitted and fuzzy pink slippers Allison had given her for Christmas. Marion always makes me feel comfortable and the cosy setting—

plants and African violets, a sturdy bookcase filled with Dickens and Iris Murdoch and the Canadian books by Margaret Laurence and Alice Munro we'd given her, a squashy chintz sofa— was just right for shared confidences. Hugh and Marion live in one of the few big brick homes in Meredith. Once you step into the front hall you leave scruffy Meredith behind.

"I just wonder why on earth she came up here, to pioneer country as it were, when she had been teaching elsewhere," Marion said.

"A sense of adventure, maybe."

"Or a bad romance?" Marion suggested. "The myth of the north is that people come here to escape the past. To drown their sorrows, although a teacher back then couldn't have done much of that and gotten away with it. Not that it's much different today."

"Let me put the kettle on for tea," I said. "I want to tell you a story."

It was getting dark when Hugh and Peter arrived. After several beers and some German schnapps, Hugh was expansive and friendly, red-faced from the drinking. He'd told the "Krauts" about my cookbooks and offered to obtain copies for them so they could serve some traditional Canadian fare along with the schnitzels and "wienerwurst" (wink, wink) to the overseas big-game hunters.

Peter went to call Miss Henderson.

"What's this I hear about a new book about the teaching profession?" Hugh asked. He had fixed himself another drink and was relaxing in his armchair.

"Oh, it's just a book," I said. "An idea I had."

"Those country teachers weren't even educated," Hugh said. "Not that those around today are much better."

"They're educated, at least."

"Pieces of paper, pieces of paper. Degrees in recreation— how to play golf, I suppose. That's what the Phys Ed fellow has got, you know. Recreation! What kind of an education is that?"

I've had some pretty good arguments with Hugh over the years.

"The teachers I'm interested in wouldn't even have had degrees," I said.

"Some of them didn't even go to teachers' college. A lot of them just went to high school and started teaching when they were seventeen."

"Probably knew more than the ones today," Hugh said, contradicting himself.

"I wouldn't be surprised," I said.

"And this friend of yours," he went on. "I told Peter you should have let me know. I don't know what he thinks Henderson can tell him. She's lucky if she remembers her own name these days. Senile. She filed a complaint about someone in her building stealing from her. Most of them can't even hobble around in there. I'll put the word out. Millicent Mulvey. Old Scottish name. Easy to remember."

"Oh yes, Millicent Mulvey, Carolyn's friend," Marion said. "The teacher the new book will be dedicated to."

Peter came downstairs and said Miss Henderson was expecting us at eight-thirty.

I was not sorry I had told Marion the truth. She was fascinated with the story and did not think it at all implausible considering what she had read about the Duke of Windsor. He was known to have had lots of affairs until Wallis came along. A dreadful woman; dreadful. The monarchy would have fallen, she said, if Edward had gone ahead and married her and stayed on the throne. And then there'd been all that shameful business about Edward's trafficking with the Nazis.

"But why don't you write to the royal archives?" she suggested. "People do, you know. We had a young librarian here in Meredith who was researching one of Queen Victoria's daughters and he wrote to the Queen. And she actually replied. Well, not Queen Elizabeth, but someone from the archives. It was something about a correct title, I believe. They sent him the information straightaway."

"This is rather different," I pointed out.

"But it wouldn't hurt to try, would it? Just to get their reaction? I'm surprised they didn't do anything about the inscription if it went on while the Duke was still alive."

"I did find out that most stonecutters wouldn't put something like that on a stone without some kind of verification."

I had called two firms for this information. Both companies had heard of Millicent's stone. And both said that although there was nothing legal to prevent such a carving, they did operate with a code of ethics.

"I wouldn't even know where to write."

"It's a shame the young librarian left here for greener pastures or I could ask him for you. Perhaps someone at the Guelph library could tell you. The information shouldn't be difficult to obtain. Oh Carolyn, it's such an interesting story! I'm so glad you told me. And I won't say a word, not to Hugh or anyone else."

"Peter thinks a journalist stole the photos. He also says that the Royals would try to stop me digging into Millicent's story. Then he says he doesn't believe a word of her claim."

"He's always been bored by royalty."

"Peter didn't even want me to tell you the story."

"You needn't worry. I shan't say a word. I wish I could have seen the photos! Imagine! Oh, I just know her story is true! Who'd put such a thing on a tombstone if it wasn't true?"

"Peter says they'd have watched Edward too closely for him to marry anyone."

"But Edward always had a mind of his own. He would have gone ahead with it and then let happen what may. He also picked his own retinue, people sympathetic to him. King George V wasn't too happy with Edward's friends. You must find out the truth. It's history after all!"

"And you told her about the break-in, too?" Peter asked on our way to see Miss Henderson.

"I just said we found the photos after Millicent's death and then that someone stole them from us. I didn't say anything about the break-in at the store or at Hendricks."

"I wish you'd simply stuck to the teachers' book. I just hope she doesn't tell Dad. If he knows, it'll be all over town. I wonder how he keeps his job sometimes."

"I'm sure your mother won't tell him or anyone else why I'm really researching Millicent."

"So you're going ahead with it."

"Your mother thinks it's a good idea."

I told him about the letter to the Queen.

"That'll really get them after you," Peter said.

"I haven't written yet."

"Well, don't. Please don't. I wish we weren't going to see old Henderson either."

"I won't ask you to help me with anything else," I said. "I promise."

Miss Henderson was waiting for us, a small woman with dyed-silver hair. Her apartment was pin-knit, all pouffy cushions and cheap ornaments. There wasn't a book in the place.

"And this is the author!" Miss Henderson gushed. "I don't believe I've ever met a real live author before!"

"I only write cookbooks," I said.

"But books just the same! I always thought Peter would turn into an author, but it seems he's married one instead! Such a clever boy, not rowdy like the others. As soon as he phoned, I dug out the old school photos."

The photos lay on the coffee table, next to a plastic arrangement of pink roses. Peter looked skinny and sad in them, one of the smaller boys in class.

"Oh yes, there he is," I said politely, as I set up the tape recorder. I'd seen similar pictures before, dragged out by Allison to Peter's embarrassment.

"A book about teachers!" Miss Henderson cried. "It's a wonderful idea, just wonderful! You'll have to let me know when it comes out. My niece is a great reader, you know. Penny, you went to school with her, Peter. She's in Windsor now and I know she'd love one. And I'll certainly buy one, or will contributors receive a free copy?"

I caught on right away. The woman thought I was writing about her. I said naturally that she would receive a free copy if the book ever came out.

"Oh, it's not definite then? I thought it was all settled."

"You never know with books," I explained. "My publisher does think it's a good idea though."

"That would be the cookbook publisher?"

"They do other books as well."

"I don't have to sign anything, do I? There's someone in the building here— oh you wouldn't know her, Peter— she moved here after you went away, not a Meredith native at all, but her son lives here— she writes poetry and she sent these poems to a company in the United States and they wrote back and asked for a hundred dollars. I told her it was a scam, but she wouldn't listen."

"You don't have to sign anything," I said. "I'll be talking to a lot of teachers and putting their stories together for the book."

Miss Henderson and I talked for forty-five minutes about her teaching career while Peter sat in silence on the couch. She had taught in various small country schools in the area before coming to the "big" Meredith school and then there had been a major to-do about the principalship, a complicated vendetta between the trustees and the Henderson supporters.

Etcetera and etcetera and etcetera.

Peter looked at his watch.

"Oh no, you can't go yet! We'll have tea!" She bustled into the kitchen to prepare tea and to bring out Rice Krispies squares.

It was only while we had the tea that I was able to bring up Millicent. I told the story about the foreword and my friendship with Millicent.

Miss Henderson said: "I have never heard of any teacher by the name of Millicent Mulvey. I'm sure she didn't teach here, unless it was in one of the unorganized schools in the municipality. We didn't have much to do with them. Why, some of the teachers weren't teachers at all, just people they hired when they couldn't find anyone else!"

"Old battle-axe," Peter said as we drove away. "She was the most hateful old sow you'd ever want to meet in your whole life. All that garbage about good boy Peter. She used to say, 'Just because your father is the Police Chief doesn't mean that you can get away with it, young man!'"

"I can't imagine you doing anything awful."

"I committed terrible crimes. Chewed gum. Forgot to do a page of arithmetic. Let's not go back yet. Let's have a drink somewhere. At the hotel?"

The Meredith Hotel, an ugly, flat-topped building on Main Street, isn't a hotel at all. At least, they haven't rented rooms since the new motel went up at the edge of town. What it is, is one of the few drinking places in Meredith, and the setting for the Saturday night brawls. Hugh's there most Saturday nights breaking up the fights, but he was off this weekend because of our visit.

At least it was cheerful, although noisy and smoky. The usual Saturday night crowd was there, young people, guys and their girlfriends, and a few middle-aged bachelors, the regulars, with a sprinkling of older women. Respectable middle-aged people and younger married couples drank at home or visited each other. I was sure that Marion had never spent an evening at the Meredith Hotel, although Allison in her heyday sneaked in there quite a bit. Hugh used to send Peter to look for her.

Peter ordered two draughts. He seemed more cheerful now and began regaling me with stories about Miss Henderson. The elastic on her slip broke one famous recess and she strapped the boys who laughed. One Hallowe'en some kids took the tires off her car, which brought a general assembly the next day. A girl named Mabel had called her an "old fart."

"The old fart is probably having a sleepless night worrying about the book," Peter said. "Wondering if it's going to cost her anything."

"If she'll get a share of the royalties is more like it!"

"Or if she shouldn't hire a ghost writer and churn out a bestseller herself."

"She'll just have to write about her own scandalous, salacious life, since she doesn't know anything about Millicent."

"And let's hope it stays that way," Peter said. "Not that she'd believe it."

"Your mother believes it."

"Would like to believe it, you mean. She hopes it's true because it's something to do with royalty."

The waiter returned, thumped Peter on the back, and placed two more draughts on the table. The juke box came on then and we couldn't talk for a while. Peter drained his beer and poured some of mine into his glass. A few couples had gotten up to dance and Peter sat watching them, but I could tell he was doing some thinking from the look on his face.

"Only people who are royalty-mad would believe that story," he said when the music had stopped. "You have to be half-cracked anyway to be interested in royalty."

"Thanks a lot."

"I knew Mom would go for it if you told her. Crazy bloody Royals."

"You're saying your mother's cracked."

"Just English," Peter said. "King and Country."

"Maybe I'll uncover something that'll change your mind."

"You're really going ahead with this thing?"

"You really don't want me to."

"You got it."

But he grinned and instead of going into all the reasons why I shouldn't, he went on about the "bloody Royals." If the beer loosened his tongue— somewhere in all this he raised his hand for more drinks— it also loosened mine, and for a change he didn't look bored when I told him tidbits from my reading— Queen Mary having this interesting habit of stealing ornaments and silver from her friends, King Edward VII's mistress Mrs. Keppel, King George V shooting thousands of little birds out of the sky.

Peter's side of the conversation involved some Monty Python imitations and soon he was regaling me with Hugh's military-style commands when he was growing up— for a while there'd been a shoe inspection every morning; some rudeness on Allison's part resulted in Peter and Allison having to call their father "Sir"; the appearance of comic books had them memorizing Shakespeare for punishment.

We were in a pretty good mood by the time we left at eleven-thirty.

It had grown chilly outside and Main Street looked deserted.

Peter was swaying as he walked, but suddenly he looked at me and said, "It's just the idea that's so dangerous, you know."

"The idea? What idea?" I held on to him.

"The idea and people believing it's true. All the royalty nuts believing it's true. A royalty nut like you," he said, giving me a big wet kiss as we reached the car.

Someone had let the air out of the front tires on the Volvo.

We walked home because it was too late to get anyone at the Texaco Centre. Marion was waiting up with tea, but Hugh had gone to bed.

Marion told us that he had, however, found someone out in the Shaw River District who remembered Millicent.

CHAPTER
SEVEN

"Neurotic. That's what I thought of your friend Millicent. Menopausal, as they'd say on *Donahue*."

Beryl Sofer lit a cigarette. A tobacco tin and cigarette roller sat on the coffee table. She was no fluttery, silly Mrs. Henderson, but a northern countrywoman with clipped grey hair, wearing jeans and a red flannel shirt. She ran the only store in Shaw River.

She lived in a new prefabricated log house with a satellite dish and a huge woodpile in the backyard. Inside, an air-tight wood stove stood in the corner, but there was a real fireplace as well. Rubber boots sat on a mat by the door. Guns hung over the hearth. They were her late husband's, but I thought it likely Beryl had shot the odd deer in her time. Bird books filled a bookcase.

Hugh had found her by the simple expedient of calling Charlie Frank, the eighty-eight-year-old retired county warden and somewhat of a local history buff, who had searched through old school records and found Millicent listed at the school in Shaw River.

"Of course *Donahue* wasn't around then," Beryl said. "Not to mention TV. I don't know what we did with ourselves. Went to bed with the birds I guess."

I laughed to show a little enthusiasm. Peter's good mood of the night before was gone. He'd woken up with a headache and then he'd had to take the car to the garage to have the tires fixed. He sat with his eyes half-closed.

"You don't watch *Donahue*? I don't know why I have it on half the time, except to see how the other half screws up."

"Millicent would have been in her fifties then," I ventured, "so she might have been going through the menopause."

"No one called it the menopause then. 'The change,' they said. Anyway, I thought Millicent was queer. Not gay, like it means today. Just weird. Fussy. The typical old school marm."

An ageing yellow lab dozed by the fireplace. We were drinking strong tea from thick mugs. Beryl had her stocking feet up on the coffee table. Peter kept clasping and unclasping his hands around his knees. Beryl pretended not to notice.

"She's not the only neurotic teacher we've had here, God knows, but she sure stood out. Teachers haven't exactly been my favourite species of humanity. My parents used to board them when I was a girl and I was afraid when Millicent came I'd be expected to take her in. Mom was dead by then and Bill and I had moved in with Dad when Bill came back from overseas. I took one look at Millicent in that suit of hers and those pearls she wore and knew she'd drive me crazy in no time, but she said right away that she understood there was a private residence for the teacher."

"That would have been the teacherage, which was a pretty fancy name for an old log house with a privy in the back and a well with a pump. So I got together a bunch of bedding for her, and Dad and Bill carted over a desk. They say she used to sing hymns in there at night."

"Hymns?"

"At night, when she was alone. That's what they said anyway."

"Was Millicent a churchgoer?" I asked Peter, trying to draw him out. "I don't remember her going to church, but I know she received a Presbyterian church magazine. I know she used to listen to services on the radio but I can't recall her going to church."

"You had to go to Meredith for the Presbyterian church," Beryl said. "All we had here was this Holy Roller Baptist thing. I don't think she went there. I never heard of her going anyway, although I think she was friendly with the minister's wife. Church is long gone, minister and wife long gone too. Just like most of Shaw River. We had more people in those days than we do now. Most of the kids Millicent taught would have moved away."

"I can't imagine her singing hymns," I said. "At night, when she was alone?"

"Just repeating gossip," Beryl said. "You know how people talk. A teacher was supposed to be holier than thou, so if they heard her singing they probably thought it was hymns. Maybe she was drunk. She never bought booze in Meredith or at the bootlegger's out here, and believe me everyone would have known if she had, but maybe she brought it with her. She had this gigantic trunk with her, and several cases as well. She was a strange one all right. Polite, but opinionated as hell. I remember one time I had Benny out for a walk and along comes old Miss Mulvey and says, 'Mrs. Sofer, where is that child's sunbonnet? Do you want your little one to get sunstroke?' Always made me feel like I was still in school. Or as if she thought she was royalty and I was the little peasant."

"I always wondered if she'd had a lost love somewhere," I said. Peter shot me a look and picked up the cigarette roller and put it down. "Someone who died in the first world war or something."

Beryl snorted. The sound brought the dog to life. He lumbered over to Beryl's chair, sank with a sigh at her feet and gave me a dismissive stare.

Suddenly he jumped to his feet, ran to the door and barked. Beryl yelled at him, "Bunny, shut up!" but the dog paid no attention. The hair stood up on his back and he snarled and pawed the door. "Bunny!" The dog ran to her and barked, dashed back to the door. Beryl got up and looked out of the window. "There's no one there! Down! Get down!" The dog reluctantly dropped to the floor, but he continued barking. "If I let him out he'll just run down the road," she said. "He thinks he's heard something but there's no one out there unless it's a ghost."

"Down, stay," she told the dog, who gave one more bark before settling with a thump and sigh by the door.

"I don't know who he thinks is out there," Beryl said, settling back in her easy chair. "Now where were we?"

Peter stood up and went to the front window.

"Don't worry. There's no one there," she told him. "Anyway, it's broad daylight. We don't even get the Sunday hunters any more these days. We're all too law-abiding. Millicent's lost love? I can't imagine a man being interested in her. Oh, you could tell she'd been good-looking in her time, but my God! Fussy! Bossy! Maybe a wimp, who knows? Not a real man anyway. Dad liked her though. Not that he was a wimp. But Mom was a teacher when they met. From away. Dad even invited Millicent for supper. I could have killed him. He was a MacIntosh. That was my maiden name, MacIntosh. They used to discuss the Scottish thing."

"Stop looking out of the window," she told Peter. "Are you ever jumpy. This old dog's always hearing things and you're just making him worse."

Peter sat down.

"So she came for dinner," I prompted. I glanced at the window. I thought of the tires, but Hugh said one Lester Saulnier was the culprit. This Lester had been barred from the hotel and our tires weren't the first damage he'd caused.

"Yup. She came." Beryl got another cigarette out of the canister and stuck a match on the wood stove. "She did indeed. It was October, her second year here. I know it was October because I cooked a deer roast. Deer roast and potatoes and turnip and peas. Her Highness in her pearls took one sniff and said she couldn't possibly eat deer meat. And turnip gave her indigestion.

"She did eat the pie, though, and she drank her tea. And then she left. Eat and run. Dad was hoping we'd play cards after supper, but Millicent wasn't having it. Wouldn't even let Dad walk her home. Wanted to enjoy the stars and the moonlight alone, she said."

"Maybe she was unhappy," I suggested.

"She could have been sociable at least," Beryl said. "Nope. She was different, that's all. Oh, she was a good enough teacher, strict, but all teachers were strict then, and some of those big boys in school were regular little hooligans. She had her hands full with them. So there was nothing said against her about her teaching."

"They talked about her? Other than the hymns?"

"People wondered. Coming way up here at her age when she left a perfectly good position down south. They just thought it was strange. This is quite the tale for your book. You probably want to know more about the school."

"You said it was a one-room schoolhouse," I said.

"With the teacherage behind it. Another privy for the school. The school shared the well with the teacherage. The boys had to bring in wood for the stove but it was the teacher's job to get a fire started in the morning."

"What are you looking at?" she asked Peter. "You have one nervous husband," she told me.

I told her about being out late at the hotel in Meredith, about the front tires being flat.

Beryl asked about the spare tire— regular size or one of those small ones? (Vehicles are always a big topic of discussion around Meredith.) Then she wanted to know what happened to the tires. I told her what Hugh had said. She knew the name.

"That would be Lester Saulnier. He'll end up with a knife in him one of these days, if he doesn't end up killing himself first with booze."

"Did Millicent get her mail at the store?" I asked.

Beryl gave me an odd look, as if the question was just too pointed, too strange.

"She probably got rent cheques. She had a house she rented in Guelph," I explained. "And I'm wondering about her ties to the outside world."

"Outside world? No one asked her to come here," Beryl said, frowning. "Sure she got her mail at the store. She'd walk over every day and talk to Dad. You say you're dedicating this book to her?"

"Don't worry. I won't include that gossip about the hymn business. I'm just trying to get an overview of her life. When I met her she was already an old woman. Her teaching days were long behind her."

Now Beryl asked questions: where and how had I met Millicent, where else had Millicent taught? I told her that I'd be looking around for people who knew her at the other places. "Although I'm not sure where exactly she did teach, not every school. I'll have to find out. She was here for two years, 1946 and 1947?"

"That's right. Bill came back from overseas in 1945 and Millicent arrived the next year. I know because we had Mrs. Ogilvy the year before and her husband returned and she had to give it up."

For a few minutes we talked about school hours, the Christmas concert, "graduation" in June. Millicent went home in the summer, Beryl said. I told Beryl that Millicent's mother had died in 1943. "Perhaps that's why she came up here, for a change. Maybe she had to stay close to Starleigh because of her mother and then her mother died and she could get away."

We were on easier ground now.

More tea? Beryl asked. She refilled her own cup. The dog whined at the door.

"Millicent was a good friend of mine but she kind of went downhill in the last years," I told her, "so it's interesting hearing about her way back when."

Small talk. Peter's eyes strayed to the window. The dog gave a quiet bark. Beryl said: "What on earth do you think is out there, Peter?"

"I think he's just anxious to get on the way," I said. "We have a long drive ahead of us."

Beryl shook her head.

"But at least have a look at the teacherage before you go. The school's torn down, but that old house is still standing. A mile down the road. Just look for it through the trees. You can make out where the schoolhouse stood."

We shook hands. Beryl walked us to the car. Bunny followed, sniffing the air, and gave a rumbling bark at the road.

"I don't know who's more uneasy, you or poor old Bunny," Beryl told Peter.

We almost missed the teacherage. It was easy to see where the school had once stood because the metal frame for the swings rose above a wilderness of alders and weeds, but behind that, what seemed to be a solid wall of firs had grown up. It was only when you came close that the squat darkness of the log cabin was visible, like pictures of the witch's house in *Hansel and Gretel*.

It was hard to picture "the teacherage" as a whole because it was so crowded in with trees. The logs were greying now, overgrown with moss, and the windows were boarded up. A rusted padlock was on the bulging front door. Maybe the entire building was no more than twenty by twenty feet, but it was difficult to tell for sure with the trees in front.

It was cool in the trees and little sunshine penetrated.

"We could break the lock," I said. I laughed. Peter didn't.

"First your headache, then that old dog spooked you," I said.

"Know what I packed in the trunk?" Peter asked.

"What?"

"My old .22. I even found some shells."

"What? Why?"

"I heard at the Texaco Centre that Lester Saulnier's been in the hospital with a bleeding ulcer since last week, so he wasn't the one who let the air out of our tires. So I took the .22. Just in case. I didn't tell Dad. I didn't want to worry you."

"This is crazy."

"Just in case," Peter said. "You never know. Don't look at me like that."

"That's why you were so nervous at Beryl's place when the dog barked."

"I woke up feeling nervous."

"You really think someone followed us here to Meredith? It could have been kids fooling around who let the air out of the tires."

"Maybe the goon saw the clipping before you took it. I just hope this is the last thing we're doing involving Millicent."

The forest was very quiet. I thought, briefly, of Millicent wearing her pearls here, the pearls "Ted" had given her, but this image was elusive. I shivered, listening for sounds in the trees, for branches snapping, birds chirping, but there was nothing. Only the stillness, and fifty feet away, the blackness of the northern forest.

A car horn tooted. We jumped.

It was Beryl, in her truck. Bunny sat up in the front seat with her. She tooted the horn again and jumped out, the dog at her heels.

"I just remembered," she said, "that Dad had a picture of Millicent standing outside the school. All his stuff's in the old house and Benny and his wife aren't home today, but when they're back I'll try and find it for you. Dad won a camera in a contest the *Readers' Digest* had and he went around snapping pictures. I'm pretty sure there's still one of Millicent around. If you give me your address, I'll send it to you."

I handed her a card. I always have cards with me in case people want to send me recipes. Beryl looked at it and stuck it in her pocket. Bunny sat unmoving beside her, but his ears were up, listening.

"This old place," she said, thumping the log wall. "Wouldn't even do for a camp now."

The dog woofed. "Quiet," she told him, "or you'll have Peter here thinking Bigfoot's in the woods. Now Sunday hunters I could believe, but Bigfoot..."

She tugged at the lock. It came open.

"Wasn't locked at all," she said. "These cheap locks, $2.99 at Canadian Tire. Looks like someone's picked it."

She swung the door open. Or, more exactly, she leaned her shoulder against the thick wood and pushed.

"Bet kids have been in here doing you know what," she said. "You might as well see what there is to see."

But even keeping the door open, it was hard to see anything at all, with the trees growing almost to the door. What struck me was that the teacherage did not have the foul, hideous odour of Millicent's boarded-up house, but that it smelled merely of old, damp wood and... something else. Something not entirely unpleasant, I thought, and then I had it: wooden matches, that faint smell I remembered from Maine, when I was twelve and sneaking cigarettes in a closed-up boat house. I could even smell the tobacco, pungent because the space was enclosed, and bitter but not unpleasant because the smell was like the American cigarettes I used to smoke.

Beryl brought her lighter out. "Just a flick of the Bic," she said, zapping the lighter a few times, so the flame shot up sporadically, revealing a rusted wood stove and an old desk, some shelves beside a window.

Bunny panted by the door.

"This place has really gone downhill," Beryl said. "This American was going to haul it away for a camp, but he had a heart attack before he got around to it. It sure wasn't this gloomy when Millicent lived here. Look."

She aimed the lighter at the floorboards.

I had been right. Five or six matches were scattered on the floor, and I could make out a cigarette butt too.

"Kids," Beryl said. "Someone should tear this place down. Before it burns down."

She gave one more flick of the Bic and then we were in darkness, just as— suddenly— Bunny started barking again, frantically this time, and then he was away from the door, thrashing through the bush.

"There's Bigfoot again," Beryl laughed.

Just before Beryl drove away, she leaned out of the truck window and said, "Forgot to tell you one thing. Millicent used to talk about going out west summers. To the farm, she said. Maybe she had a red hot lover out there!"

She tooted her horn as she left.

I drove and Peter slept. Someone at the hunting lodge had recommended a German restaurant, the Edel Haus, at Port Francis, which served venison flown in from a deer farm in Alberta, and we planned to stop there for dinner. We often have a meal on our way back from Meredith, although pickings are pretty slim. The good restaurants, the lodges, are deep in the woods, and along Highway 400, there's little beyond the inevitable fast food franchises.

Traffic was heavy with cottagers returning to Toronto after closing up cabins. I began to feel safer as the familiar tourist spots whizzed past. Knowing Lester Saulnier hadn't let the air out of our tires made me feel strange. And... there was something else I couldn't put my finger on, something that nagged at my mind but wouldn't quite come to me.

But overriding the strange feeling was the satisfaction I felt from Beryl's statements about Millicent's trips to "the farm" which of course meant the E.P. Ranch belonging to the Duke of Windsor in High River, Alberta, which he'd bought on his first Canadian trip in 1919. And if Millicent had mentioned going to the ranch, in the forties, it proved that her talk to me about the ranch had indeed been true. And why would she have kept on going out there for holidays if she didn't have some kind of real tie to the Duke of Windsor?

By the time Peter opened his eyes we were almost at the turn-off for Port Francis. His headache was gone, he said; he would drive the rest of the way.

It was a pleasant meal. The venison came with a sour cream sauce and red cabbage. Dessert was strudel. Peter had a German beer. It was a typical German restaurant, but a step above schnitzel kitsch. The beams were real wood and pewter plates stood on ledges. There was no Bavarian music. The owner waited on us. They were closing soon, she said, and going to Florida for the winter. We were the only customers.

It was almost dusk by the time we left. A car pulled into the Edel Haus parking lot as Peter drove out and a green truck idled on the opposite side of the road. Just an ordinary pick-up, the kind of truck you see around Meredith. A man wearing a cap at the wheel.

Suddenly two shots rang out. The glass in our rear windshield shattered and then we were heading for the ditch, while the truck squealed past and disappeared down the road, toward the highway.

It was all so fast; I recall the truck moving by just as we went into the ditch. That is all I know. We were both wearing seat belts and unhurt, although I banged my leg getting out of the car.

We walked— limped— stumbled— back to the Edel Haus. The owner looked annoyed. She had a table of four and Peter said, in a loud wobbly voice, that someone had shot at our car. The owner's husband came, a big blond man with a German accent who looked as if he'd just woken up from a nap. He hustled us into the apartment over the restaurant. His wife brought us coffee. The husband said the local hunters were worse than the animals they shot and called the Ontario Provincial Police.

The police came, inspected the car, and took statements. A tow truck arrived. The German watched and said he was all for getting a German Shepherd guard dog but his wife was against it. "Now maybe she will change her mind."

A reporter from the local weekly turned up just as they were hauling our car out of the ditch. The restaurant owner complained he had just bought an ad at the paper.

We arrived back in Guelph at eleven.

"This is it," Peter said. "Isn't it?"

"Yes," I said. "This is it. I promise."

We went right to bed and if this sounds as if we were stunned with panic and disbelief— we were. Finished, shocked, kaput.

CHAPTER
EIGHT

When in panic and suffering from fright and shock: do nothing. That is what we did the following week.

I did not write to the Queen. Peter took the car in for a new back windshield and body work and went to The Bookworm each day. As far as he was concerned, I was now through with Millicent's story. As far as I was concerned, I was through with it, too. At least for now.

I stayed at home and rearranged the bookshelves. I slept in until ten, eleven once. It rained. I baked bread and two kinds of apple pie, cooked a big batch of chili for the freezer. We rented videos at night. Only bills and flyers came in the mail. I got together a bag of clothes for the Salvation Army. The car was fixed and Peter took the clothes downtown and Cass asked if she could look through them first for the amateur drama group.

Peter kept the .22 under the bed, but we didn't discuss Millicent.

I decided to make a straw man for the porch for Hallowe'en. He would sit in a rocking chair. That involved buying stuffing, searching through second-hand stores for overalls, checkered shirts. Lots of the neighbours on our street, Lancaster Road, decorated for Hallowe'en. The old houses lend themselves well to this type of thing. People on Lancaster consider plaster dwarfs and black footmen tacky, but everyone jumps on the *au naturel* country bandwagon, and I spent a happy, mindless day fashioning my straw yokel. I made a soft-sculpture face and while I was sewing Marion called: had I had any luck obtaining an address for the royal archives? I was evasive. Next week,

I said; the car was still being repaired. She was reading a book about the abdication...

I walked downtown and bought orange wool for my yokel's hair, and extra pie plates, because I planned to use up the pumpkins after Hallowe'en for pies. That would take up a day.

I made fudge to hand out. I hollowed out two pumpkins, one for each side of my yokel.

Peter helped me carve the pumpkin faces and to "shell out," although he finds Hallowe'en annoying and each year suggests we go out for the night.

But this year we shared handing out the fudge wrapped in plastic wrap, bags of potato chips, miniature chocolate bars and pennies for the UNICEF boxes. Most of the kids were from our neighbourhood; we recognized their parents waiting on the sidewalk. Peter entered into the spirit of the thing, asking "Now who might you be?" "Aren't you the scary ghost?" "Going to fly off on your broomstick, are you?" without sounding too foolish.

By seven-thirty only a few older stragglers were coming to the door, and we sat down to eat our by-then limp pizza. The candy was running out. I brought up apples from the basement and Peter replenished the coins for the UNICEF boxes. We took turns answering the door.

"You go this time," Peter said.

It was eight o'clock. I looked out of the window. "There's a whole gang of them," I said. I could see five or six big kids milling around. "You give out the money and I'll do the apples," I told him.

"Let's hope that's the end of them," Peter sighed.

These kids were bigger, teenagers. We didn't do the "trick or treat" routine but they did it for us. "Trick or treat!" they cried in that kind of giggly way teenagers have, a little embarrassed but hoping to sound insolent. One kid said, "Got any razor blades in these apples?" "Only apples!" someone complained. And another: "You gonna hand in the UNICEF box? Don't be a sucker."

Then the last one held open his pillow case.

"Trick or treat?"

The voice was high-pitched and distorted, but obviously a man's. A nylon stocking covered his face and he wore a shiny black polyester wig, a long cotton red dress, and a shawl tied around the shoulders. A pearl necklace dangled over the stuffed bosom. He'd smeared lipstick on the outside of his nylon face.

As he held a pillow case out for us, I noticed he had gloves on. I dropped an apple into it. There was no UNICEF box, but Peter reached over my shoulder and threw a few coins into the bag.

"Trick or treat?" His real mouth twisted beneath the painted-on one. "Know who I am?"

"I'm sorry, I guess we've run out of candy," I said.

"Have to guess who I am! Who am I supposed to be now?"

"Lady MacBeth," Peter said.

"Guess again!" The tone was wheedling.

"Anne of Green Gables," Peter said and started to shut the door.

"I'm Millicent!" he laughed. "And what about the diary?"

Peter stiffened beside me. I grew hot, then cold. The mask leered at us.

A little goblin, accompanied by a mother, was turning in at our gate.

"Millicent" turned away, bent over in a grotesque parody of an old lady's walk. He called something over his shoulder, but the young mother was telling the child, "Say 'Trick or Treat' now. Hold your bag out, Johnny."

"I'm not Johnny. I'm a goblin!" the child cried.

"I had to work late," the mother explained to us, "but I promised I'd take him out and a promise is a promise, right?"

"Millicent" was lost in the shadows of the street.

CHAPTER
NINE

"...so I thought since Hugh'll be hunting, I could get to Guelph next week."

"Oh, next week..."

For the first time ever I didn't want to see Marion.

Peter and I were fighting. Real fighting; not mild bickering, but out-and-out war.

Without consulting him I had put several posters up around town:

Author Reading
Carolyn Archer
The Bookworm
Monday, November 11, 1985, 7:00 P.M.
Noted Guelph Writer, Carolyn Archer, author of *Country Ovens* and the forthcoming *Winter Ovens* will read from a work-in-progress, *Yesterday's Teachers*.
Come and hear about the lives of rural schoolmarms in long-ago Ontario.
Admission Free/Refreshments Served

Peter didn't yell or scream or swear at first. He just couldn't believe I would break my promise and do something like that behind his back and so on. I did the yelling: he was a wimp, he was a scaredy cat, he was a chauvinist who was trying to control my life and this control was emotional abuse.

That was when Peter yelled and called me a liar and a sneak. I had promised him and I had broken my word. And no, he was not emotionally abusive, he WAS NOT, WAS NOT. If anyone was emotionally abusive, it was I, who was endangering our lives. We had already been SHOT at, what more did I want?

But our Hallowe'en visitor had changed my mind about dropping the story. Whoever was behind everything might turn up at a reading.

And what was that about a *diary?*

By the time Marion called, Peter and I weren't speaking.

"Is anything wrong, Carolyn?"

"Everything's okay."

"Maybe next week is a bad time," she said, "but I thought with Hugh hunting, I could do a bit of Christmas shopping."

Without thinking it through, I told her about the reading, which I realized at once was a mistake. Marion had travelled down from Meredith for my one and only public reading at the Guelph library— all my other readings have really been talks in schools. Marion and I had also gone to a reading by Ruth Rendell at Harbourfront in Toronto, where so many authors read.

"A reading," she said. *Chirped* actually; at least this was how I translated her tone (annoying woman; for a minute she was the ogre mother-in-law).

"At The Bookworm actually. I'm going to read from the work-in-progress."

"You mean the teachers' book? But you've only just started it. I thought you were still researching Millicent Mulvey."

"I know, " I said listlessly. "Peter says the same thing."

She thought this over.

At last she said, "I was hoping we could go to the cemetery. If you're not too busy, that is. I'd very much like to see the stone. As far as Hugh's concerned I'm coming down to get a head start on Christmas shopping, which isn't completely a lie since I do want to look around. Did you compose a letter to the archives yet? I've found the address by the way. You write to the Queen and her secretary forwards the request to the archives."

"Not yet." My tone was sharp. I thought of Charlie's mother quizzing me on the phone: did Charlie attend church, was he eating enough, was he meeting the right kind of people or just people I knew through the newspaper?

I took a deep breath and told Marion I looked forward to her visit. She asked when the reading was and said she'd probably arrive on the weekend because someone going to Toronto had offered her a drive; Hugh would need the car when he went hunting.

Marion didn't arrive until the afternoon of the eleventh, the Monday of the reading. I had thrown together a few pages about a fictional school teacher, eighteen years old, who was teaching at her first school, boarding with a rough farm family. The "son of the house" was "sweet" on her, but she didn't want to marry; she wanted to teach. There were twenty-one children in her class; a few of the boys were almost as old as she was... It wasn't even shameless cribbing, because I hadn't been to the library; I just made it up out of my head, using the bits and pieces I knew from reading and from researching the cookbooks.

Peter and I had reached a truce, a cool truce, but a truce nonetheless. I would not mention Millicent; I would not, in Guelph, say that the book would be dedicated to her. I would not call the few newspaper people I still knew and plead for publicity.

But he was still angry and disappointed. Cornered, too. Once the posters were up, he had no choice but to go along with the reading, which Cass thought was a splendid idea, just wonderful. I was finally doing some writing with some political meat to it, was what she said.

Marion's driver turned out to be one of the Germans from the lodge. Max Halbers was over from Germany representing a group of businessmen who wanted to invest in Canada. He looked a little bit like Maximilian Schell and hadn't minded the extra miles beyond Toronto to deliver Marion to our door. Maximilian Schell or not, I wasn't in the mood for company, nor was I pleased when Marion said he'd invited us out for lunch at The Bookshelf Café, which she'd described to him.

Lunch over with (innocuous and not unpleasant), we talked about the countryside in the area and Max discussed readings he'd attended as a student, we trooped over to The Bookworm, where Max purchased a guide to southern Ontario and *Country Ovens*, which I autographed for him. Cass was in on her day off, arranging chairs for the reading, all in a dither because she didn't see how the store could accommodate the hundreds she was sure would turn up. "I keep suggesting to Peter we have story hour for kids here, but I don't see how we can have regular readings." Max said she wouldn't need a chair for him; unfortunately he had a business appointment in the evening in Toronto.

Peter was gloomy and preoccupied, and said Jake wanted me to call him. I went into the office at the back of the store.

"What's this about a reading?" Jake asked.

"How did you find out about that?"

"Peter's assistant ordered cookbooks. She wanted to have extra copies for the reading tonight. A book on teachers, Carolyn? I haven't heard anything about that before."

"It's connected to that other matter." Cass was within earshot.

"I thought for a moment you'd found another publisher."

"Don't be silly. This is just about the work-in-progress. I'll have to explain it all to you when I see you. I'm coming to Toronto soon."

"Henry would love a book on old teachers but I didn't think you'd be working on that."

"You thought right. It'll be interesting to see who turns up tonight."

"I get the drift now. You be careful, Carolyn."

At home, I told Marion everything.

"...and so the last straw was that person coming around on Hallowe'en and croaking out that he was Millicent and mentioning a diary. That was it for Peter, and probably he's right. But I just can't drop it."

She had listened passively to the whole tale, even to the story of the "break & enter," interrupting only to clarify a point, or to focus my thinking.

"Peter wants to forget the whole thing," I said. "It's just too dangerous and crazy, he says."

"I don't think those shots near Port Francis were aimed at you. Probably the fellow thought he saw a deer— you know how the deer come to the road at dusk. I really can't believe someone would shoot at you. I think the reading idea's just splendid. Peter will get over it. Am I going to see the stone?"

"We'll go tomorrow. And Wednesday we'll go to Toronto. I'm seeing Jake then. I want to explain about the teacher book to him. I couldn't tell him on the phone because Cass was right there. You don't think someone could have a bug put on our phone, do you?"

"It sounds rather far-fetched. You mustn't lose heart. Just keep telling yourself you're working on a story of historical significance. If Millicent did indeed marry Edward, she could have become his Queen and then the whole abdication would never have happened. Don't lose sight of that fact. You just concern yourself with Millicent. Just do what you set out to do— find out more about what really happened. Everything else will fall into place, I think."

As always, Marion made me feel better.

Cass was already at the store when we arrived at six-thirty, wringing her hands over the coffee-maker, moving the chairs around. She had made a display of my books and was going to introduce me, she said. She checked biographical data— born in Maine, in Guelph since 1971, married to Peter, and now working on a book about teachers long ago. "It's a wonderful idea," she said. "A lot has been written about farm wives in pioneer days but I can't recall much about teachers. In a way it was like being a nun in the middle ages, wasn't it? In the middle ages women either went into a convent where they could at least read and study, or they had to get married. And no birth control then or penicillin..."

She filled a pitcher of water for me, brought a glass. Marion settled herself on one of the rickety metal chairs, and assured Cass she would stand if space became limited.

I wore a dress Marion had made. It was more or less a copy of a Suttles & Seawinds dress we'd seen in a boutique at the Royal York— folksy and country— which I've worn for school talks, fitting the image of the cookbook writer.

Later we would go out for Chinese food and drinks— we'd only grabbed sandwiches earlier— and as I told Peter, "I can even get drunk tonight, the way poets do after they read."

The room filled. About twenty people turned up ("But we didn't advertise or anything," Cass whispered), most of them women, a couple of Cass' friends from university, a young poet whose readings I had attended. A woman asked if I minded if she taped my "talk"; she wanted to send my "speech" to her son in journalism school. I minded, but didn't like to say so.

Peter stood along the wall, beside the poet. My heart thumped. I peered at the women in their all-weather coats. There were no mysterious men present. But what if one of the women wasn't who she seemed to be?

Cass introduced me ("It gives me great pleasure...") and I took my place before the front counter, my school teacher piece ready. I would explain it was a new project, and then I would read selections from the cookbooks. And—

Answer questions.

The woman taping the reading moved out of her seat, to the front. "I have to be sure I get this," she explained. I read. Suddenly there was an echo in the room of my own voice. "Just testing," she said. I lost my place, found it; the faces watched me.

I didn't like the woman taping me.

But someone who wanted to tape me for nefarious reasons would have worn a wire. I took a sip of water. Lost my place again, coughed. People waited.

The door opened and Charlie Trott, my ex-husband, walked in. I hadn't seen him in years.

His entrance put me on automatic pilot. I had to perform now, with his beaming (smirking) face not fifteen feet away. He had gained weight, had become quite the porker in fact, and if he thought he could throw me, he had another thing coming, I told myself. I would show him, and after I finished the school teacher piece, I opened *Country Ovens* and read in a calmer, smoother voice about quilting bees and roof raisings. When I raised my eyes off the page, I looked straight at Peter, who smiled forgivingly (I thought).

I finished with a few Christmas recipes and read a passage about cutting the Christmas tree in the woods. I said my new book would have more Christmas recipes and stories in it.

"Thank you all for coming. It's been a pleasure reading to you. And I'd especially like to thank my mother-in-law, Marion Hall, who's come a great distance to attend my reading."

Applause.

Cass: "And don't forget— we have cookbooks for sale, signed by the author!"

"If there are any questions," I said.

The tape recorder woman was the first to raise her hand.

"What made you decide to write about school teachers instead of recipes?"

I answered that I'd heard so much about school teachers in doing research for the cookbooks, that the subject had more or less found me instead of vice-versa.

The woman asked if I could make a living with my writing. Her son wanted to write a novel but she'd made him study journalism. Did newspapers destroy talent? Had I ever considered writing a novel?

Then: "Have you known many old-fashioned school marms?"

I fielded that one too.

"Then how can you write about old school teachers? I thought you were supposed to write about what you knew."

The poet interrupted and asked if I wrote poetry.

Another woman wanted to know if she could get the recipes for the Dutch Christmas cookies. "Buy a book!" several people said.

Cass cut the questions off.

"We have coffee and cookies, and don't forget— cookbooks."

I had, indeed, gone into automatic pilot, but I had not forgotten about Charlie's presence. He had always been after me to "get the truth" out of Millicent. The story would be worth a bundle, he said. If I wasn't so dumb, I could get the truth out of her. Sweet-talk her; get around her; steal her secrets. Sell the story in New York; in England. Movie rights! Serial rights!

I sat behind the front counter, signing books. Cass handled the money.

Seven or eight people were waiting in line— the tape recorder woman had disappeared— and Charlie was at the end of it.

I signed and smiled. "Hope you enjoy the book." Peter and Marion were talking and neither would have recognized Charlie. Peter had never seen pictures of Charlie because I'd thrown them all out (dramatically burned them, actually). Marion knew I'd been previously married, but it wasn't something we talked about.

Then Charlie's turn came.

"Hi, stranger. Long time no see."

His round, chubby face grinned down at me. Years ago, he liked thinking he resembled Elvis Presley (he didn't), but now he was a chubby, navy "suit." His stomach bulged over his belt. His face looked greasy. When he put a cookbook down for me to sign, I thought that even his fingers appeared thicker. I could smell his shaving lotion. He was only thirty-eight, but he looked like a much older travelling salesman who enjoyed his expense account too much. Someone who liked dirty jokes, snicker, snicker.

"You can say 'For Gloria.' So how've you been?"

"Very well." I signed the book.

"I'm doing fine too," Charlie volunteered. "Bet you're surprised to see me."

"I am, rather." I pushed the book forward.

"I was in town and noticed the poster. In Guelph once a month. District Sales Manager, plumbing supplies. I thought, 'What the heck.' So here I am. Thought you would have flown the coop long ago."

"No, I'm still in Guelph."

"Saw in the Guelph paper that your friend died. That Millicent Mulvey."

"Yes, last month."

"She was how old? Ninety-five I think the paper said."

"That's right. And now— " I started to rise.

"You ever write about her? Find out anything?"

I shook my head and stood up.

"Often thought that would make a good story. Might even look into it myself. Write a book on her. I was just looking at the library file this afternoon."

"You're writing now, are you?" I said as coldly as I could and signalled Peter with my eyes.

"Just need a good story," Charlie said, as Peter reached us.

"It's like in business, you need a good idea, and I think I've got one with this Millicent thing. It's all ideas and marketing. How about going out for a drink?"

"I'm afraid not. My husband and I have plans for the rest of the evening," I said as Peter reached my side.

Charlie stuck out his hand. "Charlie Trott." Then of course Peter knew who he was. "You could say Carolyn and I go back a long ways," Charlie said as they shook hands.

Peter's face was cold, but Charlie wasn't deterred. He'd never been quick to pick up on signals.

"I was just telling Carolyn that I'm thinking of doing a book on that friend of hers, Millicent Mulvey. There's gotta be a story there. Royalty and all. Look how many people watched the wedding of Charles and Diana. Maybe it's a good thing Carolyn didn't write the story because that leaves the door wide open for me. And hey, I read someone broke into her house after she died."

I had to leave, but I knew my feet wouldn't work right then.

"Make a lot more money than with cookbooks," Charlie told me, holding up my book.

As I told Peter, it is permissable for poets to get drunk after readings. I'm not a poet, but cookbook authors have their muses, too, and I indulged myself accordingly.

CHAPTER
TEN

I awoke at ten-thirty, groggy from the night before. Two sickly, gigantic Singapore Slings and a plate of barbecued spare-ribs might have fed my muse, but they also resulted in a dry mouth and thick head.

I burrowed beneath the covers but my dream returned. Charlie had been in it and all I could see was Charlie's stupid grinning fat face at The Bookworm.

How simple it would have been if Charlie had taken the photos and committed the break-ins! Marion and I had debated that possibility in the Chinese restaurant, but I knew Charlie wouldn't have the guts. And he wouldn't have been able to keep his big mouth shut if he had the photos. Even Peter had to agree with that, although he pointed out that Charlie wouldn't have known about Millicent's death until he read about the break-in.

There'd been no obituary.

I got up and had a quick shower.

Standing under the hot water, I thought about bringing Millicent to our apartment, Charlie lolling on the couch and watching baseball on TV, a beer in hand, several empties next to his bare feet on the coffee table. He didn't get up to greet Millicent, just grunted and shot me a dirty look, because what was I doing with the old broad if I wasn't going to pump her for information? Wasting my time as usual, he would say later; just being my usual dumb, stupid self. "You don't know what he's like!" How many times had I gone to Millicent with plaintive cries of "Why did I ever marry him?"

But Millicent waited until Charlie departed the scene (with a woman from the finance company where he worked after he dropped out of school; not with the Gloria I'd signed the cookbook to) before criticizing my legally wedded spouse.

"It's time someone talked some sense to you, my girl," she told me while I wept. "Be glad you are rid of the rascal. Instead of your tears, you should be leaping for joy. That rascal has affected your brain, that's what it is. Your gaoler has taken himself away and now you are weeping!"

Charlie was a criminal, she said. He belonged in prison. The authorities should deport him back to the United States of America. I was too good for him.

Charlie was not a gentleman.

Ted had been a gentleman. Ted had never said one cross or unkind word to her. Ted knew how to treat a woman. "Whatever makes you happy, darling," Ted would say.

"If you had met him, you would know what a gentleman was," she said, "but you have been with that criminal so long I doubt if you would even recognize a gentleman today. Now dry those eyes. You've complained about that unkind husband of yours and now you're sobbing and moaning because the rascal is gone. Good riddance is what I say."

Coupled with this pep talk was Millicent's sensible advice: I was young; divorce wasn't a scandal "these days"; I had my whole life ahead of me.

Millicent, I thought, getting dressed.

Marion had coffee waiting for me. She was reading the newspaper clippings and Millicent's letters to the editor from the seventies.

"This woman is not a liar," she said. "How could anyone doubt her? Listen to this. 'I do not go to restaurants frequently, but on a recent excursion to Guelph, I visited a new establishment, Hamburger Heaven. My meal was tasty and fresh, and the price was right for a frugal Scotchman like myself, but the service left a great deal to be desired. As you know, I always stick up for the little guy and I am doing so here. In this case, the poor service was not the fault of the one waitress.

"'She was alone in the shop and had to serve the entire clientele. One customer was extremely rude and no one said "Thank you." It seems to me if the owners of this restaurant want the business to succeed, they had better not cut costs by hiring insufficient staff. I told the girl, "I know you are over-worked," and left a tip for her. She was only a poor working girl and it was not her fault that she could not keep up.'

"And she writes about the fate of farmers, about compensation for men injured on the job. I just don't believe she would have had that inscription put on her stone for no good reason. These letters have so much common sense and wisdom."

"I know. You don't have to tell me." I sipped coffee and nibbled toast.

"And the tone is entirely different in the interviews she gave. It's as if she doesn't want to talk there; as if, as she says, she's been told not to say anything."

"Did you read about the teacup? She lied about that. She told me so. She only said she'd painted the teacup because she didn't know what else to say. She was sorry about that. It was a silly thing to say."

"The reporter seemed to think so too," Marion said. "But I did find one interesting thing in the newspaper stories. In 1919 they said the Duke visited Galt— that's where the cemetery is, and wasn't Cambridge called Galt then?— and there were speculations at that time about the Prince being seriously involved with a Canadian girl. Where there's smoke there's fire, as they say. And in 1924, Governor-General Byng told Edward he wasn't allowed to return to Canada as long as Byng remained Governor-General. And it's surprising there's so little written about Edward's 1923 visit to Canada. Something must have been going on!"

After lunch Marion and I drove to the cemetery in Cambridge. "Going shopping," we told Peter, who chose not to ask questions.

The city of Cambridge is really the joining together of three smaller places: Galt, Preston and Hespeler. The total effect is haphazard, a collection of old limestone buildings near the Grand River, shady solid neighbourhoods, bungalows, shopping malls, factory outlets (Marion and I have been to a few) and down-at-the-heel taverns and bars. Once the area had been mostly Scottish, but Portuguese da Costas and O'Connors from Newfoundland have joined the original MacDonalds and MacKinnons.

Millicent had been born in Little Corners, a hamlet near Galt. "Cambridge" didn't exist when she was a girl and I enjoyed her stories of the Saturday night shopping long ago, the village fair, neighbours dropping in for tea and scones. "It sounds so much nicer then," I ventured, but Millicent was having none of this nostalgia. "Nothing stays the same. It is either backwards or forwards, and where would you have the newcomers live if it stayed the same? In the trees, I suppose," she sniffed.

But the Maple Grove Cemetery was still the same. It was a grey, overcast day, chilly, with a hint of snow in the air.

"It does bring it rather home, doesn't it?" Marion said, as we stood before the Mulvey stone. She had walked around it, reading out loud the inscriptions for Millicent's parents, her maternal grandparents, and her two siblings who had died in childhood.

Now Marion stood in front of the stone with her Instamatic and read: "Wife to Edward VIII, Duke of Windsor, 1894 - 1972."

She snapped the picture.

"I wonder if the Royals have seen this," she mused. "I wouldn't be surprised if they have."

"Perhaps they have," I said. I'd given Millicent pictures I'd taken for her. I never saw them again.

"Carolyn!"

But it was only old Alvin Fleischer, a newspaperman who'd been around the area forever. Alvin had his camera bag with him.

"Just like Grand Central here." He grinned at me and nodded at Marion. "Not much light today," he said, peering at the Instamatic. And to me: "Your better half was here earlier getting a shot. My camera jammed, had to go back for another camera body."

"Peter was here?" Marion asked.

"Peter?" Alvin looked at me.

I got it: I hadn't seen Alvin for years, not since before Charlie and I were divorced.

"You mean the ex," I told Alvin. "That's ancient history. I've been remarried for years. This is my mother-in-law, Marion Hall."

"I'm just an old fool," Alvin said. "Don't pay any attention to me. Charlie didn't say, he didn't tell me."

"He wouldn't." I could just imagine it: Charlie blabbing about my cookbooks so Alvin would talk about Millicent. "I gave a reading last night in Guelph and Charlie turned up. He said he wanted to write a book about Millicent."

"That's what he said, you and him. I wondered about you getting involved in this." Alvin was taking his gear out. He glanced at his watch. He had another assignment, he said. A damn church bazaar, and retirement next spring couldn't come soon enough for him. "No story here anyway," he said, testing the light. "If you want a reprint of my picture, let me know. Get you one. Doubt if that little camera'll pick up the details."

"You don't think there's a story here?" Marion asked.

"Nope. Just a fairy tale, but the paper wants to run something. Local interest. Beats bazaars and pie sales anyway."

We watched him taking his pictures and chatted a while, catching up on gossip. I told him about Peter's book store, and manoeuvered the conversation back to Charlie. Alvin laughed. Charlie had repeated his belief that he had a bestseller in the bag.

"I told him there was nothing in it. And then this old guy came along and Charlie collared him. Didn't mean to upset you, by the way. I had no idea you two had split."

"What old guy?"

"Just this old fellow. Little old guy. Guy in a raincoat. Charlie was still talking to him when I took off to get my other camera. And now you're here. Grand Central, I tell you."

"I just wanted to show Marion the stone. I did know Millicent, by the way."

"So you think there's anything to the story?" Alvin didn't sound very interested. Just polite.

"Oh, I don't know. She was just a friend. She never mentioned it to me. What kind of car did the old guy drive? Did you see?"

For a second Alvin looked curious.

"Millicent had an old friend in the area," I lied. "She mentioned him often. She knew him when she was young. I thought I'd like to meet him. You know, tell him I'm sorry about her death. But I can't recall his name."

"And you're going to find him from a description of his car?" He put his camera down. Marion poked me and Alvin noticed.

"Do you remember what kind of car he had?" I persisted.

An orange VW van, perhaps?

"I could ask Millicent's old neighbours about someone in a blue Pontiac, say. They might remember the name then."

Alvin looked suspicious. I knew what he was thinking, and why he was thinking it. He was due to retire soon and what if— what if— he could go out with a bang of a story? He probably didn't give two cents for royalty, but it could be a scoop. And he knew Millicent was a friend of mine.

Our eyes met. I hadn't known Alvin well in my newspaper days, but I recalled covering a local campus demonstration with him in the seventies. If he had anything, he wasn't going to give it away.

But then he proved he did not have anything, because he was telling me what he knew, which obviously, he concluded, was of no value.

"You should talk to Owen Peterson."

"Is he at the paper?"

"You kidding? Not even freelance, though he'd like to be. He's in the newsroom every other week with an idea. Off the wall, you know? UFOs in Cambridge. Lately he's been on the Mulvey thing. I don't know what he's got, but I bet it's not much."

"Owen Peterson, I'll remember that. So did you notice the car this old guy had?"

"Oh, some kind of old navy Plymouth. Shined-up to hell and back."

"Did you tell Charlie about this Owen character?"

"I thought it would serve him right to get tangled up with Owen."

I knew why Marion had poked me: pump the reporter for all you can get. Like many people, she has the touching belief that reporters have ways of getting information, that they are almost like private eyes.

But I knew Alvin had no information beyond the tidbit about this Owen Peterson. Years ago one newspaperman had speculated that the only way to prove Millicent's story would be to unearth a marriage certificate. Presumably this had been tried, possibly by a reporter telling Statistics Canada that he was a relative, and obviously, the attempt had failed.

We drove to the library, looked in the city directory for Owen Peterson, and went to a doughnut shop.

"Maybe the man that photographer saw was the Englishman who visited Millicent in the hospital," Marion suggested. "The fictional half-brother."

"Somehow it doesn't sound right. An old car, all spit-polished? I think this Englishman would have a rented car. I don't think he's anyone local. He wouldn't have represented himself as a relative if he'd been from around Guelph. Guelph isn't such a big place. The nurse said he was distinguished-looking. Somehow 'old guy in a raincoat' doesn't sound distinguished."

"Maybe this Owen fellow will know. Why don't you go and make your phone call? I can't stand the suspense."

I dialed Owen Peterson's number and found that Charlie had already talked to him.

"First the husband, then the wife!" Owen said. "Your husband just left here. It's a good thing he told me your name or I wouldn't have known you were married! But don't feel bad. You're not the only one using her own name these days. I bet you use 'Ms.' too."

Charlie, you asshole.

"You are now Mrs. Trott," I told Marion. "You are visiting from New Jersey."

Marion said it was clever I'd caught on right away. It was a game with her. But not with me, I thought, as I drove across town to Owen Peterson's highrise apartment. I knew Charlie's thought processes. I was somewhat known locally; my cookbooks, on display in so many stores in the area, would give him some legitimacy; he could claim, rightly, that I had been a good friend of Millicent's. I could picture his fat face when he related these details and hear his smug voice saying, "Yes, my wife and I are in this together. With her knowledge and my marketing know-how..."

I was going over the speed limit, half-listening to Marion's idle chatter ("...I'll have to remember, from New Jersey. I've never been to New Jersey, have you?" and so on), and I almost missed the orange Volkswagen van tailing us at first. I stepped on the gas, pushing the speedometer up to seventy, twenty kilometres above the city speed limit.

The van was two cars behind. I couldn't make out the face of the driver, but he was wearing dark sunglasses.

I signalled right. The right side blinker on the van flickered. But would someone tailing me be so noticeable? I remembered from thriller movies that cars following would often go ahead, then backtrack and return to where the first car had turned off.

I veered right and squealed into another doughnut shop lot. Marion was still talking. "What's wrong? Are we lost?"

The doughnut shop was on a corner lot. The VW drove by on the street, and I followed.

"Watch for an orange van," I told Marion.

The driver was going slowly. For a minute, I caught dark glasses in the reflection of his side mirror. And a broad face.

"Hold on," I said and pulled off to a side street.

We were in an industrial area of factories and warehouses. There wasn't much cover here, and I drove into the parking lot of a company that manufactured windows. Our car was partially shielded by a large semi.

"Are you sure we're really being followed?" Marion asked.

I started to answer, but the van was coming along the road now, the way we had come. The driver must have realized he'd lost us and turned back. He was driving slowly, looking to the right and left, turning those awful sunglasses from side to side.

And now he was driving past us, past the Volvo behind the large semi.

He saw us. The van veered but he righted it and stared right at us and stopped, idling the motor.

My impression had been right: a broad, fleshy face, half-hidden by very dark glasses, almost like glasses the blind wear to hide scars. His collar was up and I glimpsed heavy hands, big hands in dark leather, on the steering wheel.

The driver, unmoving, stared at us from behind the black glasses, as if he wanted to memorize our faces.

This wasn't an old guy in a raincoat. There was strength, malevolence, in the thick face, in those large hands.

Someone banged on the window.

A truck driver.

"You ladies okay?"

"Just lost our way. We took a wrong turn back there. We're from out of town," I said, as the orange van emitted a blue cloud of smoke from its exhaust and drove away.

Owen Peterson was too full of himself to realize we were nervous.

He was a small man, mid-fiftyish, on a disability pension from the post office. An amateur historian. Struggling writer. ("Your husband said he'd get information about a literary agent from you and now here you are!")

My story was that Charlie and I were splitting up the research on Millicent. We had obviously crossed our wires because I thought Charlie wanted me to contact Owen and now Charlie had already been here.

"Unfortunately I don't have my address book with me, but I'll send you the name of some literary agents," I told Owen. "I'll get it in the mail to you first thing tomorrow morning. Did Charlie say where he was going after here? I won't be in touch with him until this evening."

Marion fidgeted beside me on Owen's flowered sofa. His apartment was dreary, littered with coffee cups, newspapers, books of the unsolved mystery variety. The flowered sofa and dowager drapes didn't go with the clutter. I wondered if he'd had a wife once. There was a thick layer of dust over everything and the room reeked of stale cigarette smoke.

"A two-city marriage, I understand," Owen said. "Him in Orillia and you in Guelph. I hope he finds a house soon so you can move."

"So do I," I said.

"When you talk to him tonight, tell him I've considered his proposal."

"He'll be glad to hear that." I had no idea what Owen was talking about. "He'll be glad you've made a decision."

"Well, I've had the experience." He got up and went to the cardboard filing cabinet by the window, in front of the pulled drapes. A single philodendron sat on top, and even that hardy plant was yellowed and dying from the lack of light.

He pulled the drawer open and read out what were obviously the titles of articles he'd written: "MacKenzie King's Boyhood: A Prime Minister's Childhood in Kitchener"; "The Post Office in Rural Ontario"; "The Future of Unions"; that kind of thing.

"I've got a dozen queries out at all times," he said happily, returning to his lazy-boy chair. "That's been my philosophy all along and soon or later someone'll bite."

"Charlie's lucky to have your expertise," I said.

Owen nodded. "My expertise and your husband's organizational abilities." Suddenly he looked at Marion. "You did say you're from New Jersey, didn't you? I've got an article on Atlantic City, if you'd like to see it— "

I thought he was going to head over to the files again, so I opened my purse and took out a notebook.

"And my part in this is supposed to be keeping track of everything, so that we don't all run around doing the same thing," I said.

"And your contacts," Owen added. "Your invaluable, wonderful publishing contacts. You have to admit you are a published author."

"But just cookbooks," I said.

The conversation had a surreal edge to it. My hand shook as I opened my notebook.

Owen was too wrapped up in the prospects of fame and fortune to notice. I let him blather on for a few minutes before I cut him short.

"I just want to check if Charlie did talk to that old gentleman he met in the cemetery today. We had coffee afterwards and he was going to call him."

"The old fellow. In the Thistledown Seniors' place, down by the Grand? He was on his way there, you won't have to bother. The old guy said he knew her too, just like you did. Amazing, isn't it, how we'll all be working together? Maybe next time this year we'll be drinking red wine in Paris together. On the left bank. Oh my. Wait till you hear about what I dug up. Those fools at the paper are going to be sorry, but they wouldn't listen to me. And it was there all the time, right in her mother's obituary."

This time I didn't stop him when he went to the files.

"Right here. Have to remember to get it photocopied tomorrow for when Charlie gets back. Said I'd send it on to Orillia, but he's moving out of his motel, he said."

"You could send it to me. I'll leave my card."

I put it on the table, shoving over a pile of newspaper clippings on the Loch Ness monster.

"...and survived by a daughter, Miss Millicent Mulvey, of Campbellville, and a foster son. A foster son! Of course that would be Millicent's child. I always thought she had a child with the Duke."

And here he did an incredible thing, which only added to the unreal aspect of this visit: he put his arms together, as if rocking a baby.

And they would not let me have my babies. She only said that once and I thought she meant she hadn't been married long enough to have children.

I held my hand out for the clipping.

"I could have this photocopied for you. I'll do it right now if you like and get it back to you."

But he didn't like. He'd be going to the library himself before too long. Maybe even tonight. He practically lived at the library, he said.

He hovered anxiously over my shoulder while I studied the clipping. I could smell his sweat and dirty clothes.

"I'll get you a copy, don't you worry," he said, taking it back.

It didn't matter. I'd seen the date on the clipping.

"What did Charlie say that old fellow's name was?" I asked Marion. "I should write it down before I forget."

"Looks like you've forgotten already," Owen said. "I should let you have my article on 'Improving Your Memory in Thirty Days.' I just wrote to the *Readers' Digest* about that. I'm thinking of writing to the *Saturday Evening Post* too, but I hate to do multiple queries. Not professional, the writers' books say."

"Wasn't he called— ?" Marion looked at me. "I must be getting Alzheimer's. It's just on the tip of my tongue."

"McDrew," Owen said, pleased with himself. "George McDrew. Old friend of hers. Do I detect an English accent there? From New Jersey?" he asked Marion.

Marion said she'd been a war bride. Owen Peterson slapped his thigh. "Bingo! I've got an article on war brides too! We really are all in tune, aren't we?"

Owen rummaged in the files. I pocketed my business card.

We returned to the library and found the address for the Thistledown Seniors' Home, which we found listed as the Thistledown Arms.

It was almost four now and a few snowflakes were starting to fall. Some of the stores had Christmas lights on. I felt weary. The decorations didn't give me that tingling, expectant pre-Christmas feeling, but looked tawdry and sad, the way they do in January.

I should have been excited about seeing George McDrew, but I kept expecting to see the orange van again.

CHAPTER
ELEVEN

George McDrew lived in apartment 807 of the Thistledown Arms, a highrise near the Grand River. I buzzed the number.

"Yes?" Ya-ess: an old man's quavery voice, cautious and suspicious. Sleepy, as if he'd just woken up.

"Mr. McDrew? You don't know me. My name is Carolyn Archer and I was a friend of Millicent Mul-"

The intercom shut off. There was no buzz to admit us through the security entrance.

"Now what? I guess we wait," I told Marion.

I buzzed again. There was no response, but two women entered the lobby, their arms filled with parcels. One wore a mink coat. This wasn't a nursing home, but simply an apartment building for seniors. And a pretty pricey one at that, I judged. A sign at the back read "Whirlpool and Sauna." There were comfortable chairs beside the elevator.

"It is rather chilly out, isn't it?" Marion said.

It's as Peter says: an English accent gets you far in rough-and-tumble Canada. The woman in mink took a key ring out of her alligator purse, unlocked the door, and admitted us with a smile.

Marion kept up the chit-chat in the elevator. From Toronto, she said; visiting her uncle. The women believed her. "You're not driving back tonight? They've forecast snow. You know what the 401 is like, and at night too." "Florida can't come soon enough."

"You realize I didn't tell them whom we're visiting," Marion said, after our companions got off on the 5th floor. "It seems that the less one says in this business the better."

Then the elevator doors opened on the 8th floor and a man stood there who could only be George McDrew. For a minute he studied our faces and then he pulled a gun from his pocket.

With his other arm he reached behind me to hold the elevator button. Marion's face turned white. We moved out of the elevator and to the side, away from the gun.

"I've had enough of this foolishness," he told me. "I've had it up to here. And you," he said to Marion, "I don't know who you are, lady, but you just turn around and go down the way you come up. This don't concern you. So git."

He motioned with the gun, but in doing so his hand came off the elevator button and he tottered. For a minute I thought he would trip. The gun was large, black, and, I judged, old. It looked too heavy for his hand, which barely fit around the butt. The elevator doors slid shut behind us.

"Certainly not," Marion said.

"You don't see this?"

He showed her the gun.

"I certainly do see that you have a gun. They'll think you are senile and put you in a nursing home with the Alzheimer's people."

He mumbled something I could not catch. We could hear the elevator descending.

"You had better put the gun away, hadn't you?" Marion said. "Before anyone else sees you with it."

"She's the one I want, her." George McDrew muttered, looking at me, but he lowered the gun to his side.

He made a move to grab my arm, but it was easy to evade him. He was about as big as a twelve-year-old child, and the wrists that protruded from his stretched-out grey sweater (very much like one Peter keeps in the store) were frail and sad. He was wearing brown plaid carpet slippers. But his clothes were clean, he was shaven, his thin white hair was brushed. His eyes, behind thick glasses, were milky blue.

"I know you're not going to use the gun," I said quietly. I wasn't afraid of him. I had never seen him before, yet he seemed familiar. "It's probably not even loaded. I only want to talk to you."

His eyes gauged me. They were more reserved than threatening. Yet there was steel in that milky blue. And anger, too.

"Don't you know I was a friend of Millicent's? A good friend. I adored her," I told him. I kept my eyes on his.

He swallowed. His adam's apple moved in his wattled throat.

George McDrew dropped his gaze first.

He stuck the gun in his pocket.

"She's got nothing to do with Milly." He looked at Marion. His voice changed when he said "Milly." I had never called her that and I didn't know of anyone else who had. "How do I know she's not one of them from the old country?"

"She is my mother-in-law, Marion Hall, and she lives in Meredith, Ontario. Millicent taught there once, long ago."

"Sure," he said, "and that fellow today was your husband. I set him straight all right."

"Charlie and I were divorced a long time ago. Millicent didn't like him. You know whom I'm married to now, don't you? You know Peter. You've seen Peter. You saw him when you came to our house on Hallowe'en, for one thing." I had made a wild guess, but it worked. George led us down the hall.

Unlike Owen Peterson's apartment, George McDrew's place was neat and orderly. There was no dust, the carpet looked clean, an African violet flowered on the window ledge.

A tintype photo of a sour-faced woman I took to be George McDrew's mother sat on a small bookcase filled with a few brightly jacketed books, book club selections probably, next to old volumes that looked like school books. A stack of *Readers' Digest* was on the little table next to his recliner. A Hudson Bay blanket covered the sofa. The blanket was rumpled, but he straightened it before we sat down. A newspaper opened to the crossword puzzle lay on the coffee table, and next to it, a magnifying glass.

It wasn't a bad place. Only a few touches— a tin plate from Florida nailed to the wall, a plastic placemat under Mama's photo, a windmill constructed out of popsicle sticks— showed that "a woman's touch" was missing.

We all sat and looked at each other. George had the good manners to look embarrassed. This was probably the first time in his life he had threatened women with a gun.

He reminded me of old men in Maine, tough, silent, taciturn fishermen, gnarled with arthritis, who wouldn't give up the sea. My grandfather had been like that, a fisherman who'd married "above himself." He died not long after I went to live at my grandmother's. The memories I have of him are of a small man getting up at dawn to light the fire before setting out for the shore. By the time I was up, he was back, having his tea and eggs. He always poured some of his tea into my glass, diluting it with lots of sugar and milk. When he went to town to have his hair cut, he came back with his pockets filled with candy. He liked to take me to see the ducks on the water. But I can't recall a single word he ever said to me.

Once Millicent wrote a letter to the editor about an old neighbour who had done her a favour, which she called "a great goodness." Men like George McDrew— and my grandfather— would do "a great goodness," I knew, and as I looked into his pale pale blue eyes, our eyes locked again.

Finally he excused himself and went into the other room. I heard a bureau drawer being shut. He was probably putting the gun away.

"You must have grown up in Galt with Millicent," I ventured, when he returned.

"Never met her till Starleigh. Then it was in Guelph. But then I went and moved over to Galt to be near Eva.

"My sister," he added, "but she's long gone."

We sat some more.

George McDrew broke the ice. "Trying to put one over on me, that fellow."

"But I had nothing to do with Charlie coming here today! You met him at the cemetery, didn't you? And there was a man from the paper there too, taking pictures. I worked with that reporter a long time ago. He was there again when we went to the cemetery, and he told me about Charlie being there, and Charlie saying we were still married.

"Charlie wants to find out about Millicent and for some reason he thinks if he says he's still married to me, it'll improve his chances. Because of the cookbooks I write, you see. He wants to make a lot of money out of Millicent's story."

"He's not finding out anything from me!" George McDrew said with vigour. "I was fool enough to let out where I lived and then he come here but I didn't let him in."

He didn't sit like an old man, all crumpled together in his recliner, but pushed forward, with his elbows on his knees.

"I did not let him in, no I didn't! He's having no part in this."

"But why point a gun at me? Why did you think I ought to do something with the diary?" I didn't want to mention Hallowe'en again directly. "What—" What diary, I was going to add, but he cut me off.

"You have it, don't you? I saw you take it. You and your husband."

"You were there that night, in Starleigh?"

"I saw you. I was there. At the end of Governor, right where it makes a curve. Didn't have to follow you or nothing. Know your car. I've seen it before, many a time. Maybe Milly and I were on the outs, but I kept an eye on her. She knew it, too. But she wouldn't have anything to do with me after I took the diary. 'You just give it back and then we'll see,' she said. But I wouldn't give it back. Not for her to burn. So we didn't talk any more."

"When was this?" It wasn't at all clear to me what he was talking about; "when" seemed a good point to start with.

"Longer than I care to remember. The only reason I'm talking to you now is because you have the diary. What did you do with it, burn it? The way Milly wanted? Is that what you did?"

"I didn't burn it. I wouldn't do that." I decided to let him think we had found the diary too, but did he know about the pictures?

"Then why're you keeping it secret? That's what I want to know."

"If you had the diary, why did we find it in Millicent's house?"

"Ask a question and you get a question back," he said.

"I guess we're all asking them," I said. "There are enough questions to ask."

He looked at me impatiently, as if I didn't understand a thing. And I didn't.

"Questions," he said at last. "That's what I can't have, questions from all the nosey parkers. Poking in and asking questions which ain't no one's business but Milly's."

"But you wanted the diary found. You put it there."

"Right in back of *his* picture. I figured someone would come along. All that talk in the paper about documents she had. And I didn't have to wait very long, did I? Not even an hour. What with her gone, I knew someone would come to find out what it was all about. I told Milly: 'You've gone and put the thing on the stone and it's time you told the rest.' But she said it wasn't her idea to have it put on. Not her idea at all. And they'd said not to tell. But they had to let her keep the papers so she could have it put on the stone. Then she was to give over the papers, but she still had the diary. They knew she had something written down, but she didn't want to hand that over to them. Not for them to read. So she told them she burned it. But she didn't, not then. Wanted me to burn it. And I wouldn't let her do it. So I took it. Never thought it would come between us like it did."

"But it did?"

"I wouldn't give back the diary, would I? Not for her to burn. I stopped her once. That was enough. She said, 'George, you throw the match in,' and I looked in the barrel and there was the little book I give her back in '19. She was in Starleigh a couple of years then. That's when she went on her trip, the war being over. To Halifax, like she wrote about, and where she met him. The truth would come out, she said. *They* would look after it, after she was gone. That's what they told Milly.

"I had this letter, could I come. So of course I come, I was only living in Guelph then, Milly was back in Starleigh. Just a hop, skip and a jump. 'I just can't burn it myself, destroy all those memories. You do it, George,' she said. So I grabbed the book out of the barrel and she tried to grab it back. But I wouldn't give it back. It's all she had left. They made her get rid of the other things."

"Other things?"

"Pictures, she had. Her and him. On their wedding day and out at the ranch there, in Alberta. I recognized it right off. Some by the house, out in front, and others under the trees with the two of them and some of the high-and-mighty folks from the old country. Wouldn't I know Milly in pictures to see her? And him— I'd know him anywhere. Met him once too, overseas in the war. In France, there. Shook his hand. Not that you had to meet him to recognize that face. In all the papers, all over the place. So there they were in the pictures Milly had. And the one of them after they got married, Milly in this fancy dress."

"You saw these pictures?"

"Milly had them, didn't she? Saw them with my own eyes. She brought 'em back from Alberta with her, when I went and got her.

"After all she went through I wasn't going to let her come home all by herself, was I? I just got on the train and went and brought her back. But you know all that, from the diary."

Marion spoke for the first time. "I haven't read the diary if it'll make you feel any better. I wouldn't think of reading it."

"But that's the point of it! You're supposed to read it! Without the diary they'll say she's crazy like they wrote in the newspaper. An old lady with her dreams, they said. Like none of it happened. And sure as I'm sitting here, it happened. That's what I've been telling you. I saw the certificate too, all signed, legal and proper. Only he didn't use his real name, didn't sign it 'Edward' which is what he always signed."

He spoke awkwardly, all in a rush, as if he had this big story in his head that he had to tell, but he didn't quite know how to do it. He had probably rehearsed it many times during the night hours when he couldn't sleep for worrying about the diary, which had been the cause of the loss of Millicent's companionship and friendship. He reminded me of when I taught a creative writing class once for Adult Recreation and people writing their life stories would say, "You know what I mean," because the story was so big and complete in their heads, so all-consuming, that they did not know where to start.

"Royalty don't sign with their last names. No they do not. Only he couldn't sign like a prince so he signed 'Ted Renfrew,' for Baron Renfrew, which is what he called himself sometimes. That was in the diary, too."

"Yes, I know," I said, trying to keep the facts straight in my head: Millicent asked George McDrew to burn a diary, but he took it instead. *They* had taken the marriage certificate after she had the inscription put on the stone at their request. But George McDrew had seen the certificate and photographs.

And someone must have gone to Millicent's house just before I got there and removed the diary, I thought. How had they done this without George McDrew seeing them? Had they left in such a hurry that they didn't have time to find the photographs? I wondered.

"I told her and told her she should hang on to the certificate, but they said she had to hand it over after the inscription was on the stone and they would look after the rest. Bring her story out when she was gone, they said. I told her not to trust them. But she wouldn't listen, Milly wouldn't. She could be one stubborn woman, I tell you. And there's many a time I wished I could just give her the damn diary back and to hell with them and we could be friends again. But I knew she'd just go and burn it, and then there'd be no proof to her story, none at all. I wasn't going to have any part of making her the laughing stock of the whole entire world.

"Just because she wasn't royalty, they said. That's why they couldn't let the marriage be. And then they made her have it on the stone. Burns me up to think about it. And look who he took for his second wife. That American Jezebel. Poor Milly."

"That must have killed her."

"Damn near."

He fell silent and traced a pattern on the carpet with his slipper.

"Wallis Simpson," Marion said.

"That's a name I don't care about hearing," George McDrew said.

Silence again.

"She knew it was coming," he said at last. "Milly knew. He wrote her. She knew before the newspapers or anyone. She told me, too. No one else. Except her mother. I read the letter."

"Can you tell us what the letter said?"

"No, I don't think I can. I gave her my word. I burned that one all right. Put it in the stove. You know those stoves people had?"

"They still have stoves like that in the country around Meredith," Marion said. "Up north."

"Then you know what I'm talking about. I just took the letter and dropped it into the stove in my place in Guelph. Had Milly over. Just had a feeling things wasn't right and they wasn't, neither. So I went over and took her for a drive like I sometimes did and then we went to my place and she showed me the letter. Still have the kitchen table where we was sitting."

He waved his arm to the rear of the apartment. I could see a refrigerator through the archway.

"Same table," he said, "and she sat there and watched when I put the letter in the fire. And didn't say a word, neither."

"You must miss her," I said. "I know I do. She helped me a lot when Charlie and I split up. If it hadn't been for her, I don't know what would have happened to me."

Incredibly, I found myself telling the story of Charlie's girlfriend at the finance office. I told everything, not caring that Marion, who'd never heard the story, was hearing it now.

"You stick to that husband of yours, the one you're married to now," George McDrew told me, when I was through. "Yes, that husband of yours is a good one. He's a gentleman all right."

This brought tears to my eyes. George McDrew was a gentleman. He pretended not to notice my quavery voice when I asked why he hadn't just given the diary to a writer, someone at the newspaper, for instance.

"It's like I said, I can't have all these questions. They'd ask and I'm such an old fool, I might say something I'd feel sorry for afterwards. You don't know who you can trust these days. It wasn't the diary, but me. All the questions. I didn't want to be the one having the questions put to me. And what if they was like that fellow this morning? In it for the money. Liar, too. I knew right off he was lying when he said he was married to you."

"You could have just given the diary to me. You knew about me. You knew I did some writing."

"I thought maybe you wouldn't want a whole lot of questions neither. And what if they asked you where you got it? I thought of it, don't think I didn't. Drove around with the diary, right by your front door I did. But then I figured if I put the diary behind the picture, whoever come along, going to all that trouble, wasn't going to chuck it out. And no one would be bothering me with questions I wasn't going to answer. Not when I give Milly my word about stuff she never told anyone else."

"You took a chance." Perhaps the diary included the secrets George McDrew was speaking about. I thought of the "foster son" in Owen Peterson's clipping.

"I did, I did. But I was watching. When you come along, I was easier in my mind, you being Milly's friend. And the whole thing wouldn't lead back to me. And if no one'd come along I was going to get the diary back from behind that picture."

"So you saw us that night."

"First you come walking along and then your husband come around in the car. I saw you carried something out."

I nodded.

"You went to see her in the hospital, didn't you?"

"Hospital? I didn't even know she was in there! First I knew, this girl in Starleigh called me up. And then it was too late, Milly was gone. It was all over. And there wasn't a thing I could do. I'm lucky that girl thought to call me. Who went and told you I visited that hospital?"

"No one. I just thought— they said this elderly English gentleman was there." As soon as I spoke, I knew I'd said the wrong thing. I'd forgotten about the English accent.

"I sure don't sound like any Englishman I ever heard speak. If any Englishman turned up, it was one of them."

"Them?"

"One of them. Those English. One of them that caused all Milly's problems. But where are they now? Not out telling the story. If it hadn't been for me and the diary—"

He sounded bitter. I thought of how he must have felt bringing a heartbroken Millicent back from Alberta. She was probably on the verge of a nervous breakdown and George McDrew, solicitous and kind, could only have irritated her with his attentions. And who had his rival been, but "the golden Prince" everyone loved, the most famous bachelor in the world? George McDrew wouldn't have been human if he hadn't seethed.

"They even paid for the inscription," he said.

"They did?"

"Sent Milly the money. I saw the cheque with my own eyes. That's how much they wanted it done." He shook his head. "So what about Milly's diary? What about it? If you're the friend to her I think you are, what're you going to do?"

"I'm going to see my publisher in Toronto tomorrow." I knew then I would do as George McDrew asked: I would somehow bring Millicent's story out. I would do more than just find out the whys and wherefores. The break-ins and the other things were just obstacles to overcome.

"I thought I'd of heard of something by now," he said.

"These things take time. I've already discussed it with the publisher. We'll make definite plans tomorrow."

"And what would those plans be?"

"Publish Millicent's story." I hoped Jake would go along with it. I knew I'd have to talk to George McDrew again. I'd have to find some way of letting him know I had found just photos, not the diary.

"You mean a book?"

"Yes, a book for the world to read. I just wish I knew more after the diary ended," I said, making a guess that Millicent hadn't kept the diary up.

"There's nothing to know. Milly come home and after a few years she went teaching again. They said she didn't have to, that they'd give her money, but she said she was getting another school and she did. I give her credit for that."

"Oh yes."

"She wasn't one to sit around, not Milly. Anyways, she said she'd of gone crazy, sitting around and thinking. So she got herself a school in Campbellville. And that's what happened. Nobody knew the story except those of them involved. Not a single soul outside of her mother and myself."

"And that's all?"

"That's all I can tell you."

He was lying.

"But I can come and talk to you again? About dates, background information? The stone, for instance. You said 'they' said she could have the inscription about Edward put on the stone and that they paid for it."

"Well, she couldn't have it without their say-so, could she? Not to have it stand. Not with *him* still living. She'd never of thought of such a thing on her own. Knew it wouldn't be allowed. And wouldn't of wanted it even if she'd thought of it herself. She knew reporters would come nosing around. What kind of position did that put her in, now I ask you? But she went and did what they asked of her, same as she always did."

"Why would *they* want it on the stone?"

"You tell me. So she'd look foolish. Or so he'd look foolish. She said they never liked him or wanted to let him be king. And then he went and visited Hitler. And they sure didn't like that other one he married. I do not know! I never could figure that one out. But she went along with them."

"Can you tell me when she wanted to burn the diary?"

"Right after the thing went on the stone. Would of been 1968, thereabouts. You believe there's anything after?"

"After?"

"After we go." His eyes glistened. I think in his mind the fact that he had told me the story, unburdened himself, freed him to be intimate with me, to say things to me he would not dream of telling anyone else. I think now, if I had pushed harder, stayed longer, if perhaps Marion hadn't been there, he would have told more— not only the things in the diary I was supposed to know already, but other secrets. I wish now I had "pushed," but at the time I was already planning to pay another visit, hoping we could become friends. Once he trusted me, I could confess the diary had been stolen by someone else.

"Yes, I think so."

"Then you won't be thinking I'm off my rocker if I tell you that I feel Milly's around and she wants me to do something with the diary. She knows what's going on, I know she knows. So you *have* to do something about it."

107

"I will, I promise you. I'll make sure her story gets told."

He stretched his hand out. I took it. It was frail and thin, but warm. We shook.

"Now you've given your word," he said.

"I've given my word."

"And I'm a witness," Marion said.

It was time to go. The sky outside the window was dark, and the snow was coming down.

Did he think *they* (the English obviously, powerful spies) were poking around?

"I wouldn't put it past them. It wouldn't surprise me. They always kept tabs on Milly. Writing letters and a few times this fellow come to see her. That would of been in Guelph. Don't know about Starleigh, but sure as I'm sitting here they kept their eyes on her. Knew what she was up to, right to the end. Even when she wasn't– " he searched for the word. "Well," he said finally, instead of "going downhill" or "senile." "She wasn't good at the end."

"Someone broke into Peter's store. We wondered if *they* had anything to do with that."

"Hard to say. Lots of criminals and thugs all over the place these days, but it wouldn't surprise me one bit either. And maybe they're thinking she had the odd photograph around the place. Nope. You got the diary in a safe place?"

"In the bank," I lied. "We rented an extra big safety deposit box. That should ease your mind. I haven't just been doing nothing."

"And Meredith," Marion reminded me.

"Yes, we found someone Millicent knew up north."

"Oh, she had a miserable time of it up there. Cold the whole winter long, but she wanted to get away. Ted– that's what she always called *him*– was back from the Bahamas then. You heard about the Bahamas? That Harry Oakes that got killed? Well, the Duke was back and Milly didn't want to think he'd be visiting around Ottawa and not come see her, so she took off. That was at the bottom of it, but he never did come to Ottawa, not so far as I know. They wouldn't let him. Once he was at the ranch but that would of been in '41 or

'42, in the fall. And Milly was out there in the summer. Used to go out, you know. After she got over it, but that was Milly's stubbornness, I guess. And then she wouldn't go no more and don't ask me why. I figure I knew Milly better than anyone else but she still had a few secrets she wasn't telling, not even to me. Sometimes I could not figure her out. But that's men and women for you."

He might have been describing a woman he was married to, the way old men say, "We've been married fifty years but I still can't figure out what she sees in going shopping."

After pulling old-fashioned galoshes over his slippers, he walked us to the car. I said I hoped we'd meet again soon, and this time he nodded his assent. I gave him my card. He told me to be careful driving home.

"Can I ask you one more thing?"

"You've asked enough, so one more can't hurt."

"How come you met us carrying a gun?"

"I didn't know who was coming up. I figured one of the old women would let you in. And after that— fellow— this morning— I didn't like the sound of things. Said he had connections, like in the movies. You wanna know when I got the gun? When I went to bring Milly home, but I never have used it. Never even went hunting after I got back from overseas in W.W. One."

He said that he was sorry about Hallowe'en. He felt like a "gol-darn fool" whenever he thought about it, he said.

And then he asked if "Milly" had ever mentioned him to me.

I lied and told him yes; and that she had said she missed him.

"When Millicent's mother died, the newspaper mentioned a foster son," I said. "If I could talk to him... You wouldn't know where I could find him, would you?"

"Dead. Car accident. That would be Ernie, from over London. An orphan boy. Family of kids."

I could tell from his face that the foster son had no connection to Millicent. So that's one for you, Owen Peterson, I thought.

"And it all began in Halifax," I mused. "On that trip she took."

"Closest she could get to the old country, she said. New Scotland it was. Never could see it myself, that trip."

"And then she met the Prince."

"Stole off the boat, he did. *The Renown* it was. He got away from his watchers and Millicent just happened to go for a stroll that night over to this park they have there." He shook his head. "Ruined her life, I always said."

The ground was blanketed with snow. The Christmas lights seemed cheerful now. Meeting George McDrew hadn't been what I expected. Other than the things he had told us, the facts which I'd write down later and sift and puzzle over (and the omissions I'd wonder about), the story of his long devotion to Milly, which was more binding and fierce, more lasting and real than many marriages, made all the orange VW vans in the world and petty robberies seem insignificant and unimportant. I was glad I had not told him that the diary was stolen before I got to it, but I wondered if I should have mentioned the photographs.

"Christmas," Marion said. "You know, with everything that's happened today, I almost forgot I promised Hugh that I would pick him up a couple of flannel shirts at that factory outlet we went to last year. You don't think we can stop there, do you?"

I thought we could, and we did. I bought Peter a shirt too, and as I paid I fantasized that by Christmas I'd know George McDrew well enough to invite him to have Christmas dinner with us. If we went to Meredith this year, maybe he could come along... and... he'd tell me everything.

I told Peter about Charlie's ploy, but I said nothing about George McDrew, to whom I had given my word that I'd tell Millicent's story to the world.

I had no way of knowing that George McDrew had less than a day to live.

CHAPTER
TWELVE

Getting a phoney letter from Jake was Marion's idea. He'd write me a letter saying Hendricks wanted to do the book on teachers "dedicated to Millicent Mulvey." I could then show this letter to people I interviewed.

We told Peter we were going Christmas shopping in Toronto. I think he didn't want to know what I was up to. He probably reasoned that we couldn't argue about what he didn't know.

We went by train. More snow had been forecast. It's only an hour's trip and we wouldn't have to worry about parking, but more than that, I liked the idea of a *train* that morning, as if riding through the snowy, suddenly Christmasy southern Ontario landscape would bring me closer to the reality of George McDrew going out to Alberta to escort Millicent home.

By *train*. A brown cardboard suitcase, money taken from the bank. A hip flask for the three day journey to the west? Maybe not, so as not to dull the outrage, so as not to detract from the mission, as he watched the miles pass through the bush of northern Ontario, over the prairies, all the way to High River, Alberta. The gun in the pocket of his overcoat. Wanting only the trip to be over, but knowing that before that happened, there would be heartbreak, moods, nerves, illness, Millicent crying in the privacy of the Ladies'.

And arriving at the ranch, at Pekisko (a hired car; more money gone; there was that about it too): "Just pack your bags, Milly girl. There's a train that leaves at five and we're going to be on it."

Millicent would have been... glad to see him. Now it was all over. The Prince— "Ted"— would soon resume his former friendship with Freda Dudley Ward, his mistress of many years and the woman King George called "the lace-maker's daughter." "Ted" would meet Thelma Furness, the American socialite who would be his mistress until Mrs. Simpson came along. Hunting at Balmoral Castle, a safari to Africa, sailing with Mrs. Simpson to Greece and Turkey...

While Millicent... closing my eyes as the conductor passed with trays of coffee, I imagined her and George together, returning to Starleigh. I could see George's small hands folded in his lap, while Millicent stared out of the window at the granite cliffs and forests of the Canadian Shield.

As Marion and I were speeding to Toronto, George McDrew, as I learned later, was in the lobby waiting for a taxi. Two men in the building were expecting a van to take them to the seniors' centre for lunch and cribbage. George McDrew carried a navy overnight bag. When the taxi drew up, they asked if he was off to Florida. Had he won the lottery? His ancient car and reputation for counting pennies were something of a joke. George McDrew taking a taxi? "Hit the jackpot, did you, George?" "Your horse come in?"

George McDrew muttered something about business, and that was the last time the old men in the lobby saw him alive.

His body was found at four that afternoon in Riverside Park in Preston, by kids cutting through the park on the way home from school. It had started snowing again and the boys were throwing slushy snowballs. One landed on the hunched-over body of an old man lying in front of a bench.

The zip-in lining was in his raincoat and he was wearing a white shirt and navy tie, as if he'd he'd gone to meet someone important. He had a large bump on the head, but this could have come from the fall. The navy bag was gone. His wallet was missing.

The police found my business card in his *shoe*. On it was written and underlined twice: Call her!!!

We had a good day in Toronto. Marion purchased gifts for Allison's family at the Eaton Centre and bought herself a new dress and two books on Edward VIII. I took the subway north to St. George and met with Jake, who agreed to give me the phoney letter, and said Hendricks would consider a book about Millicent if I gathered enough facts.

"So you're really going to go ahead with this?"

"It's something I have to do, Jake."

"It's not going to be easy. You'll have to build from scratch. You no longer have the photographs and you never saw the diary George McDrew says he had. Re-construct her life. Gather evidence, talk to people. See what you can find out. Build a case, like a lawyer or detective."

My cookbook had been rushed to the printer for release in December. Orders were already coming in from advance mailings. Jake still believed Igor, now fortunately back in hospital after undressing in the subway, was responsible for the break-in at his office.

"You'll have to mention that in the foreword. People could say you're lying but there's nothing wrong with a little controversy. And they'll say that diary the old fellow left at Millicent's house never existed."

"You haven't discussed Millicent with Henry, have you?"

"I told you I wouldn't tell anyone. Why should I tell him?"

"I don't know. Maybe you should mention the teachers' book idea to Henry anyway. In case anyone calls here checking up."

"You mean as far as he's concerned you are writing a book about the little red schoolhouse?"

"Exactly."

"Peter still against the idea?"

"We said we're going Christmas shopping today and I guess that's what he wants to believe."

"Oh boy," Jake said.

"I think I'll just quietly go on with the research— do my own thing. I'm not even going to discuss Millicent with him for the time being. He'll change his mind when I uncover the truth."

"It's too bad you didn't find the diary," Jake said.

"Someone got there first. That in itself has to tell you something."

I met Marion at one in the Elephant & Castle, an English pub-style restaurant in the Eaton Centre. She'd called Max Halbers, the German who'd driven her to Guelph, at his office, and met him for coffee because she was knitting a sweater with a "Canadian moose" on it for his nephew in Germany and she wanted to check the size, but he was gone when I arrived and we ate a leisurely ploughman's lunch.

Max had offered Marion the use of his company condo at Harbourfront if we wanted to spend a few days in the city, a prospect which I could tell she relished.

"We'll tell Peter we're doing the town," she said.

After lunch we went to the provincial archives on Grenville Street— no one followed us, I didn't see any orange VW vans— and found that the archives had directories listing teachers and schools going back to 1912. Searching through these was a tiring process. We had to obtain the books from the librarian three at a time, and wait for each request to be processed. By the time we traced Millicent to West Montrose and Starleigh it was four o'clock and we called it a day.

We decided to return to Toronto the following week— Marion was all for using the condo— and we took the subway back to Union Station and had coffee at the Royal York Hotel, where I bought bread-dough Christmas ornaments in a boutique.

The only remarkable thing that happened all day was in the archives.

Bending over a dusty book, I heard Millicent's voice saying, very clearly, "Carolyn!" as if she was glad I was pursuing her story. Her voice sounded just as it had the night when we found the pictures, only now I thought of how happy she used to be when she gave me something— a candy dish that had been her mother's, an address book I still used, a picture she had made from dried flowers. This time, she seemed to be giving me another gift: encouragement to tell her story.

Unaware that at that moment the boys were coming across his body in the snowy park, I thought of George McDrew saying, "Do you think there's anything after?" And as Marion and I drank coffee, the ambulance had already carried his body to the morgue at the Cambridge Hospital.

It was still snowing when we got to Guelph and Peter was waiting for us on the station platform.

Peter of the grim face.

"They found a dead man in the park in Cambridge and he had your card in his shoe."

"What're you talking about?"

"Some old guy. They don't know who he is. The police want you in Cambridge. What's going on?"

"George McDrew," I said, quaking. "An old man we talked to yesterday about Millicent."

"Well, he's dead," Peter said.

He turned his back and headed for the car.

Once I was over the shock, I explained to Peter about meeting Owen Peterson and then George McDrew. I couldn't cry.

The atmosphere in the car was tense and Peter didn't say very much.

"If he had no ID he must have been mugged," was the only thing Marion said.

Peter said there was a story about the teachers' book in *The Meredith Times*. And: "A dead man's the final straw. I didn't even know you'd seen him. I felt like an idiot talking to the cops."

With the snow and the bad driving, the police station was deserted except for the dispatcher and a young constable. It was eight-thirty before a detective showed up to interview Marion and me.

Detective Miller was a short, rotund man of about fifty, wearing a green plaid blazer.

"Detective Miller," he said, shaking hands. "Like Barney Miller, in the show."

He took us to a cubicle at the back of the station and withdrew a plastic bag holding my card and a twenty dollar bill, along with a bad polaroid of George McDrew's face.

"An old hobo trick," Detective Miller said. "Put some money in your shoe. This your card?"

He shoved the plastic bag across the desk. I could see "Call her!!!"—underlined twice— written on my card in a shaky hand.

"Yes, that's my card." I couldn't bear to look at the picture, but I recognized George McDrew. "I gave it to Mr. McDrew yesterday when I interviewed him. My mother-in-law, Mrs. Hall, was with me. She's visiting us from Meredith, up north, and she wanted to shop at some of the factory outlets here in Cambridge. We were in the area anyway, so I decided to see Mr. McDrew."

The detective produced a yellow legal pad and took down our names and addresses.

"All right. Let's get his name first."

I told him and he wrote that down; I said George McDrew lived in the Thistledown Arms.

"When did you interview Mr. McDrew yesterday?"

"It was about four, I think. It had to be about four. We went to the library to look at the city directory and then we stopped for coffee and it was just about four before we got to Mr. McDrew's apartment building."

"What did you interview him about?"

"For a book. I'm a writer— I've published some cookbooks— and now I'm doing a book about school teachers in the twenties and thirties in rural Ontario. The book's dedicated to an old friend who just died and Mr. McDrew had known her since she was a young woman. I just visited my publisher today about the book, actually."

I produced Jake's letter. The detective read it and passed it back to me.

"I'm only mentioning Miss Mulvey in the introduction, which will tell about her teaching days. That's the teacher, Millicent Mulvey. Actually, she's buried here, in the Maple Grove Cemetery. She has that thing on her stone, about Edward VIII."

Miller looked up.

"The Duke of Windsor," I said. "The one who abdicated. But she was old when she had that written on the stone. She wasn't always neurotic."

The detective tapped his pen.

"I'm not even mentioning that in the teachers' book," I said. "I'm not getting into that. People would think I'm nuts."

"He was the one who married that American divorcee," the detective said. "Mrs. Simpson. My wife watched the show." He frowned with distaste, as if he'd had to forego a Blue Jays game so his wife could see the program.

"Yes, Edward VIII," I said. "But I'm writing a book about teachers. There's enough there to research. We were at the provincial archives today." Marion and I had each received an ID card at the archives. We could show them if we had to. "Actually, my ex-husband was always talking about doing a book about the royalty thing. I ran into him just the other week and he mentioned it again."

I'd just remembered Owen Peterson. He would notice an obituary for George McDrew and not only call the police, but go back to the newspaper with this "new angle." It was better to cover my tracks right now. And what about Charlie? What if he had anything to do with George McDrew's death? It would be like him to pressure and threaten an old man. "I know books on royalty sell— my husband Peter has a bookstore— but I'm just interested in the book on teachers and that's what I talked to George McDrew about. I was hoping to come back to talk to him again. He was a nice old man."

"Looks like he was planning to call you," Miller said. He peered at the card in the envelope.

"And to stick it in his shoe," I said.

"So he wouldn't lose it," Miller said. "Old people forget things. I've got a mother-in-law in a nursing home who keeps her pocket money in a pouch around her neck. It's a good thing he put your card there or we might have spent days getting an ID. We'll be checking with the neighbours, of course. Routine. And try to find the next-of-kin."

"Didn't he say his one remaining sister was dead?" Marion asked. "Maybe there's no one."

Miller shrugged. Terrible to grow old, he implied.

"You don't think Mr. McDrew met with foul play, do you?" I asked.

"Hard to say. We didn't find a wallet, but he could have lost it, grown disoriented. Wandered into the park. Sat down to get his breath, had a heart attack. There'll be an autopsy. I can drive you to the hospital, or do you want to follow me? It's never pleasant to identify a body. We might as well get it over with."

But he didn't get up. He fiddled with his pen.

"That's the only time you ever met him, yesterday?" he asked me.

"The only time. Miss Mulvey lived in Starleigh. Mr. McDrew was originally from Starleigh, but he moved to Cambridge to be near his sister and for the last few years Miss Mulvey was in a nursing home. I only found out where Mr. McDrew lived yesterday."

"You spent today in Toronto?"

"We just got back by train. I saw my publisher in the morning while my mother-in-law shopped. After lunch we went to the provincial archives. And then we took the train back to Guelph."

He wrote that down.

"They gave us ID cards at the archives. Do you want to see them?"

I thought he would say this wasn't necessary, but he didn't. I produced mine, and Marion hers, and he looked at them.

"You have to sign in and out at the archives," I explained, "and you have to leave your purse and bags in the foyer."

"Makes sense. Well– do you want to come with me in my car then?" Miller asked. "Your husband can wait here if he likes."

But he still didn't get up. He rubbed his chin, removed his glasses and cleaned them on his jacket. His forehead creased. I could hear the buzzing sound of the electric clock on the wall. Crackling static from the dispatcher's radio came from the front of the station. A door opened. Footsteps. Miller tapped his pen on the desk. Finally, as if he didn't know what else to do, he read over what he'd written on the pad.

"I've put down your statement, if you want to sign," he said.

I read the thing quickly: I'd met Mr. George McDrew for the first time yesterday when I interviewed him at four o'clock (approx.) for a book I was writing. I left my business card with him.

I had not had any contact with him since that time. I had identified the card found on the body. I had spent the entire day in Toronto with my mother-in-law, Marion Hall.

I signed. Marion added her name.

Miller tossed the pen down and finally got up.

"So, your car or mine?" he asked.

I said we'd follow in our car so we could drive straight home. "It's been a long day and we're all tired. We haven't even eaten yet."

Peter didn't say a single word as we drove to the morgue.

Just like in the movies, the morgue was in the basement of the hospital and the body was in a kind of tray. The attendant pulled back a sheet. Marion and I stood side by side. Miller was behind us, jingling loose change in his pocket.

"Yes, that's George McDrew," I said. Marion agreed.

Marion turned away, but I forced myself to look.

His eyes were closed, and he was wizened, gaunt, and his lips looked black. There was a purplish swelling on his right temple. He looked at peace in a strange, determined way. His chin seemed to thrust forward, as if to say, "There, I've had my way, I've done what I had to do."

Marion heated a can of tomato soup, made tea and toast. It was hard to eat, but I got down some of the soup and tea and went right to bed.

I couldn't sleep and it was a long time before Peter joined me. He turned his back and pulled the blankets around him.

"I'm not asleep," I said.

"I wouldn't sleep either in your shoes."

"I should have told you about seeing George McDrew, but it would have just been something else to argue about."

Peter sighed.

"At least put your arm around me," I said; he did.

I started to cry, and Peter tightened his grip. After a while, I told him all about finding George McDrew and what he had said. Peter listened and he didn't argue. He didn't say that he didn't believe George had told the truth about going to the ranch, about seeing the marriage certificate, having the diary.

"And now he's dead," Peter said.

"I gave him my word that I'd tell Millicent's story."

Peter could have said I'd also given him my word to drop the story, but he didn't. What he did say was, "And where does that leave you?"

"Telling the story, I guess."

"I wish you wouldn't."

"You said the idea of Millicent marrying the Duke of Windsor was dangerous, but think how much more dangerous the truth would be," I said.

"I don't think that old man would want you to risk your life."

"He could have just been mugged," I said.

Peter didn't answer.

"I still don't believe Millicent really married Edward," he said at last. "Not a real and valid marriage. But let's not talk about it any more tonight. Just get some sleep."

"We've all had a shock," I said.

"I shouldn't have been so tough on you tonight," Peter said, "but it was so embarrassing hearing from the police and not knowing what to say."

"What did you tell them?"

"I said you interviewed lots of people and didn't always tell me all the details. The detective probably thinks we're just another couple on the way to divorce."

"That'll never happen," I said.

"That's right. Let's try and get some sleep."

Just before he drifted off, Peter said Beryl Sofer, from Meredith, had left a message that she couldn't find a photo of Millicent.

The oblivion I sought didn't come. I went over and over the thing in my mind. Who had gotten to George McDrew? Why? Thugs, I told myself firmly one minute, and closed my eyes only to think of the Royals and British Intelligence and Charlie. Finally I dozed off to a half-wakeful dream about the Prince and Millicent and something about Queen Elizabeth. Peter was sound asleep.

I turned the light on, reached for the telephone on the night table, got Charlie's number in Orillia from directory assistance, and dialed. The phone rang twice and then it was picked up. A sleepy woman's voice answered, "Hello, hello?" I hung up. Peter mumbled something in his sleep.

I felt better for having done it, but even as I dialed, I knew Charlie wasn't involved in George McDrew's death. I could imagine Charlie lying beside "Gloria" and muttering, "Oh for chrissakes." Maybe he would accuse Gloria of having a lover.

I got up and found Marion in the kitchen with a pile of books on the table.

"Can't sleep," I said.

"That's two of us, then. I was lying in bed thinking about what happened to Mr. McDrew, and I had to get up. I know it sounds callous but I just had to go over my notes. Just listen to this.

"Edward asked the queen in 1968 if he and Wallis could be buried at the royal burying ground at Frogmore. That's at Windsor Castle. She didn't give him permission until August, 1970, two years later. And by that time, between Edward asking permission and the Queen granting it, Millicent's inscription was on the stone. And if the Royals paid for the carving, it makes sense that they had an ulterior motive, which has to be their hatred for Wallis."

"But that would mean they wanted Millicent's story told. Why did they take the diary then?"

"Wallis is still alive. I think they want the whole thing kept secret until Wallis dies. They probably hoped Wallis would go first, but she's still hanging on. Her lawyers would squawk if the story came out now. That's what I think. They never let her use the title Her Royal Highness. And something else. When the Queen's cousin, Princess Alexandra, married, they had a souvenir genealogical chart printed. Everyone's spouse was listed except for Edward's. Even another cousin who'd been divorced had his former wife listed, but the program simply gave Edward's date of birth and the fact that he abdicated in 1936."

"It sounds so evil, so— so machiavellian."

Marion raised an eyebrow in acknowledgement.

"But they wouldn't let him stay married to Millicent," I went on. "And then he met Wallis and once he was king he thought he could marry her. I don't care about Wallis. I care about Millicent. That's all George McDrew cared about too. I don't care about British Intelligence. Or the Royals. I'm not going to let this go. Jake said I have to build a case, and that's what I'm going to do. And then I'll put it all in a book."

"Did you know that in 1927, Baldwin— the British Prime Minister— compared Edward to George IV when he was talking to MacKenzie King? George IV had a morganatic wife of many years, but they forced him to marry someone else. When George IV died, he asked that a picture of his real wife, Maria, be buried with him. MacKenzie King wrote about the incident in his diary. We should read King's diary."

"Which is at the University of Waterloo library! I've consulted it before for the cookbooks. Why didn't I think of that? We can go there tomorrow."

"After what happened? Are you sure?"

"I'm sure. And I think Peter's beginning to believe me. I told him what George McDrew said."

But how would Peter react when I went ahead with Millicent's story? I worried.

"I also wrote a letter. A draft of one anyway."

Marion's letter was addressed to The Royal Archives, c/o Her Majesty the Queen, Buckingham Palace, London, England.

CHAPTER
THIRTEEN

In a way, George McDrew's death cleared the air. No more secrets, we agreed. Peter wasn't happy that I was still determined to research Millicent's story, but I promised research would be just that: research in libraries and archives.

And soon, I told him, I'd have to stop anyway because I'd be busy with all the hoopla that came with having a new book out.

So it was that I felt much better as I sat down to the microfilm reader in the basement of the Dana Porter Library at the University of Waterloo.

If MacKenzie King had been a British instead of a Canadian Prime Minister, he would have been Monty Python material. Vain, pudgy, fussy, secretive, suspicious, self-congratulatory, King was a lifelong bachelor who revered and idolized his mother and communicated with her after her death, sometimes via his little dog Pat.

Luckily for history, he was a fervent diarist, writing copious daily accounts about speeches, slights, kudos.

I found August, 1927, when the Prince of Wales had travelled to Canada with his brother and the British Prime Minister. It was Edward's fourth trip to Canada, and the purpose of this one had been to open the Peace Bridge between Canada and the U.S. Baldwin accompanied the Princes until Alberta, when the official part of the trip was over, and the Princes went to the ranch and the P.M. continued to the Rockies.

August 3: the Prince of Wales, his brother Prince George (later to be the Duke of Kent), Baldwin, MacKenzie King and various dignitaries, had gone to dedicate the Peace Bridge between the U.S. and Canada. A most impressive ceremony, MacKenzie King wrote. King wore a frock coat. Lunch at Government House, and then they all— except for the two princes— trooped to see A POULTRY SHOW!!! Dinner that night...

Then, on August 4, Baldwin and King were on "a ramble" alone at Kingsmere, King's estate. This was what Marion had talked about.

"On our ramble Baldwin & I talked over many matters." What if, Baldwin said, the royal family were to "throw up a sort of George IV... Let your fertile mind work on that."

George IV had had a morganatic wife.

"He expressed strongly the wish that H.R.H. wd. get married, & hinted at this being possible after his return."

Married to a proper wife, of course, I thought. A foreign princess or a titled lady from the British aristocracy.

The Prince of Wales played golf while this talk went on.

"At 8:15 I had dinner for the Prince of Wales & Prince George."

King and the Prince of Wales had a "very interesting & intimate talk together." The Prince wanted to visit the U.S. but Baldwin said no. The Prince told King "... that people did not understand what it was to be always on a job, that he needed a little relaxation & that he meant to do his part properly when the time came, & wd. be careful, but that he needed some change from the restraint of it all."

Chicken and ducks were on the menu, courtesy of the Quebec Minister of Agriculture, but King had contributed his own lamb for lunch... The Prince drank sherry & champagne and "had brandy once or twice..."

The next day they went on a cruise to Kingston. A Miss Jones sat at the

Prince of Wales' right. She spoke, King said, "in a cheap and cheeky way, &
I think the prince felt a little ashamed of her."

August 6, there was a dinner and dance given by the Ontario Government
at the King Edward Hotel in Toronto. The Prince of Wales gave a speech,
made a better impression than at Ottawa.

"I was afraid he might skip duty dances but he did not."

At twelve-thirty a.m. the Princes slipped out "to a little dance on the quiet."

To see Millicent?

I decided to request King's diary for the abdication period and right away
I found something significant. Talking to the cabinet about the abdication
crisis, he tells them about his after-dinner talk with the Prince in 1927. The
Prince "...had told me that evening of his intention to marry and that he would
send me the name of the lady later on..."

His intention to marry.

King had omitted this surely important information in his diary in 1927—
the diary he planned to leave for posterity. Yet here it was revealed in 1936.

The Prince, warmed and exhilarated by champagne and brandy, by thoughts
of escape from eventual Kingship, had let down the barriers. I imagined the
winsome, slightly sad smile I had seen in photographs, could see the backdrop
of society people and candlelight. "I shall be married, Mr. King." Or did he say,
"I shall be married, Prime Minister."? The indiscretion would have been followed
by something like panic. By caution, certainly: "But you must give me your word
not to reveal what I have told you, Prime Minister."

And King had kept his word, until the abdication, when he told the entire
cabinet.

And in 1936, grappling with the abdication, this revelation by King might
have influenced the Cabinet Ministers' feelings. Perhaps he revealed that a
marriage had taken place and been annulled. Now that the Prince was King,
another marriage, resulting from a famous romance, could not be annulled, and
so they must decide what to do. An earlier, aborted marriage would strengthen
the King's resolve to have his own way, so that there was no turning back.

I found Marion in the fourth floor reading lounge of the Dana Porter
Library, talking to a white-haired man.

"Ah, Carolyn, here you are." A book on Edward VIII lay on her lap. "I'd like you to meet Ewan MacLeod. He's a student at the university."

"One of the senior citizens blessed with free tuition," Ewan MacLeod said, shaking hands.

He did not have an English accent. He looked like a retired insurance executive in his camel hair overcoat and polished shoes.

"It's wonderful being able to return to school," Marion said. "If I lived in Waterloo I'd take some courses too. And to think they're free!"

"For seniors," MacLeod said. "But I hardly think that term applies to you."

"It will before too long," Marion said. "It's marvellous anyway to have the opportunity to learn new things."

"If an old brain can learn anything," MacLeod said. "I wonder sometimes." He smiled at me. "Your mother-in-law was telling me you're the cookbook author. My wife has some of your books. She'll be thrilled when she finds out we've met. I suppose you're here researching a new one."

"I'm writing a book about country teachers years ago."

"Went to a country school myself," Mr. MacLeod said. "Back in Oxford County. The building's still standing as a matter of fact. Young people live there. Hippie types. She's a potter or something. Completely renovated the thing. It's amazing how the old things are catching on. My wife found a recipe for bean soup in your books by the way, exactly the way her mother used to make it. So you're a student of history over and above matters culinary."

"Oh, I enjoy history."

"Fascinating stuff." He tapped Marion's book. "I suppose you're a monarchist too, like your mother-in-law?"

"Oh no. Not me."

"So many young people don't give two hoots about them, not that I entirely blame them. Imagine the Queen with all her billions, not paying income tax. I remember seeing the Queen Mother and King George when they passed through this way on their tour in 1938. The railway station was packed, everyone had to see them. I can still hear my mother talking about the abdication. What a shock that was when MacLeod— he nodded at the book— "abdicated. And they're still writing about it today. I don't suppose you've ever thought about writing about that?"

I shook my head.

Marion put the book in her bag and stood up.

"I'm still interested in them," MacLeod said. "Illogical as it may seem, my wife and I got up at the ungodly hour of five in the morning to see Charles and Diana's wedding."

MacLeod walked us to the elevator.

"I have to admit I am one of the ones who rose at dawn to see it too," Marion said. "And here I've bought a book about Edward VIII, although it was only $5.99 on sale."

"One of those— what is it called?— remaindered books," MacLeod said. "Not a good thing for authors, I understand. There was something in the press about that just the other week. Is that a problem you've encountered?" he asked me.

I said as far as I knew my cookbooks had never been remaindered, and then, thank goodness, the elevator doors slid open and Marion and I were alone.

"What was that all about?" I asked her.

"He just came over and started talking to me about my book. I thought he was a professor at first."

I snickered.

"Actually, I think he was trying to pick me up."

"Pick you up."

"He wanted to buy me coffee, but I said I was waiting for you. You thought he was the famous Englishman, didn't you?"

"The thought did cross my mind."

The elevator came to a stop.

"He's a retired jeweller, he says. His son manages the store in Kitchener. His wife is crippled with rheumatoid arthritis," Marion said, as we stepped into the first floor lobby.

"I thought he was pretty ingratiating," I said.

"They hoped to travel when he retired, but his wife's almost in a wheelchair and he's taking courses instead. Russian history this year. He believes the Romanovs escaped the slaughter."

Outside, the sun was shining and the snow was melting.

"You don't think a spy or someone in intelligence could change his accent, do you?" Marion asked.

"I suppose it's possible, but MacLeod strikes me as nothing more than what he says he is."

"Mr. McDrew's death has me thinking the most incredible thoughts," Marion said.

"Forget MacLeod. Wait till you read what I found in King's diary."

Marion read the photocopies of the microfilm in the car.

"But it all ties in! The Prince tells MacKenzie King he intends to marry in 1927, but King keeps it out of the diary until the abdication. Baldwin must have known too, or suspected something, considering the comparison to George IV with his morganatic wife. If Edward confided in King, he must have told Baldwin too. He knew Baldwin for years.

"And remember— I think I mentioned it to you— Edward's secretary, Lascelles, threatened to resign in disgust at exactly that time. He would have resigned but his wife worried about their financial future. So it all does fit together!"

The Kitchener Public Library was our next stop.

A stranger to the area would think that Kitchener and Waterloo are one city. The same street, King, runs through both. Suddenly you've left Waterloo and are in Kitchener and you're not even aware of the fact.

Kitchener was called Berlin until World War I, when anti-German sentiment prompted the name change. The German influence is still strong. The Old Order Mennonites speak German and after World War II, more Germans settled there, many of them ethnic Germans from Eastern Europe. Country inns serve schnitzel and sauerkraut. Kitchener's Oktoberfest is supposed to rival Munich's.

I'll forego Oktoberfest and schnitzel, but I love the old Farmers' Market in the Kitchener downtown where Mennonites sell vegetables, preserves, apple schnitz and summer sausage. I like to go in the early fall and again just before Christmas, when the stalls bulge with ornaments and crafts.

Millicent's first teaching position was at West Montrose, just outside of Kitchener.

The library is a few blocks from the market. When my second cookbook came out, I gave a talk about it at a "Noon Hour Book Review." I've done research there in the Grace Schmitt Room, the repository for local history records.

The Grace Schmitt room, in the basement, had a file on Millicent, but it was disappointing. Except for an item from the local paper, the *Kitchener-Waterloo Record*, which mentioned the break-in and speculated that Millicent and the Prince might have gone through a morganatic marriage, there was nothing we hadn't found in the Guelph library. The clipping about Meredith wasn't there.

The first person we saw when we walked up the stairs from the basement was Ewan MacLeod.

He was checking the computerized catalogue, and I hoped he wouldn't notice us, but we had to walk past him to get to the rear exit and the parking lot, and he saw us right away.

He told Marion: "We shouldn't keep meeting like this!"

I decided to drive up King Street to see if I could find MacLeod's Jewellers. I figured Ewan MacLeod would name the store after himself.

It was there, three blocks away. "MacLeod's Jewellery and Fine Watch Repair."

"Let's drive out to West Montrose," I suggested to Marion. "Just to see where Millicent taught. I don't think you've ever been there. There's a covered bridge and a charming general store. I think they have a post office where they stamp letters 'The Kissing Bridge.' We can ask if there are any old-timers around who go back to the days when Millicent taught there."

I was pleased to see that the store carried two of my cookbooks. Marion bought postcards and mailed them to Allison's kids. I introduced myself to the clerk, autographed the books, and was informed they would be ordering my new one.

I asked about Millicent.

"West Montrose was her first teaching post. I was hoping to find someone here who knew her then. I know it's about seventy years ago, but someone who's eighty or ninety now could possibly remember her."

A young Old Order Mennonite woman, accompanied by a small girl and wearing the distinctive black coat and shawl, came in as I was talking and waited behind us at the counter.

"I'll write her name down and leave my card," I said. "Miss Mulvey was from Galt so she could have boarded with someone here if she didn't go home each night."

As we were getting in the Volvo, the Mennonite woman came out and glanced our way. She looked as though she wanted to talk to us, but walked to her buggy.

I rolled down the car window.

"Excuse me?"

She was probably thirty, but looked ten years younger with her unmade-up, round-cheeked face, and friendly, if hesitant, smile. I introduced myself and explained about Millicent. The woman's name was Lucretia Schantz.

"I know she wouldn't have taught at a Mennonite school—"

"Oh, but in those years there was one school for all." Lucretia's voice had that melodious accent the women at the market had. "You are not the first to ask about Millicent Mulvey. We have read about her in the *Record*."

I felt guilty lying to her. Mennonites believe a simple "yes" or "no" is enough in a court of law. They don't swear oaths and they're pacifists.

But— *someone else had been around asking questions.*

"I've seen the *Record* article too," I said, "but she was an old friend of mine. I'm writing a book about teachers in the early days which I'm dedicating to her. The foreword will be about her. That's why I was hoping to meet someone who knew her when she taught at her first school here in West Montrose."

"My husband's grandmother knew her," Lucretia said. "We look after her. She was ill and sleeping last week when the man came to our place. She's better today. Would you like to see her?"

"I would like to very much."

Peter couldn't fault me about talking to Mennonites, I thought as we followed the horse-drawn buggy to a farm several miles up the road. A sign at the beginning of the long, tree-lined lane read, "Summer Sausage. Eggs. No Sunday Sales." Old Order Mennonite farmhouses don't have electricity and there are no curtains at the windows. Lucretia's place was no exception, and it looked prosperous and cosy. A large barn was right behind the two-storey white farmhouse, with the traditional "doddy haus" for the old people attached to it. A black-and-white border collie barked at us, but Lucretia shushed him away.

The inside of the house was immaculate and traditionally plain. The linoleum gleamed. Geraniums bloomed on the window sill. A scrubbed wooden table with six chairs arranged around it stood in the middle of the room. The wood stove shone.

An old woman dozed in a rocker. She wore the traditional white prayer cap.

Lucretia removed her bonnet, shawl and coat, and took off her little girl's covering.

"Oma, people have come to see you," Lucretia said. The old woman's eyes fluttered open and she began to get up, but she stayed put when Lucretia spoke to her in German.

She introduced us quite formally and Mrs. Schantz extended a paper-thin hand.

"Sit yourselves down," Lucretia told us, indicating the chairs.

"I understand you knew Millicent Mulvey," I said to Mrs. Schantz.

"I have explained about the book," Lucretia said.

"She was a good teacher," Mrs. Schantz said, and spoke in German to Lucretia, who replied in the same language. This seemed to reassure the older woman.

"I was fourteen years old. It was my last year in school when she came to West Montrose, but I saw her many times after. I went to the Martins for six months to help with the baby. She was on the next farm where the English lived."

"English" meant non-Mennonite. Mrs. Schantz's accent was strong, but her voice was clear.

I felt more and more like a criminal as I listened to the elderly woman reminiscing. They had driven Millicent in their buggy to St. Jacobs. Millicent liked reading stories and gave the young Mrs. Schantz a book about England.

I asked the questions that would have been expected had I really been writing a book about teaching. What was the school like? How long was the school day? How many students were there? How did they heat the school?

And: "You must have missed her when she left West Montrose," I said to Mrs. Schantz.

Mrs. Schantz said something in German to Lucretia who said, "Now you must speak English. These ladies don't speak Deutsch."

"She visited after I was married," Mrs. Schantz said. "She did not know I was married. I had a baby and she did not know. Then she came one or two more times, before she went to Alberta. And once more, years after that. She bought apples from us and we gave her a little grey cat. Did you know they wrote about her in the newspapers?"

"Yes, I've read the papers."

Silence. Marion complimented Lucretia on the lush geraniums.

"You must have been surprised by the story," I told Mrs. Schantz.

"I was not surprised. Now they are saying it is lies." She said something else, in a low voice, in German, to Lucretia, who translated: "She has given her word she would not repeat what Millicent told her."

An uncomfortable feeling filled the room. We were all uneasy: Marion and I because of our duplicity, the grandmother because she could not be open, and Lucretia with something like embarrassment. Marion tried to save the day by talking about the sunny weather, which led to talk about Meredith. Lucretia said cousins of hers who used cars had gone camping near there...

"In any case," I said finally, "I'm really interested in Millicent's early teaching days. I almost never discussed the royalty thing with her."

"Millicent was honest," Mrs. Schantz said.

She spoke matter-of-factly, the way she would have said that Millicent had blue eyes.

It was time to go. I thanked Mrs. Schantz and Lucretia walked us to the car.

"You know, it's curious that someone else has been asking questions about Millicent," I told her. "A few other places I've gone I've heard someone's been around too. An older gentleman with an English accent."

Lucretia surprised me by saying, "Like Michael Caine?"

"Oh, before I joined the church I saw some movies," she explained when she noticed my surprise. "I always liked Michael Caine."

"I'm from England, too," Marion said.

"I knew that," Lucretia said. "But you don't talk like the man who was here. He didn't have an English accent."

"I wonder how many people are asking questions about her?" I mused, hoping Lucretia would tell me what she knew. "The one with the English accent was elderly."

She didn't disappoint me.

"This one wasn't old. He was young. In his thirties, I would say."

Charlie? She answered that too.

"He was thin and he looked like he might work in an office."

So there was another mystery, then.

CHAPTER
FOURTEEN

The Queen
Buckingham Palace
London, England

Your Majesty:

I am writing to Your Majesty about a Canadian woman called Millicent Mulvey.

Miss Mulvey died recently at the age of ninety-five. She lived in Starleigh, Ontario. In the late sixties she had the following inscription placed on her family tombstone in Maple Grove Cemetery in Cambridge: Millicent A.M.M.M. Mulvey, Wife of Edward VIII, Duke of Windsor.

I met Miss Mulvey in the early seventies and we became friends. She seldom spoke about her supposed marriage, but she told me that she had married the Duke, then Prince of Wales, in western Canada.

I am a writer presently working on a book about school teachers. As Miss Mulvey was a teacher for many years, I am dedicating the book to her and mentioning her in the foreword. It was not my original intention to describe the mystery surrounding the stone, but recent speculation in the press and new information which has come my way have convinced me that I should at least look into the story of a possible marriage to the Duke of Windsor.

People who knew her years ago have expressed their belief that Miss Mulvey did indeed marry the Duke, but that the marriage was annulled. One person mentioned seeing a marriage certificate and photos, and said that "the palace" paid for the inscription on the stone.

My purpose in writing to Your Majesty is to ask if there is any mention of Miss Mulvey in the Royal Archives at Windsor Castle. Would it be possible, Your Majesty, to forward this request to the archivist?

Thank you very much for your consideration.

Yours sincerely,
Carolyn Archer

"I think it's a good letter," Marion said. "I hope I've worded it correctly. I would have written 'Your humble and obedient servant' but that's not required any more, apparently."

"I feel silly. I'm sure they won't tell us anything. The Queen's not going to write and say that it's all true."

"You're not asking the Queen to tell you what she knows," Marion said sensibly, reading it over again. "You're not putting her on the spot. You're asking her for information from the royal archives."

"I don't think the archives will tell us anything even if they have any information."

"We might be surprised. It's definitely worth a try. They may be hoping someone will investigate the story. You can type this up first thing in the morning and we'll post it straight away."

After we went to the post office in the morning, we walked over to The Bookworm. Peter was at the bank and Cass was decorating for Christmas.

"It comes earlier every year," she complained. "And we're having that same old plastic tree again." She pointed at the spindly thing in the corner by the children's books. "Even with books underneath it'll still look crass."

Marion patted Cass' arm. "Why don't I get the ornaments and do the tree for you?"

She left and Cass asked me if Peter had given me the news.

"The news?" I was sure she didn't know about George McDrew.

"About the man who was in asking about books by this woman you knew, Millicent Mulvey. I overheard what your ex-husband said about her— I wasn't listening but I was right there— and that's why I remembered the name. Anyway, Peter said he'd tell you."

"I guess it slipped his mind," I said. "Who did you say was in?"

"This elderly fellow with a British accent. I'd never heard of Millicent Mulvey until the night of the reading. Who is she anyway? If she's a local author I've never heard of her."

"She's not really a local author. She wrote children's stories but I don't think she ever had anything published. It's curious that someone was asking about her. Maybe she had something published and I don't know about it. I'd like to find out."

I knew Cass wouldn't know about Millicent's story because she never read the local papers.

"I checked *Books in Print* and I didn't find anything."

"Maybe she self-published. You've never seen this man before?"

"Sorry. I would have taken his name but we were busy and he didn't hang around."

Marion came back with the box of ornaments.

The doorbell dinged. The customer was Charlie.

Marion and Cass discreetly went to the back room.

"What're you doing here?" I felt the blood rush to my face.

"Buying books." Charlie grinned, pleased with himself. He was wearing what looked like a new and expensive navy cashmere winter coat and a paisley scarf. The man had dressed-for-success today.

"Why don't you take your business elsewhere? And what right did you have to tell those people in Cambridge that we were still married?"

The grin spread.

"At least I found out you're investigating Millicent's story too," he said. "Just as I thought."

"I'm not investigating her story. I'm writing about her in the foreword!"

"Sure you are. Anyway, I could accuse you of the same thing."

"What do you mean?"

"You didn't tell Owen Peterson the truth. You let him think we were still married."

"Go to hell." I turned away. "Get out of here."

I walked to the door and opened it, but Charlie didn't move.

"I found out something," he said.

"You and Owen I suppose. He's an idiot."

"That's not very nice. Don't you want to know what I found out?"

"I'm not interested."

"You should be. It's pretty good."

"If you don't leave, I'll call the police."

"I have a right to be here. Just a friendly customer." The grin remained, but his teeth clenched.

"Just go!"

"We could trade information," Charlie said. "We could even collaborate."

"Get out."

Peter walked through the door.

"I want him to leave," I told Peter. "Call the police. He won't go."

"I'm just here looking for early Christmas presents," Charlie said, but the grin was gone.

"If Carolyn wants you to leave, I think you should go," Peter told him. "We can be civilized about this or I can call the police."

"I was just going to give her information," Charlie said, as if I wasn't there. "But she doesn't want to know what I know."

"If she doesn't want to know, she doesn't want to know," Peter said.

But I wanted to know what Charlie knew.

"What I suggest," Charlie said, "since you've mentioned the word civilized, is that we act like civilized human beings and talk about this over a cup of coffee. My treat."

Peter looked at me.

"It's up to Carolyn," he said at last. "But before she answers I'm going to tell you that I know you let people think you were still married to her. I didn't appreciate that one bit. And I don't want it repeated."

"I can understand that. Yes I can." Charlie nodded. "But it was a misunderstanding. I met that photographer years ago. When he assumed Carolyn and I were still married, I just let him go on thinking it. I see now that was a mistake. I understand how you feel."

Smooth old Charlie.

"I'll have coffee with him if you come along," I told Peter, who couldn't very well refuse.

We went to a Tim Horton's, where Charlie made a big production of wanting to buy doughnuts for us ("Come on, it's on me. You don't want a cruller? How about a raspberry-filled? You have to have something...").

"Fifteen minutes," I said.

Charlie licked sugar off his finger from his lemon-filled.

"Right. Got you," Charlie said, "although I think we can all be friends here." He took a big bite of his doughnut. "I sure wish I could persuade you folks to have something with me. You don't know what you're missing.

"You know, this could be a really big story, really big. I'm talking money here. First rights to the highest bidder. Tabloids. Film rights. Anything to do with royalty is a big seller."

"So what did you find out?" I asked.

"I knew as soon as Owen said you looked him up that you're thinking the same thing I am. No, you don't have to deny it. I know you're interested."

"For the teachers' book," I said, but Charlie ignored that, and went on to say that I was in a unique position for having known Millicent such a long time. Surely I knew things, he said, things probably no one else knew, although he knew a thing or two as well. He was just sorry that I hadn't listened to him long ago regarding Millicent, but that was water under the bridge.

"You have to admit," he said to me, "it was my idea in the first place. I thought we could collaborate."

"I don't think—"

"Let me finish here, okay? Don't dismiss it out of hand. There's going to be a lot of footwork involved. Time's of the essence. I bet you we're not the only ones chasing down this story now that she's dead. It's an open field. A contest, if you like. Every man for himself, just like in business. This is no different."

"Get to the point."

"All right. Okay. We get together on this, pool all our resources and talents and split fifty-fifty."

"What about this Owen fellow?" I asked.

"He's in it with me. He's doing research for me around Cambridge. I've got him interviewing someone this afternoon as a matter of fact. Fifty for me, out of which I pay Owen for his help. What you do with your fifty is up to you, of course."

"Just tell us what you have," I said.

"I think we'd have to have an agreement first," Charlie said. "But it's good stuff, that I can promise you."

"I wouldn't get mixed up in this if I were you," Peter said.

"I'm really only interested in the teachers' book," I said.

Again, Charlie ignored this. "Have you had any strange occurrences?"

I just looked at him.

"I've had some strange phone calls. Breathing and hang-ups. My wife thinks I have a girlfriend."

He smirked, letting us know just how dumb his wife was.

"Is that what you wanted to tell us?" I asked. "That's it?"

"That is *not* it!"

"If you're not going to tell us, we'll just go."

"Then you'll never know."

"Let's go. This is nuts," I told Peter. "Let's get out of here."

"Next thing you'll tell us is that your buddy Owen is interviewing George McDrew today," I said.

I had spoken sarcastically, ready for the punch line that George McDrew was dead, but Charlie looked startled, as if I'd hit on a big, dark secret.

I smiled at him.

"So Owen is seeing George McDrew. I spoke to him, too. It looks to me that I beat you on that one."

Charlie considered what to say.

"We might as well leave now," I said. I pushed my cup away. "George will tell Owen he told me everything there was to tell."

"I guess the old man's lawyer called you, too," Charlie said.

Now I didn't know what to say.

"His lawyer set up an appointment with Owen," Charlie said. "His *lawyer*. This wasn't just an old man talking, but a *lawyer*. They're meeting at three-thirty this afternoon. We're going after an affidavit. Did you get an affidavit too?" he asked me.

"Why would I need an affidavit for an old man's reminiscences about his school days?"

"You went to a lot of trouble to find him just to talk about old school days, didn't you?"

"I guess Owen'll be seeing the lawyer soon," I said. It was just after two. "Well, I hope he gets his affidavit."

Peter and I stood up.

"Your loss," Charlie said, and he added an expression I remembered from years before when he had issued ultimatums: "The bell isn't going to toll again."

"I'm going to Cambridge," I told Peter. "You know I have to go, don't you?"

"Going to Cambridge to tail this Owen character isn't my idea of reading books in libraries," Peter said.

"But the chance won't come again. We could find out who's behind everything."

"I don't like this 'we.'"

But he couldn't talk me out of it, and he had no choice but to come along, although he tried to argue that people like Owen and Charlie were just idiots who didn't know anything.

We didn't go back to the store. I called Marion from a pay phone and Peter and I took the back road through the countryside to Kitchener, and continued from there to Cambridge. Peter was glum and disapproving, but I was glad he was there.

By five to three we were at Owen Peterson's apartment, where I buzzed Owen from the lobby. He answered the buzzer. I dashed back to the Volvo.

Owen came right downstairs and looked up and down the street. I ducked down. He wouldn't recognize Peter.

I kept my head down when we parked along the street to wait. Luckily, Owen lived on a one-way street and would have to pass us when he left. It took half an hour before a dirty brown station wagon with Owen at the wheel came out of the garage.

"I don't believe I'm doing this," Peter said.

We tailed Owen for two blocks, but then another car cut in and we were two cars back. Owen was a nervous driver, slowing down inappropriately and causing the driver in front of us to lean on his horn, and speeding through a yellow light. We had to wait for the red to change, but Owen slowed down again, and by the time we came to the next set of lights we caught up with him.

Owen's destination was the Holiday Inn near Fairview Mall, Kitchener's biggest shopping centre. I made Peter park at the back of the lot so I could stretch my muscles. Owen got out of his car carrying a briefcase.

"What now?" Peter asked wearily.

"I guess we wait. Or we could sort of hang around inside the lobby."

"We?" Peter raised an eyebrow.

"I'll go alone then."

"Say 'Hi' to Owen is more like it. Not that it matters. The guy must be a real idiot."

"You wouldn't go alone, would you?"

"Me?"

"He wouldn't know who you were."

"You want me to go inside? And what're you going to do?"

"I could just sit here."

"Sure. Alone."

"You could go in and I could go to the mall. Fairview's just down the road."

"And what am I supposed to do? Pretend to be the lawyer or what?"

"Just see who comes along."

"We're really playing spy here. Cops and robbers."

"If you don't want to do it you don't have to."

"What choice do I have?"

Peter said he would meet me at the Hudson Bay restaurant.

If he wasn't there by four, I said I'd call the Holiday Inn and have "Peter Malone" paged.

"I just don't believe I've agreed to do this crazy thing," Peter said.

At the mall, I soon gave up window shopping and took the escalator up to the restaurant in The Bay, where I ordered their "English tea." I managed to drink some tea, but I couldn't eat the scones and dainty sandwiches. I wished I still smoked. I hadn't even brought a book.

At four, I had "Peter Malone" paged. Peter wasn't there.

I ran to Woolco and bought a black mohair beret and purple tinted glasses. In the car, I pulled the beret down over my forehead and ears. With the purple glasses, I did look different, and I was wearing my green jacket, not the trench coat I'd worn when I met Owen.

A police cruiser was parked in front of the Holiday Inn.

CHAPTER
FIFTEEN

Owen was far too angry to recognize me, even in my flimsy disguise.

"I tell you someone did not take my briefcase by mistake!" he was saying to the police in the lobby. "It's no good to assume it'll be turned in when that person realizes his mistake! I had important, valuable documents in my case. I demand that you search for the perpetrator!"

One of the cops asked what paper Owen worked for.

"I'm independent! I'm working on a story that has far-reaching implications! An international story! Instead of standing here and wasting time, I suggest you look for the man. Blonde hair and black leather jacket! Go out and find him and don't waste time! I know my rights and I demand you do something!"

Peter. Peter had been wearing his black leather jacket.

"We'll do what we can, sir. But I'm sure your case will be turned in."

"And if it's not? What then? My documents can't be replaced. You don't know what you're dealing with here. And not only do you have the description of the man, you know where he works." He held up a blue case marked "Bank of Montreal."

The case wasn't Peter's. I had never seen it before.

"We'll check it out, sir."

"Check it out! When? Tomorrow? I have a good mind to call in the RCMP!"

"You're free to do so, sir."

Owen refused to provide the police with a list of "documents" in the case, saying only they were "private papers." He had been sitting at the bar, waiting for "a contact." The man in the black jacket had been next to him having a beer.

Owen looked around. I darted out of the front door and drove back to the mall.

Peter wasn't in the restaurant. Still wearing the beret, I ordered coffee and sat by the railing of the balcony overlooking the mall. Peter did not appear.

At quarter to five, I drove back to the Holiday Inn. The police cruiser was gone and so was Owen's car. I headed back to the mall, parking by The Bay so I could dash up to the restaurant again.

And there was Peter, getting off a bus. Peter of the black leather jacket and Owen's brown briefcase, which swung against his side.

He had taken Owen's case and simply walked out of the hotel with it. A bus was coming along and he got on. Downtown, he had found a copy centre near the bus terminal, photocopied the papers, and took a bus back to the mall.

But if I thought these actions meant a change of heart on his part, I was mistaken. He'd read the "documents" on the bus and knew right away they were "garbage."

"Owen's nuts, Nothing in those papers of his. When you read the junk he had you'll see what I mean. And now let's get back to the Holiday Inn."

"The Holiday Inn? Are you crazy?"

"I should just throw the whole thing into the garbage, but I might as well return the case so he can go on dreaming. Of course he'll think someone's copied the papers, as indeed they have."

"But what are you going to say?"

"I'll say I took a briefcase by mistake. Very sorry and many regrets and so on. He's totally out to lunch. And no one turned up. Maybe that asshole Charlie played a trick on him."

"Owen's probably been on the phone to Charlie already, but I guess Charlie isn't going to tell him about you, is he? Not without admitting I'm no longer his wife."

"I don't care what Mr. Owen tells Charlie," Peter said. "I can't believe I went along with this."

In the Holiday Inn parking lot I scrunched down again while Peter returned the case, although Owen's car was gone.

They told Peter at the hotel that the police had threatened to arrest Owen if he didn't cool down.

Owen had cooled down.

"The whole thing was nothing but a joke," Peter said to me as soon as he was back in the car. "I bet Charlie's behind it. The bastard just wanted to see how far you'd go."

"George McDrew dying wasn't a joke," I said.

"Aren't you assuming a lot? He could have just had a heart attack and died."

"But what about what he told me?" What had happened to Peter's sympathy now?

He didn't answer right away. We were hitting rush hour traffic. Peter shifted into third with a crash.

"I don't know," he said. "I just don't know. It's a bad business as far as I'm concerned."

There were messages at home: someone from the Meredith paper wanted to interview me about the teachers' book and I was to phone Detective Miller of the Cambridge Police.

The papers would have to wait until the morning, but I called Miller.

"It looks like your old friend did die of a heart attack," Miller told me. "I thought you'd like to know."

"There was no evidence of foul play? What about the bump to the head?"

"The coroner thinks that was from the fall against the base of the bench. So, unless you know something we don't, the old fellow wandered into the park pure and simple."

"I've told you all I know," I said, "but thank you for calling. What about his wallet? Did they ever find that?"

"You sound like a detective yourself," Miller said. He didn't laugh. "Yeah, someone found his wallet and turned it in. Money still there, too. No credit cards. A kid found it. There's a niece flying in from New York to see to the funeral, but she won't be here until next week. Just reached her today."

"You couldn't give me her name?"

"How about if I tell her to call you?"

"I'd like to attend the funeral," I said.

"No reason why not, unless it's private."

"So you're closing the case?"

"There never was a case," the detective said.

I had read Owen's papers— just an essay— on the way home. It was nothing but a re-hash of morganatic marriages in the history of the royal family. He concluded with descriptions of the Prince's visits to Canada, and surmised that Millicent had met Edward in Alberta, where Owen thought she'd taught.

Wrong, Owen, wrong!

But I was intrigued by a scrawl— "son/England/western Canada"— in the margin.

"Of course they'd never let her bring up the child herself," Marion said, "since the child could be seen as having a claim to the British throne. They'd have had the child adopted, brought up by a well-to-do family. England could be right, although I read about the child of a Royal Duke being brought up in the States. If I remember correctly, it was adopted by a wealthy publishing family. I'd say Owen's guessing."

We were in the kitchen. Peter was staying determinedly in the living room.

"He was wrong about the foster son," I said.

"Exactly," Marion said.

"And a child would have been another reason George McDrew didn't want to talk to journalists. And maybe that's why he had the gun. Maybe he thought someone would try to kill Millicent. But I am curious about that notation. I wish I could ask Owen about it."

"You can't. You're not supposed to know about that."

"What if George McDrew really did have a lawyer who contacted Owen?"

"Owen has a propensity for talking. You'll likely hear before too long."

"Except he doesn't know where to reach me. The phone's in Peter's name and he doesn't know Peter even exists."

"All we can do," Marion said, "is go on with our own research. We still have to finish at the archives in Toronto. We could stay at Max's condo."

"Peter will be thrilled," I said.

The phone rang. Peter picked it up in the other room and called out that it was for me.

"Yes, this is Carolyn Archer."

"Let me speak to Charlie!"

"I beg your pardon?"

"Don't play games with me. I know he's there. Tell the son-of-a-bitch to come to the phone! I'm not some dummy like you were! Don't try and fool me. Just put Charlie on!"

"Is this Gloria?"

"Gloria!!!" It was a scream. The phone went dead, but it rang again almost at once.

"What do you know about Gloria?"

"Charlie bought one of my cookbooks and I autographed a book to Gloria." Why protect Charlie?

"The son-of-a-bitch! The fucking bastard! Gloria! That asshole!"

"I'm sorry. I thought you were Gloria."

"No, I am not Gloria! This is Sandy, his goddamn wife! I'm going to kill that bastard if he ever shows up!"

"He did drop into my husband's store this afternoon."

"What do you mean your *husband's* store? Charlie said you never got married again and don't you dare say you're writing a book with him!"

"I'm not writing a book with him. And I am re-married, happily so. How did you get my number?"

"Charlie had it in his goddamn book. What an asshole!"

After a bit more swearing, with some weeping thrown in, she told me that Charlie was supposed to have come home by seven, but he'd never shown up. Gloria was this woman he worked with and a total, five thousand per cent bitch. Sandy wanted to know why Charlie had come to the store. I told her he had tried— unsuccessfully— to persuade me to collaborate on a book with him.

"He told me you were begging him to return to you."

"I'd rather be dead," I said.

"The son-of-a-bitch!" she cried. "And he had me thinking you were still in love with him. What time was he in Guelph?"

"Around two."

"He was going to stop in Toronto to see this editor at some tabloid. He said that they'd go for it if you were involved— like, they printed some of your recipes or something. And then he was going to come home. But he's not here."

She finally hung up ten minutes later.

I didn't have to tell Peter that his mother and I were returning to Toronto and probably staying at Max's condo. Marion did it for me.

"And I'll be able to finish up my Christmas shopping too," she said. "There's no point in travelling back and forth between Guelph and Toronto if we have a place to stay, is there?"

"You're both crazy," Peter said.

"We'll only be going to the archives," I said. I sounded like an apologetic teenager and felt like one.

"Why tell me?" Peter said. He went right to bed and when I joined him he was either already asleep or pretending.

In the morning Marion called Max and arranged for the condo.

Max would even pick us up the next day. He was just leaving for Windsor and would get us on his way back to Toronto. He had to go to Ottawa, but after he came back he was off to Alberta and we could borrow his car.

So that was that. I hated feeling Peter was so angry with me and got busy on the phone.

I returned the call to the Meredith paper and told a reporter about the book on teachers, and mentioned Millicent, saying I would like to hear from anyone in the area who had known her.

I phoned Beryl Sofer, who still had not located the picture of Millicent.

I phoned Jake to keep him up-to-date and to let him know that I'd be in Toronto the next day. Jake said he'd just been going to call me himself. He had a message for me from Owen Peterson, of all people.

"He says you interviewed him but he can't find your card, so he phoned here. Who is this guy? He wants to sell me on a book of travel essays. The low-down on package tours, he says."

"He's an idiot. He thinks I'm still married to Charlie and he didn't lose my card. I pocketed it so he wouldn't call me. The whole crazy thing isn't worth going into."

"Sounds like it to me. I didn't think it was true he was helping you with the Millicent book."

"Are you kidding? No way, José. Listen, I'll explain it all when I see you. It's just a crazy misunderstanding."

"He told me the FBI, CIA and British Intelligence are after him," Max said. "He must be related to Igor."

"Just ignore him. You'll have to drop into our swank headquarters in Toronto. A condo at Harbourfront. Someone Marion knows is lending it to us. A businessman who's out of town a lot."

"I'll bring the champagne and caviar," Jake said.

I called Sandy, but there was no answer.

Against all rational judgement and common sense, I called Owen. The phone didn't even finish ringing once before he picked it up and told me he'd get back to me. Presumably he thought his phone was bugged.

I lied that I was calling from a pay phone— on my way out of town, I said, to do a workshop in London— and ten minutes later I called him back at the number he gave me. Complications! Complications! but when you have the CIA and FBI after you...

He breathlessly filled me in on the fact that an intelligence network had stolen his briefcase, copied the contents he was sure, and the man who returned it disappeared into thin air.

"What's going on? I was supposed to call Charlie last night but I couldn't reach him. And they haven't heard from him at work."

"Charlie was in Toronto last night. That's why you couldn't reach him. He told me George McDrew's lawyer contacted you."

"I was supposed to meet him at the— I'd better not say on the phone. He didn't turn up. Intercepted, I'd say. There's a lot of curious stuff going on, I can tell you. And I'll tell you something else too. The package I was supposed to deliver wasn't all there, if you get my drift. Did Charlie get to the Toronto people?"

"He's going to see them on his way north today. I know he had some business out of town, and I was out last night myself at a—" I improvised quickly– "writers' meeting, so I'll probably hear from him today."

Owen latched on to that right away. What kind of writers' meeting? Could he attend the next one? There was nothing in Cambridge but a bunch of old hens getting together. I said I'd let him know about the next meeting.

"So what do you mean you didn't have the complete package?"

"In my briefcase," he lowered his voice, "I had a document saying that a certain party had a son, but so far as I've found out, she had a *daughter!*"

"A daughter?"

"Pretty smart, eh? Did you get the contract in the mail yet? Charlie said you'd be getting it any day now. Don't worry, I didn't mention the contract to your publisher when I spoke to him in case there was a hitch or something. Seems like a nice guy. He and I might be doing business together, by the way. Other than the other thing."

"There's no problem with the contract," I said, wondering exactly what Charlie had told him.

"Wouldn't mind seeing a copy," Owen said. "I know a thing or two about contracts myself."

I said I would send him a copy (I could say later that the deal fell through; I'd think of something. Say I had leukaemia).

"That was a good idea you had, writing down son instead of daughter," I told him.

"Knew you'd think so. And not only that, but I put the wrong place down too."

"The wrong place?"

"England, I said, and Vancouver. England's right for sure, but when you think of Vancouver, what's the exact opposite you can think of?"

"The east coast?"

"You just about got it. Charlie thought it was pretty good too. It's just too bad the lawyer got intercepted."

"Don't you have a number for him?"

"He was calling from out of town, but I know it was from an office because a secretary came on the line first. He'd be carrying a book of Robert Frost poetry, he said. His name was Jackson. You know, I could help you with the editing, too. Cut out the extra words. When you write yourself you can't see your own mistakes, but I can."

"There's just one thing that bothers me. Now you're saying a daughter, but what about the foster son?"

"Not on the phone. Let's say Owen put his thinking cap on."

"The trouble is, you have to substantiate things in books." Why was I even talking to him? "You have to back up your claims. Something isn't true just because you say it is."

"Don't you think I know that? But there is such a thing as logic."

"Maybe Charlie'll find out something definite from that tabloid in Toronto. The— I've forgotten the name."

"I was going to ask you the same thing. If he wasn't your husband I'd say he was holding out on us. But I guess you can trust your own husband."

"I'd say so. I'd recognize the name if I heard it. But I've been doing some last minute things with the new cookbook. This guy definitely said he was George McDrew's lawyer?"

"He didn't mention names, but it was clear who he meant."

Owen putting two and two together again.

"He wasn't a local lawyer?"

"Toronto. That's why I was meeting him at the Holiday Inn, 'cause he knew where it was."

"Maybe he had an accident on the way."

"I would have heard, wouldn't I? Nope, he was intercepted. Or this guy who took my briefcase was acting for him. I tried the old fellow's place but there was no answer. I even went there and rang his apartment, but he wasn't home. I'm not leaving any stone unturned."

Sooner or later, Owen had to find out George McDrew was dead, but what did Owen matter anyway? I hadn't even gotten any information out of him. I was sure he didn't know anything.

Well, almost sure.

CHAPTER
SIXTEEN

Max was at the door at ten the next morning. He drove his leased Mercedes like an airplane and we were in Toronto by eleven. Marion said the condo was "lovely." We were on the seventeenth floor with a magnificent view of Toronto harbour. Swedish furniture, impressionistic prints, state-of-the-art stereo equipment. Fridge stocked with wine, fruit, cheese, gourmet frozen dinners, and Danish beer.

Marion contained herself until Max left and then she went from room to room, opening closets, inspecting the glassware, turning on lights. There were two bedrooms, each with a king-sized bed and a feather duvet. There was even a bidet in the main bathroom.

"It's like another world," she said, and she was right. Guelph seemed a million miles away. Peter, too. We hadn't really made up the night before. Although I awoke once and felt him holding me, in the morning he was gone before we were up.

In this new setting it was easy to think like the liberated career woman who might live in a place like this: what right did Peter, or any man, have to dictate what I should do and not do? On the other hand, there was this little gnawing feeling that I hated. In some way I couldn't explain, I knew Peter was right. There could— would?— be trouble and more trouble, but even more, I hated this new lack of warmth between us.

In the morning Marion and I awoke to driving snow. The building seemed to sway with the wind, which whistled and blew in the elevator shaft as we went down.

We had planned to take a bus to Union Station and the subway from there to the archives, but the doorman, Tom, the elderly Irishman Max had introduced to us, insisted on calling a cab, as if he thought that anyone who stayed at that address was rich. But it felt pretty wonderful to gaze out at the poor working slobs shivering at bus stops from the inside of the cab.

We were in the archives by ten-thirty. This time we were better organized. Marion and I divided the years between us. I took the twenties, she the thirties.

There was no voice from Millicent.

By three o'clock we had both finished and decided to press on to the forties, although we were starving. We were through by four-thirty.

We found Millicent teaching, from 1913 to 1927, at Starleigh, Etobicoke, Lambton Mills; in the thirties at Malton and Campbellville; in the forties again at Campbellville and Meredith.

As far as we could discover, she did not teach after the spring of 1927 for two years. 1923, when she had taken a year off, was blank too. There were also some years missing in the middle of the thirties.

Everything tallied, even the missing years in the thirties, when George McDrew had burned the letter from the Prince. If she had been depressed and ill at Edward's relationship with Mrs. Simpson, it made sense that she hadn't been able to teach.

The wind had died down when we got outside, but it was still snowing. Rush hour meant a crowded subway. We took it as far as the Eaton Centre, where we gratefully sank into a booth at the Elephant & Castle.

We bought wine so we wouldn't use up all the good Moselle at the condo and went home by taxi.

There were messages on the machine, but they were all for Max. We opened the wine and played Beethoven's *Pastorale*. Marion got out her knitting to remind herself "That this isn't real life and I might as well get going on the sweater for Max's nephew. You must admit it's fairly cheap rent."

I started to re-read— again— Frances Donaldson's *Edward VIII*.

I called Peter at eleven.

"The idiot phoned the store twice."

The idiot?

"That damn Owen Peterson."

Owen had been calling Guelph bookstores trying to find out my home number.

"He didn't connect you with the briefcase business?"

"I didn't even talk to him. Cass answered the phone. She wouldn't give out your number," Peter said wearily. "He's calling all the bookstores to find your telephone number."

"I hope she didn't say that I was married to the bookstore owner."

"No, but he told Cass he was your writing partner."

"I hope you set her straight on that."

"Why should I do that? Let her think what she likes."

"Peter—"

"What's a little more craziness anyway? For all I know you'll end up teamed up with Owen, the way this is going."

"You're upset."

"Why should I be upset? Just because you choose to go on a wild goose chase which could be dangerous doesn't mean I have to get upset."

"No one even knows where we are except you."

"Don't forget the royal spies."

"Oh Peter. Do you want me to come home?"

"Are you?"

"No. I just wish you'd understand."

"That's the trouble, I do understand."

"I'm not going to call Owen."

"You'd better, before he turns up at the store and recognizes me and reports me to the police. That's the last thing I want."

Peter sighed. I told him I loved him; he said he loved me too. I suggested he come to Toronto on Sunday; he wouldn't commit himself.

The real trouble with calling Owen was that it was getting complicated keeping the story straight, trying to remember what I had last told him about Charlie. What if Charlie gave him a different story?

But I didn't have to worry. Owen answered on the first ring again and once more there was that business of him wanting to go to another phone, but I said I was calling from a friend's place and just on my way out.

"You're always on your way out," he said grumpily, and added that he'd at last heard from "our friend." "Our friend" had stayed in Toronto last night.

"I know. That's why I decided to come to Toronto this afternoon, to catch up with him. Someone at this bookstore in Guelph said you were trying to reach me. It's a good thing I dropped in there. I have to see my publisher tomorrow anyway."

"A meeting at the publisher's, did you say? I could come in for that if you want."

"We're just getting together to iron out a few details about the new cookbook."

"I sent him a batch of my stuff today. They say you shouldn't send it without a query, but since I've discussed it with him, I thought it would be okay to send it in. He should have it by tomorrow. Used Purolator, by the way. Cost me an arm and a leg, but I don't trust the post office. Maybe I should come in tomorrow. Meet the guy."

"Don't you think it would be best to give him a chance to read your material first?"

Owen sounded doubtful. Strike while the fire is hot, he said.

"I included some of the other material as well," he added meaningfully.

"Did you?"

"Why don't you give me the number where you're staying and I'll get back to you later?"

"I'm afraid I don't have the other number with me. It's unlisted so I can't even get it from directory assistance. I could call you back later."

Owen hummed and hawed. He wanted to speak to me on another phone soon. He might be snowed in later. "I sure wish I had the number where you're staying. There's no way you can get it?"

I promised to call him back and to give him the number of the friend I was staying with.

"So how'd our friend do at the– the– ah– client?" he asked.

The tabloid?

"He was checking into that today. I haven't heard from him yet. Maybe he'll call me later."

"I guess he doesn't mind you going out on your own."

"He trusts me," I said drily.

"Damn," I told Marion. "There's no way I can get out of it. If I don't call

Owen back, he'll get suspicious and maybe even turn up at Hendricks tomorrow. Or go to Guelph. Won't Peter be happy then."

"You could accidentally reverse two of the numbers."

"Then he'll turn up at Hendricks tomorrow. What will Max think if Owen keeps calling here for me after I'm gone?"

"You'll think of something," Marion said serenely. "He's European. He'll assume Owen is your lover and he won't say a word."

I wished I'd never met Owen. I phoned him back half an hour later and gave him the number of the condo. Then I had to wait for the call-back.

"You put in a good word for me tomorrow," he said. "Although I still think I should come in and meet the guy. Haven't you ever heard that story about Thomas Wolfe turning up with a big package of manuscripts? Say Wolfe didn't go to the office but mailed it instead. Maybe he'd never have been published."

"I don't think that's a good idea, Owen. Aren't you afraid they'll think you're being pushy?"

"I know how to act. I'd just play it by ear."

"I really have to talk to Jake about the new cookbook. This is a business meeting I'm talking about, Owen. I don't think it would be at all appropriate for you to tag along. I'd even say you'd be hurting your chances with them. But I'll put in a good word for you. Actually, though, I've been thinking about your work. Remember what you said about putting two and two together? That's not going to cut any ice with a publisher. They'll want to know your sources."

"Who says I didn't name my sources? You're talking about that east coast article." He paused to let the meaning sink in. "I guess you want to check that out for yourself."

"All I'm saying is that if I go to bat for you, I don't want to be in for any surprises down the line."

"We're partners, aren't we? You, me, and Charlie?"

"That's what I understand."

"All right then. You're suggesting I'm hiding something from you."

"Listen, Owen, if you're not happy with the situation, just say so."

"Who's saying I'm not happy? Just a minute here. I thought we had an agreement."

"I know we have an agreement," I said, wondering how much crazier this could get.

"All right then. I've got nothing to hide from you, nothing. And I'll prove it. Can I ask you something?"

"Go ahead."

"If I send something to a publisher, will his code of ethics permit another writer to see it?"

He was so *stupid*.

"I guess it all depends. Once or twice Jake has asked my opinion of something. I critiqued a children's manuscript for him once."

"That's your answer then. Do you see what I mean? You get my point?"

I did.

"Now you've got me worried about sending stuff out. What if another writer steals your work? Don't get me wrong. I trust *you*, but tell them not to let anyone else see my work."

"Will do."

"And hey— what about the contract? How's that coming?"

"I'll ask about it tomorrow."

"You're sure they're really interested?"

"As far as I know."

"I kind of thought there'd be a contract by now. I know they don't like to take a chance with a writer who doesn't have a book to his credit, but I thought since you were involved..."

"I'll see what I can do."

"It won't be real for me until I see it in black and white. Signed, sealed, and delivered. It's almost too good to be true."

"I know how you feel."

"This is my chance and I don't want to blow it. I worry about that contract."

He went on like this for some time.

We were at Jake's office by ten, but Purolator hadn't yet delivered Owen's package.

Jake looked tired and hung over. Every once in a while he drowns his sorrows when he gets together with one of his old friends. He drank four cups of coffee while I filled him in on Owen and the crazy complication with Charlie.

Jake didn't like the idea of giving me a phoney contract to show at all. Not one bit.

"A letter's one thing," he said. "But a contract? If he has a copy. who knows where it might lead? He sounds crazy to me. Why don't you just tell him to get lost? Tell him you're doing the book on your own."

"Of course I'm doing the book on my own! The partnership business is just an idea Charlie put in his head. I'm simply playing along," I said. "I know it sounds nuts."

"Nuts isn't the word for it," Jake said. "Get out of it. Tell him you're doing the book alone. Period, end of problem. Oh, my head."

Jake mumbled that the Owens of this world believed little green men lived in the middle of the earth and that the world was flat.

"Once I get the information, it's good-bye Owen. Good-bye Charlie, too," I said. "Don't worry about the contract, Jake. I don't know why I even brought it up."

"Henry signs the contracts anyway." Jake sounded bleak. "And now you say this guy's sent a whole pile of junk here. It'll go right back with one of our friendly rejection letters."

"Just hold on to it for now. Don't forget he included information about Millicent as well."

"Henry would strangle me with his bare hands if I drew up a phoney contract," Jake said.

Molly buzzed. Purolator had delivered the package.

"I guess Tolstoy sent us something," she sniffed, lugging it in.

It was a big box, a grocery carton of material. Jake took one look and excused himself. Marion and I were welcome to it, he said. He was going to the drugstore for nasal spray.

The box seemed to contain every article Owen had ever written. A lot of the stuff was about Florida: "Florida on a Shoestring"; "Florida for Seniors"; "Blue Cross and Florida"; "An Afternoon at Busch Gardens." There was a humorous essay on obtaining a passport, another on curling. "Your Apartment Cat."

And so on.

He had written a two page letter of introduction, and attached a bibliography, listing every letter to the editor and every minor newspaper article he'd ever published. He'd written for two mystical magazines...

The material on Millicent was in a separate envelope. He had included the essay from the briefcase, and another piece entitled "My Investigations to Date," which spelled out the library research, books he'd read, the mysterious non-meeting with the lawyer, strange phone calls... And: "Recently this writer had a fortuitous meeting with a visitor to the Cambridge library. While photocopying material, Mrs. Grace Littlehurst of Willowdale happened to be waiting for the machine. Noticing my endeavours, she commented that she had known Millicent Mulvey years ago. Mrs. Littlehurst did not know that Miss Mulvey had died.

"Likewise, she did not know of the inscription on the stone.

"Mrs. Littlehurst met Millicent in Malton, where both boarded at the same establishment. Mrs. Littlehurst mistakenly opened an envelope addressed to Miss Mulvey, Littlehurst's maiden name being Muller, thus explaining an honest error, and learned of the existence of a child. Being an honest individual, Mrs. Littlehurst told Miss Mulvey what had occurred. Miss Mulvey then swore her to secrecy and said she had had a child by an 'important personage.' Said child had been taken to England. Years later, Miss Mulvey and Miss Miller, by then Mrs. Littlehurst, met at a school reunion. Miss Mulvey informed Mrs. Littlehurst that the above-mentioned child, then grown up, was living on the east coast. Mrs. Littlehurst believed the child to be female.

"I have no reason to doubt the veracity of Mrs. Littlehurst's story. I plan to contact Mrs. Littlehurst again. I should mention that Mrs. Littlehurst's purpose in being at the Cambridge Public Library was to research her family tree, her grandmother having come from Galt, which is now part of the City of Cambridge."

Jake returned as I was calling directory assistance. He gave a dismissive stare at the box and slumped at his desk.

There was no listing for a Littlehurst in Willowdale.

Jake asked if we had what we wanted.

"Found something. It's— " I started to read it to him, but Jake held up his hand. "Not this morning. Later."

"Come to the luxurious condo then?"

We made a date for Sunday night.

"Take the box downstairs when you go," he said. "We'll keep it for a few weeks if it'll make you happy."

I left the box with Molly and used her phone to call the reference desk of the Toronto library. They did not find the Littlehurst we wanted.

I took the Millicent material with me.

At the condo, I phoned in ads to weeklies in various towns where Millicent had taught, mentioning the book about teachers.

Then it was time to tackle the Grace Littlehurst lead. I called Owen, told him the package had arrived, but of course (of course!) I had to wait for him to get to another telephone.

Ten minutes later he was back on the line. I had to assure him that the line I was using wasn't bugged. "No one even knows I'm here except for you."

"And your husband."

"Of course my husband. I read the material, but there's no Littlehurst in Willowdale."

It wasn't a helpful call.

"That's the name she gave me," he said querulously. "I know she lived in Willowdale because she had a book from the Willowdale library on searching out your roots. I saw it with my own eyes. I recommended another book to her."

Did he have a phone number for her? No, he didn't. She'd told him it was in the book.

"I'll have to keep looking then," I said.

He was more interested in the other material he had sent to Hendricks. I assured him it would be strongly considered. "As long as it doesn't end up in the slush pile," he said. "What about that contract?"

"The fellow who signs them is in England," I lied.

"In England!" (On Mars!)

"Sorry."

"I knew it wouldn't be today. I had a feeling it wouldn't come through."

And more of the same. Etcetera and etcetera.

Littlehurst, Littlehurst. I looked in the phone book again and found one "G. Little" but I got a musical voice on the answering machine: "Hi, this is Gerry."

"Maybe she lives with a married daughter," I mused.

"Yet she told Owen she was in the book. She must have given him a wrong name."

"What's the opposite of little?" Marion asked. "Try 'big.'"

No Bighurst either.

But there was a G. Greathurst. I dialed.

Grace Greathurst answered. She was the right party.

"This is she." A snooty voice.

This was both too easy and too hard, I thought, as I explained my purpose for calling.

She knew who I was. Owen had said he was working on a book with me.

"He showed me some of your cookbooks. I'm afraid I'd never heard of you, but I don't do much cooking any more. Never did. I've been a businesswoman most of my life."

Could I see her?

Usually, the cookbooks are winning tickets. But not this time.

"I told your friend all I know," she said.

"It wouldn't take long. I'm in Toronto for a few days on business. I'd really like to see you."

Sighs. "Very well. Let me consult my book."

We made arrangements for the next day, Saturday, at one. She didn't sound like the friendly, inquisitive woman Owen had encountered at the Cambridge library.

We spent the rest of the afternoon Christmas shopping. Marion bought Hugh a book on Winston Churchill and a new bird guide, miniature wooden trains from Germany for Allison's boys, and gloves for Peter. I got Peter a framed woodcut of an English bookstore I thought he'd like and bought pink dessert dishes for the house.

It wasn't exactly elegant dining with our big parcels, but we splurged on mustard chicken at Le Chapeau de Pierrot, a bistro off Yonge Street.

It was even less elegant straggling back with our arms full of packages. We couldn't find a taxi and had to take the subway. Worse was to come. Transferring to the bus to take us to the condo, I dropped the bag holding the dishes and heard glass shatter.

I peered into the bag. Two were broken. At least they weren't crystal.

"You can buy some more tomorrow," Marion said, as we came to our stop half a block from the condo. "That's what's so wonderful about being in Toronto. Everything is right here. If I'd bought something here and broken it in Meredith, it would be months before I could replace it."

An orange VW van was parked illegally in front of Max's building.

"Remember Owen's paranoia," Marion said, as we crossed the street. "Anyone who's tailing us isn't going to park in a no parking zone. They'd be towed away."

"Unless they're scrunched down in the seat and know they can get away quickly. I'm going to get the license plate number."

"Just walk by," Marion said, but I stopped and resolutely looked inside.

The front seats were empty but *black leather gloves* lay on the dashboard. The license plate was covered with what looked like mud.

I reached into the shopping bag, took out glass shards, and placed them in front of the tires. It wasn't much and probably the tires would just press the glass into the snow, but I felt better for having done it. Marion said nothing.

There was no doorman in the lobby.

And what if someone got on the elevator and...

But the elevator took us straight up and no one got on.

I called downstairs to the lobby. The doorman answered, but he wasn't Tom. I identified myself and said I'd noticed the orange van. I'd been expecting company, I explained, and the person sometimes drove an orange van. I was concerned because the vehicle was parked illegally. My friend might have gone to a convenience store for cigarettes.

"Could you look and see if the van's still there, please?"

"Just hold on."

The van was gone.

"I was here all the time, except when I checked the sauna. I never saw any van," the man said.

"A coincidence," Marion said. "It has to be a coincidence. And I still say someone tailing us wouldn't have parked in a no parking zone. It doesn't make sense. There must be thousands of similar vans in Toronto."

She made coffee. I called Peter, who said that George McDrew's niece had telephoned and left her number in New York.

Her name was Peggy Lovely and she lived in Manhattan.

Peter still hadn't decided whether he'd come in on Sunday or not.

Peggy Lovely sounded glad to hear from me. She had a faint, barely perceptible, southern accent, explained by fifteen years as a professor of Victorian Literature at a university in Georgia. She was on sabbatical this year and had just returned from England.

"I'm so happy you called. I never kept in touch with Uncle George as much as I should have, I'm afraid. We used to visit Canada when I was a girl, but since my father died we've more or less lost touch. Lucky I sent Christmas cards or maybe they'd never have reached me."

So the police had searched his apartment, I thought.

We talked for half an hour. I explained who I was and how I had gotten to know her uncle. I decided to be honest and to tell the truth about Millicent.

If Peggy was amused or amazed by the story of Millicent and the Prince, she didn't show it.

"Millicent, Millicent. The name does ring a bell. Was she a short woman with a prominent jaw? I may have met her as a girl, but I can't be sure. It would have been in Guelph, I think. But don't hold me to that."

The memorial service would be late Tuesday afternoon. The body would be cremated.

By the end of the call we were on such friendly terms that I offered to pick her up at the Toronto airport on Tuesday and drive her to Cambridge.

CHAPTER
SEVENTEEN

Yonge Street is supposed to be the longest main street in the world. It starts in downtown Toronto and if you follow it all the way you end up in northern Ontario. To get to Willowdale you just follow Yonge Street. I guess you could call Willowdale a suburb of Toronto. When I first came to Canada you had to go half the way by bus. Today the subway goes all the way out, and you really can't call it suburbia any more, built up as it is with highrise apartment buildings and office towers.

Grace Greathurst had said to walk a block north of the subway stop, turn right, and her house would be on the next corner. Her place turned out to be a small brick storey-and-a-half. A shiny black cat sat in the window.

No one was home. Now what? If we'd had a car we could have waited in comfort, but the air was chilly and we couldn't very well perch on the cement steps.

We walked back to Yonge Street, had coffee in a pizza shop, and returned half an hour later. Same story.

"For heaven's sake. She knew we were coming!"

"Let's try the back door," Marion suggested. "Perhaps she's in the kitchen and can't hear. Maybe the doorbell doesn't work."

We trooped past the garage to the back, where I pounded on the door. There was no response. Pink kitchen curtains were pulled across. A tied garbage bag sat on the back steps. In a detective novel, I'd read about a private eye going through the garbage, but that was at night. In the next yard a boy was putting bird seed out. I rapped on the door again and put my nose to the window.

Next door, a face appeared at the window. The boy gave us a furtive look and darted inside.

"We could ask the neighbours," Marion said. "They know we're here anyway."

"I just talked to her yesterday. She knew we'd be coming all the way by subway for crying out loud!"

We returned to Yonge Street and looked around an East Indian store and a leather shop, where Marion bought a hand-tooled wallet for Allison's husband.

Back to the lady's house. This time I rang the bell at the neighbour's. A woman yelled, "If it's the Jehovah Witnesses again, tell them we're not interested!"

The little boy we'd seen in the yard finally answered the door. He called his mother, who said, "We're not interested. We have our own religion."

She wasn't any friendlier when we explained who we were.

"Grace had to go out of town all of a sudden. I don't know where she is. We're looking after her cat for her."

It was a long trip back to the condo.

A wasted afternoon.

"You could call Owen," Marion said. "Maybe there's been a mix-up somewhere."

"No, definitely not. Absolutely not. The asshole. I bet he put the wrong name down on purpose. What a wild goose chase."

"You think Owen told this Greathurst person not to talk to you?"

"I wouldn't put it past him. Who knows what he told her? Maybe he said I was a CIA agent or something just so she wouldn't talk to me."

"But do you really think he'd deceive you and spoil his chances of getting a book published? Wouldn't he have known you'd find out?"

"Oh, I don't care. I'm through with him."

"But wouldn't he have realized you'd find out if he lied to you? It doesn't make sense." She had her knitting out and stopped to count stitches. "Mrs. Greathurst might have given Owen the wrong name."

"Then why mention Millicent at all?"

"To see if Owen knew something, perhaps."

"Then she would have wanted to know what I knew."

"But you're not Owen, are you? You're an intelligent person, a real writer. Perhaps she told Owen more than she planned to— without thinking it through— and that's why she gave a wrong name, so he couldn't find her. But she didn't go far enough inventing an alias. Have you considered that she might be trying to find out more about Millicent herself?"

"The whole world wants to write about Millicent. Charlie and Owen and now this Greathurst bitch! I can just imagine what Millicent would think of all this! She would have hated Owen and I know what she thought of Charlie. And this Mrs. Greathurst spilling out her guts to a complete stranger in a public library! Repeating intimate details out of a private letter!"

Millicent. I had brought copies of her letters to the editor with me. Re-reading them restored my sanity. I fell asleep picturing her the way she was when I first met her: a tiny, Scottish-Canadian woman with bright eyes and a heather brooch pinned to her sweater.

I dreamt, but it was not about Millicent. It was— something else. I woke up in the dark and at first I didn't know where I was. The dream... I knew I'd had it before and it was something important, something I should have known but couldn't recall.

Something I was missing.

I called Mrs. Greathurst's number but (of course) there was no answer. It took me a long time to fall asleep again.

Peter didn't show up on Sunday. Marion called Hugh, not really wanting to in case he'd shot a deer and wanted her to come home to wrap the meat.

But Hugh didn't want Marion to come home to wrap venison (he had shot a deer, but Allison and Joe had done the honours). The news wasn't good.

"Oh no!" I heard her say. "Not really. I don't believe it! Are you sure? Yes... I know... I just can't believe it... You got home at one... Of course I locked up. I always lock up... But if nothing was taken... Just let me tell Carolyn."

"Our house was broken into!" she told me. "The back window was broken but Hugh says nothing was taken."

Hugh thought that Theriau fellow he'd mentioned before had broken in, looking for illegal game in the freezer, Marion said after she hung up. Two weeks earlier, Hugh had arrested him for a similar offence. The freezer was the first place Hugh checked because he'd gone to take a steak out for dinner. Everything was moved around in there, Hugh said.

As someone had ransacked our freezer.

"But nothing else was disturbed," I said.

"That Hugh knows of. The window in the back door was broken. He didn't think any of our papers were missing, but I always file those things in the desk drawer. My jewellery's all there, the television wasn't taken, the silver wasn't touched. Just the freezer, as far as Hugh knows. I suppose it could have been that Theriau fellow..."

"But you had no papers there about Millicent."

"Only a draft of a letter to the Queen," she said, "in my desk in the sewing room."

"Well, then."

"It's just the thought of someone breaking in and looking. Maybe I should go home..."

"You can't go home! How often do you come to visit us? Just because some redneck looked for illegal game at your place you want to leave!"

"It's such a frightening feeling that a stranger was in our house, looking around. I don't know."

She was still preoccupied when Jake arrived at eight, toting a bottle of (cheap, Canadian) champagne and a six-pack of beer.

He was in a better mood than he had been on Friday and dug into the bagels and cold cuts. He wasn't impressed with the condo. He and Henry lived in their parents' elegant old home in Rosedale which had been converted into two separate apartments. "Expense account place," he pronounced, opening a beer for himself after pouring champagne for us.

"Better than a poet's garret," I teased, and we talked about our journey to Willowdale, which led to the notorious Owen, which led to speculation about Millicent's child and possible complications which could have arisen for the crown if the child had been legitimate. The British crown business turned the conversation quite naturally to England. Soon Marion and Jake were chatting away about "over 'ome" as Jake called it, and Marion began to relax.

Marion was telling Jake about a doddering aunt of hers who sounded like Jake's landlady in London, when a key turned in the door and Max walked in, carrying a garment bag.

He looked surprised— and not too pleased, I thought— when he saw Jake sprawled out on the leather sofa and the two empty beer cans on the coffee table, but his good manners asserted themselves, and he strode across the room and extended his hand to Jake, who had already risen to his feet (and tucked the back of his shirt in).

I introduced them. I think Max was mollified by the fact that Jake was my publisher, and not some scruffy poet (or auto worker).

"I am afraid I have startled you. I must apologize. My meeting ended sooner than expected. I shall sleep on the sofa tonight. I am intruding, but my flight leaves tomorrow for Winnipeg at eleven."

"Don't be silly," I said. "It's your place, and I will certainly take the sofa for tonight."

"I should be going." Jake was still standing.

"No, please. I do apologize."

Marion asked if Max had eaten.

"Chicken cutlets at six, but I will have a beer. I see you are not drinking the Danish beer," he told Jake. "Will you join me?"

"Sure. But have one of the Canadian too."

"I'm afraid I'm not a great fan of your beer. Nor your cigarettes for that matter." Max lit one. "They are two things about your country I do not admire so much."

Things improved after that. Max had a Canadian beer, Jake a Danish one. Max praised the lox, and after some discussion about Hendricks, the conversation drifted back to England. Millicent wasn't mentioned, but Max noticed Marion's books on Winston Churchill and Edward VIII.

"Ah yes," Max said. "The Duke of Windsor. The magazines my sister buys have written about him. The Duke of Windsor visited Germany before the war, I believe. He never thought England and Germany should go to war."

"So the books say," Marion said. "He even visited Hitler at his mountain retreat with Mrs. Simpson after he abdicated. I've read that the Germans tried to kidnap him and Wallis, and put Edward back on the throne, but they went to the Bahamas instead. There were all these secret meetings going on. Apparently the Germans told him that the English would bomb his ship. I think Churchill had to threaten him with a court martial to get him to leave Europe for the Bahamas. Even when Edward was back in Europe after the war, he made no secret of his admiration for Hitler."

"Nice fellow," Jake said.

"I cannot think why anyone would admire the madman Hitler," Max said.

"Some people even say that the real reason for the abdication wasn't Wallis but his Nazi sympathies," Marion said. "And you say you've read about Edward in German magazines," she prompted Max.

"About Edward and Princess Grace and Queen Elizabeth and the daughter— Anne— who loves horses so much. It is all so much hoopla-la, stories written to sell the magazines. I do not pay much attention to the articles."

"But you read them," Marion said.

Max laughed.

"When I visit my sister and the children make too much noise, I amuse myself as best I can. The magazines are there and the children make noise and so I look at the pictures."

"Give me the noisy kids," Jake said.

"You are very interested in Edward, I think," Max told her. Marion replied that she liked history, and read a lot of it.

"Edward always said," Marion went on, "that if he had remained king there wouldn't have been a war."

"Yes, and the Nazis would have ruled the world," Jake said.

"Thank God that did not happen," Max said.

"Anyway, Edward never wanted to be king," Marion said. "He would have made a wretched king. I've read the government stopped sending him official documents because he either didn't pay attention to them or just left them lying around for his house guests to read."

She went on like this for some time. Jake and Max were bored and I saw a look pass between them: older women and their royalty-madness.

Jake left at eleven (by bus, although Max offered to drive him). I walked him to the elevator. "Watch out for lover-boy," he told me. I poked him in the stomach.

Max absolutely insisted on taking the couch, but I wished I'd made him sleep in his own bed. The light burned in the living room and I could hear him lighting cigarettes. The TV was on, turned down low, but I could still hear it. Usually noises don't bother me, but I'd had a lot of coffee and was too wired to sleep. If Max hadn't been there, I would have gotten up myself and watched TV or read, but he was there, and all I could do was lie in bed and listen to his movements and think about the break-in in Meredith.

It was possible that this Theriau had it in for Hugh, but I knew— *knew*— that *they* had broken into Marion's house looking for something. What? *What* were *they* looking for? They had the photos, the diary, and who knew what else? Maybe they had ransacked George's apartment by now.

I even had the thought that *Grace Greathurst* had broken into Marion's house. Maybe *Grace Greathurst* had killed George McDrew...

At the same time, there was that strange thing I was missing, that thing I had dreamed about the night before. I had more or less forgotten about the dream during the day, but now it came back, and I was sure that if I could just remember what it was, then everything would become clear.

I think I dozed off briefly, but suddenly the phone was ringing and I was wide awake again.

I picked up the receiver, but Max had already answered.

"It is for you, Carolyn," he said. I heard a click as he put the phone down and then there was Owen's voice on the line.

"Owen! For heaven's sake! Do you know what time it is? It's two-thirty in the morning! Are you crazy?"

"Who answered the phone?"

"The man whose condo this is. He just came back from a business trip and is flying out again tomorrow morning."

"How do I know he's not listening? Does your husband know about this?"

"I think both questions are rude. I found Mrs. Littlehurst, by the way."

"Be careful!"

"It's not her real name anyway, is it? But she wouldn't see me. She ran away!"

I slammed the phone down.

Max knocked on the door, wanting to know if there was trouble. Marion was behind him.

"Just a crazy writer," I lied. "I hired him to help with some research, and I've regretted it ever since. I can only apologize, Max. And you have to be up so early in the morning."

"Ah, the book on teachers. But there is no need to apologize. I was still awake. I hope I did not disturb you. I am one of those fortunate people who require little sleep. Tomorrow I will have a sauna and that will refresh me."

"I wasn't asleep either," Marion said. "Too much coffee late at night. I'm not used to it. We have really imposed on you, Max."

"That is nonsense. There is camomile tea. Shall I make some? It will help everyone to sleep."

So at two-thirty a.m. we all drank camomile tea.

Max was right when he said he required little sleep. The clock radio read seven when I awoke and found him taking suits out of the closet and shirts from the armoire in my room. I closed my eyes, and when I opened them again it was almost nine. I was supposed to leave for the airport at nine-thirty! I jumped into the shower and pulled on slacks and a sweater.

Max, fresh-faced and shaven, was leisurely drinking coffee, as if he had all the time in the world. Marion was still in her bathrobe.

"My God— I'm sorry Max. I overslept. We'll leave right away!"

"You must not worry, Carolyn." He was all smiles. "There is always another flight. Airplanes fly at all hours."

"I overslept too," Marion said. "I think I'll pass on the airport if you don't mind. I've a bit of headache this morning. Can we go to Malton this afternoon?"

"Malton? Is that not where the airport is?" Max wanted to know.

I explained that Malton used to be merely a small village where the woman I was dedicating my book to had taught.

"But we should get going. I don't want you to miss your plane."

It would only take fifteen minutes to get to the airport, but I was worried about the traffic and driving a strange car. Max lit a cigarette. I put my coat on, and then I couldn't find my purse. I was worried I'd left it in the deli, until I remembered the condo keys were in it, and I'd used them when we came back.

I finally found it jammed under the bed— it was my big quilted bag and it was stuck there— and then I had to practically push Max out of the door.

I made him drive to the airport. They were announcing final boarding when we got there. I said I'd pick him up at ten-thirty on Friday.

Marion was asleep on the sofa when I got back and the phone was ringing. Owen. He had to see me right away.

"For heaven's sake, Owen, what's wrong with you? You wake me up in the middle of the night and now you think I have to jump when you say jump. I don't have time to see you today. I have plans for this afternoon. I'm busy."

"Busy with Charlie, I suppose," he said.

"Not busy with Charlie. And it's none of your business."

He said he was in Toronto. "I came purposely to see you."

"Fine. Then you can find your Mrs. *Bighurst!*"

I slammed the phone down.

Marion was sitting up, rubbing her eyes. The phone rang again.

I didn't answer it. "I'm going to tell Owen to get lost. The man is nuts. It's all Charlie's fault." The phone continued to ring. "I'm going to tell Owen the truth," I said, "and get him out of our hair."

His voice was wheedling. He'd driven to Toronto only to see me in a car that wasn't road-safe, he was paying "top dollars" for parking, and he thought we had an agreement. I said we didn't have an agreement. Not any more.

He didn't know what to say to that. Finally he asked about all the material he'd sent Jake.

"I have nothing to do with that," I said.

"But I thought..." I could picture him sweating, turning white. "I... went to Orillia yesterday. That's why I called so late. I found out you're not married to Charlie any more..."

He was apologetic, uncertain now. He sounded like he was going to cry. But he tried to assert himself. "I think you owe me an explanation. I haven't slept in over twenty-four hours."

"What about this Bighurst/Greathurst dame?" I asked. "Talk about not sleeping. You sent us on a wild goose chase. First you give us the wrong name and then she isn't there. What'd you do, warn her?"

"Bighurst?"

"Greathurst," I said. "That's her real name."

"Mrs. Littlehurst, you mean."

"That's not her name, but you don't have to be very smart to figure it out. Fortunately I was smart enough. Her name is Grace *Greathurst*, you liar!"

Ranting had a good effect. He said in a small voice that the name she had definitely given him was Littlehurst. And what did he have to gain by lying to me? he wanted to know.

He didn't say that I was the one who had lied.

What he did, instead, was to— cry. Everything— sob— was— sob— finished— for— him.

It was all over. What was the point in living? He would never make it as a writer now. He was getting older, he'd never had any real happiness in life...

I should have hung up, but I listened to his crying. *Wept* is a better description of how he sounded. Not he sobbed. But— *he wept...*

I agreed to meet him in an hour at the Elephant & Castle.

Owen did look pathetic in the restaurant. It was lunch hour and crowded, and he was squashed into a corner. Stirring tea, pale and sweaty in his bulky overcoat. He looked ten years older.

There was no large table available and we had to crowd around the small table. Close up, Owen looked even more awful. His wispy hair stuck to his greasy forehead, and his hands shook as he lifted his cup.

Nothing ever worked out for him. He wasn't surprised. It had all seemed to be too good to be true. But it was the same old story, he said. His wife had left him too. For another man. A lawyer, a successful person. And then his dog had died, a wonderful dog...

It seemed as if he had nothing to lose after I'd heard him coming apart and that he might as well let everything else spill out.

"So you went to Orillia and found out the truth," I said.

He nodded bleakly. He was suspicious that he hadn't heard from Charlie, and called the C. Trott number again. This time he didn't hang up when a woman answered, but asked for Charlie. Charlie came to the phone. Owen hung up, and decided "right there and then" to have it out with Charlie, to confront him. He knew something fishy was going on; Charlie had lied to him. Owen drove to Orillia "and I don't remember a single thing of that drive. I didn't think of the bald tires on my car or anything. I just knew I had to go there."

Charlie's car was in front of the house, but it was Sandy who answered the door. "I thought she was his girlfriend, but it turns out she's his wife, and then Charlie came and I had it out with him. The wife was yelling that she was sick of his lies and Charlie told me to get lost. I didn't even get my foot in the door. So that's that, I guess. It's all over now."

His eyes were magnified behind his thick glasses. I hated those beseeching, sad eyes. The fact that he didn't berate me for lying to him made him seem even more pathetic. He listened passively as I told him how Charlie had led people to believe that he and I were still a team so people would talk to him.

"And I'm afraid I let you go on thinking that," I concluded. "I am sorry about that."

"Nothing's gone right for me since my wife left me. We were married for twenty-seven years. I moved to Cambridge to start over but my health went and I had to retire from the post office. I thought I'd have time to do my writing, but that's amounted to a hill of beans. I might as well face it." He looked at me. "My wife's name was Shirley. She lives in Toronto."

I crossed my fingers and said Jake would still consider his work.

He brightened at that. Did I really think so?

"But I think you've been less than honest with me about that woman you met at the library."

"No! I swear to you that I was telling the truth! She obviously gave me the wrong name!"

He reached for my hand, to shake it, but I put my hand under the table.

"And the business with the lawyer phoning you?"

"That was the truth, too. What can I do to make you believe?"

"George McDrew is dead. He was already dead when that 'lawyer' called you to meet him."

I could tell from his face that he hadn't known this.

"I think someone was playing a joke on you," I said.

Owen stared into his coffee cup. I turned away. Perhaps I had gone too far. I was sure he was crying again.

"But I will put in a good word for you at Hendricks." He didn't— couldn't— say anything. "Don't worry. Your writing wasn't put in the slush pile." Technically, this was true. "Of course I have no control over what they actually decide to publish."

At last he spoke in a wobbly voice. He even smiled a bit, a childlike imploring smile: I'm sorry I was bad, I'm sorry you had to hit me.

"I guess that's something. I want you to know that I haven't kept anything back from you over Millicent. You know everything I know. I hope you believe me. I realize I don't actually know that much. I could poke around Cambridge. And if I find out anything..."

"You'd share it with me?"

"Yes, if you like."

"What about this tabloid business with Charlie?"

"I don't know the name of the paper. Charlie talked to several people and then he found this fellow with a magazine who once used some of your recipes in a column or something."

"Some of my recipes."

"A while ago. That's why this fellow talked to Charlie, because he knew you. Or knew of you. Charlie was going to get back to me on that, but I guess now he won't. Maybe I shouldn't have gone up to Orillia."

"You had to find out the truth sooner or later."

"Sometimes it's better not to know the truth. I could have been happier for a longer time if I hadn't found out so soon."

This was the most pathetic thing he'd said.

"You know you can always work on Millicent's story by yourself. There's nothing to prevent you from going ahead on your own," I said.

"I don't know. I wouldn't mind sharing anything I learn with you."

I didn't like this idea. I was sure Owen wasn't lying, but he was so irritating.

"I'm too upset to start out on something big on my own right now. It's dangerous, you know. Believe me, I'm not lying. I have had some pretty strange things happen since I got involved in this Millicent thing. Someone's been in my apartment. I've been followed a few times. People phone and hang up. You may think I'm imagining this, but I'm telling the truth. This orange van's been around."

Luckily, he didn't look at me. He didn't see my reaction.

"Even if you're not interested in anything I find out, I want you to watch it. You can't get tangled up with digging out dirt about the royal family and not have trouble," he said. "I don't care if you never want to see me again, but I don't want you to get hurt."

"But if you're frightened, why go on with it?" I asked. "You can always drop it."

"I'm interested in it, you see. Just like you are."

"But I'm only dedicating my book to her."

"Yet you're interested in this tabloid business."

"Yes, but—"

Marion spoke for the first time.

"Something has just occurred to me. You don't know who I really am, Owen."

He looked up, dazed.

"We said I was Charlie's mother, but I'm not. And I'm not from New Jersey. I live in northern Ontario and I am Carolyn's mother-in-law, only my last name is Hall."

"My husband's name is Peter Hall," I said. Now Owen could get my home phone number, but I doubted if he'd call me. I had a feeling that he'd be too embarrassed to ever call me again.

"It's so much to take in," Owen said. "Last week the world was fine and now it's all different."

"Just remember Hendricks will consider your work," I said.

Owen nodded.

"Thank you for giving me hope," he said, quite formally. "May I call you if I uncover something about Millicent around Cambridge? Just to tell you, with no obligation whatsoever?"

Reluctantly— against my better judgement— I agreed. Tears swam in Owen's eyes.

It was Marion who located the tabloid, *British Press*, not in the yellow pages but in the main telephone directory. The editor's name was Edgar Brighton and he had recently talked to Charlie.

Edgar Brighton was English, semi-retired (I judged the magazine's office was in his home), and glad to speak to another English voice.

Edgar Brighton had written to the Duke of Windsor in 1971 about the inscription on the stone, and to ask the Duke if he had been married to Millicent Mulvey.

The letter was sent by registered mail.

The Duke of Windsor never replied.

Marion would call Edgar Brighton, after we returned from Cambridge, to set up an appointment to see him.

CHAPTER
EIGHTEEN

I knew I'd like Peggy Lovely the minute I saw her striding through the customs' barrier at Pearson International Airport. My first impression was of a small, lithe, tow-headed young woman. The image that came to mind was of a sporty English woman who loved horses. She was dressed casually in a camel hair sports coat open over wool slacks. Loafers, shoulder bag.

It was only when you got close that you could see the lines under the eyes, around the mouth. By the time her luggage arrived on the carousel, we were chatting as if we'd known each other forever.

I asked if she rode.

"No; do I look as if I do?"

"That's what I thought when I saw you."

She laughed. "I thought you looked exactly like a cookbook author. A little artsy, like someone who also writes plays." She smiled at me.

We drove straight to Cambridge. Peggy was going to stay in George McDrew's apartment. ("Or isn't it habitable? Is the refrigerator in the living room, for instance?") The memorial service was to be at a funeral parlour at four, followed by a reception in the common room in her uncle's building. The funeral director had arranged the catering.

"Like pizza, everything's been ordered over the phone," she sighed.

Real grief wasn't evident, but she showed a quiet, rueful regret. George McDrew was her father's baby brother. "By the time George came along, Dad was already sixteen and out working. And when he was eighteen, Dad moved to Boston." Her father had gone into banking and done quite well. "In those days you didn't need an M.B.A. He didn't marry until he was forty-three and he was almost fifty when I was born. He didn't return to Canada for a visit until I was five or six. George was living in Guelph and Aunt Eva, George's sister, was in Cambridge. We stayed with Eva— I think Mother preferred her to George, who tended to be outspoken. George was wonderful, kidding around with me, giving me candy, unlike Eva who I remember as a real dragon— didn't like kids, had none of her own, and spilled milk was a real disaster. George used to send me a dollar for my birthday every year. And a present at Christmas. He sent me five hundred dollars when I married! I should have visited him, I know. I invited him to my wedding but he wrote saying he wasn't one to travel much."

"But he said he went out west to bring Millicent back," I said.

We were in George's apartment, drinking tea without milk because there wasn't any.

"Yes. Millicent. I've been thinking about what you told me. I think she had a cat, a great big grey cat. I have this picture of myself sitting with a cat on a porch. I wish I could tell you more, but we didn't get to Guelph that much. We'd drive over to spend an afternoon with George once or twice each visit. We stopped visiting when Father died and during the war gasoline was rationed. It's sad when you think of it. George was my only living relative. Except Brad of course." Brad was her twenty-five-year-old son. Peggy was divorced. "I wish Brad had met George. Isn't it sad the way families grow apart?"

There was a knock at the door.

It was a neighbour, bearing a casserole. "A covered dish" as I call it in my cookbooks. She introduced herself as Sophie Kopernick "from next door," and she intended to have a visit. I made more tea as she gazed with great curiosity around the apartment. It was probably the first time she'd ever been inside it.

It was from Sophie that we learned George had taken a taxi and carried a small bag with him the day he died.

After she had conveyed sympathy and not so discreetly found out who we all were, she said:

"If only George had taken his car that day, it mightn't have happened! No one could understand it, George taking a taxi. He never took taxis. I shouldn't say this, but he was careful with the dollars. Not that I'm criticizing. It was just the way he was. Going through the Depression and all.

"And he went everywhere in that car of his. Still driving, at his age, but he passed the test every year so I guess it was all right. And I heard he had a bag with him. One of the fellows asked him if he was going to Florida. They were waiting for the van to the seniors' centre, but George never went there. And to end up in the park like that! It was a shock for all of us, but you know what the world's like these days."

"I thought he had a heart attack," I said.

"After being robbed is more like it! They say that bag of his is missing."

After Sophie reluctantly left, we filled Peggy in on the search for Millicent's story and all the things that had happened.

She did not think the break-ins, the orange van following us, the strange happenings were coincidences. In her opinion, the royal family would do anything to protect their image and reputation.

"There are some who believe that Queen Victoria had masked bandits find a marriage certificate in Quebec that proved her father, the Duke of Kent, had married his mistress, Madame St. Laurent."

Marion knew the story; I did not. Queen Victoria's father had been ordered to marry to provide an heir to the throne. He had married a German princess, but in doing so he'd had to relinquish his mistress of many years with whom he'd lived in Canada.

"I hate to think Uncle George met with foul play," Peggy said.

"The autopsy definitely said a heart attack," I reminded her.

But she already knew that.

"And what about the taxi? And the bag that Uncle George had with him? Where is that? Let's see if we can find anything here."

There was just enough time to hunt around before she had to get changed for the service. The top drawer in the dresser held papers— insurance forms on the car, the cards and letters Peggy had sent, and miscellaneous photos, none of them of Millicent. There was a bank book showing a balance of $23,598, George's birth certificate, his mother's death and marriage certificates, and his discharge papers from the Canadian army. A tin box held his will, which left everything to Peggy.

The gun was beneath socks and underwear.

And— in the bottom drawer— a silver cigarette case with the Prince of Wales feathers engraved on it.

A present from Edward, or on his behalf, for George's help?

But there were no papers relating to Millicent.

I'm sure the strangeness of George McDrew's death and the arrival of the niece from New York accounted, partly, for the large attendance at the funeral parlour. The room was filled with senior citizens. We sat in the front with Peggy, in the family pew, and I was aware of curious eyes on us throughout the service.

Owen, thankfully, was not there, but I hadn't told him about the service and as far as I knew, no notice had been in the paper. But I was pretty sure that even if he'd known, he wouldn't have attended in case he'd see me there. Owen was a wimp, but even wimps have pride and he'd cried in front of me. I doubted if I'd ever see him or hear from him again.

As Peggy was shaking hands and receiving condolences, I noticed Detective Miller, wearing a bedraggled overcoat over the same old blazer he'd had on when we talked to him, watching from the corridor. I went over to speak to him.

"I see the niece called you," he said.

"Yes. As a matter of fact I picked her up at the airport. I've been in Toronto for a few days. I had to drive by the airport anyway. It's a good thing Mr. McDrew saved her Christmas cards or you wouldn't have found her."

"Her name was listed as next-of-kin on the lease."

"Oh."

"Did you think we searched the apartment? You've been reading too many detective thrillers."

"A neighbour told us Mr. McDrew took a taxi the day he died. He never took taxis, apparently. And the neighbour said he had a bag with him," I said. "I guess the bag wasn't there with the wallet."

Miller shrugged. Rumours, he said. He went over to speak to Peggy.

The reception at the building— in the common room— was even better attended than the service. I have to say it was a jovial affair, with a large assortment of squares, cookies, little sandwiches, cheese and fruit, and large urns of coffee and tea. From what I overheard, the old people didn't waste time talking about death, now that the service was over. George was dead, but they were alive and catching up on gossip.

I recognized one of the women Marion and I had seen the day I interviewed George McDrew. She had a plate loaded with goodies. Sophie from next door went one better, putting together a care package for later.

By six-thirty, only morsels of crumbly cheddar cheese and a few grapes remained. The last mourners— translate party-goers— straggled out.

"You must be exhausted," I told Peggy. "It's been a long day for you."

"Exhausted, but something's occurred to me. Everyone I talked to mentioned Uncle George's pride in his old car. That's one place we haven't looked. Let's go down to the garage. The car keys should be with the apartment keys the super gave me."

We took the elevator to the garage.

George's old navy blue Plymouth was shiny clean, as if it had just been waxed. The interior was spotless and there was nothing in it except a map of Ontario and insurance papers in the glove compartment. The trunk held a bag of salt, a spare tire, and an old but clean and carefully folded car rug.

"Poor Uncle George," Peggy said. "He bought this car when Brad was born. He wrote and said maybe he'd even drive down to visit. I'm afraid I wasn't very encouraging. Brad was a colicky baby and I was just finishing my doctorate. My husband wanted me to drop out. It wasn't a good year. Uncle George never suggested visiting again. He probably thought I didn't want to see him."

She slammed the trunk down with a bang. The noise must have covered the sound of the door opening, because when I raised my eyes I saw a man standing in the doorway to the stairwell. For a minute the red neon exit light illuminated his face. He wore a fedora and his face was— bland.

And then he was gone.

Peggy and Marion hadn't seen him.

I could only whisper and point at the door. It was Peggy, after a moment's hesitation, who opened the door, but the staircase was empty.

The elevator didn't come. We pressed the button again and again, but the indicator light remained firmly static for the lobby.

"He's holding the button," I said. "He's waiting for us to come up the stairs."

"But if he's waiting for us, why doesn't he just let us take the elevator? He could even get on the elevator," Marion said.

"But he wouldn't know if we took the stairs or the elevator. This way we have to take the stairs."

"No we don't," Peggy said. "We don't have to do any such thing. Let's go for a little drive. We'll be safe in the car. I should buy some milk and bread anyway."

We had our coats with us because we hadn't returned to George's apartment after coming back from the funeral home. We got into the car, Peggy inserted the ignition key, and the motor turned over at once.

The garage door opened automatically. Outside, Max's Mercedes was still parked safely in the visitors' space. I noticed Peggy looking in the rear-view mirror, but we weren't followed as I directed her to a nearby variety store, where she bought a carton of milk and a package of rolls.

Back at the building, she parked the Plymouth next to Max's Mercedes.

"No garage this time," she said, trying to make a joke of it, but she hesitated before walking into the lobby.

"If you don't want to stay in the apartment tonight, you're welcome to stay in Guelph, or to come to Toronto with us," I offered.

But she had things to do, she said. She wanted to take the will to a lawyer in the morning, for one thing. And she'd have to sort through the clothes and other things to clean the apartment out. It had already been rented for the first of the month.

"Maybe I'll have a sale for the things I don't want," she said, as she unlocked the apartment door. "That might draw someone out."

"I tried that too. I gave a reading in our bookstore but no one unusual showed up, unless you count one ex-husband."

"Beautiful creatures, ex-husbands, aren't they?"

"Mine was gloating, I'm afraid. I can't picture Charlie working for the Royals."

Nothing appeared to have been touched in the apartment. The cigarette case was where Peggy had left it.

"I'm almost disappointed," Peggy said. "Relieved but disappointed."

"If I hadn't told you about Millicent, you'd think nothing was wrong. Perhaps I shouldn't have told you. Maybe I've worried you for nothing."

She shook her head.

"At least you haven't scoffed at Millicent's story and your uncle's involvement in it. Most people would have," I said.

She took a moment to answer.

"As soon as you mentioned her name something clicked. I knew I'd met her and I remembered the cat, but I don't know. There's something I can't remember. Something I can't put my finger on. Something someone said once? I don't know. I'll try to remember. Maybe staying here for a few days will bring it back." She picked up one of the sofa cushions and smoothed it absently. "I've been thinking and thinking, but I just can't come to it. I wish I could remember..."

I wished I could remember that missing something too.

"What I don't understand," Peggy said, "is that George said the Royals wanted the inscription on the stone and now they're trying to stop anything from getting out. I really don't understand it, unless George was mistaken about that. Don't the detectives in novels always say you have to find the motive? That's what you're missing— the motive."

"Isn't the motive to prevent Millicent's story from being told?" I asked. "George was quite clear that the Royals paid for the stone. He didn't understand it either, I think."

Marion repeated her theory about the inscription being a vendetta against the Duchess of Windsor.

"It could be seen as some kind of blackmail. And who else would be involved except for agents acting on behalf of the royal family?" Marion asked.

No one had an answer. It was almost seven-thirty and time to go. We had a long drive ahead of us back to Toronto, and I wanted to drop in at home on the way. Peggy walked us to the elevator, which arrived at once.

We were about to get on when she grabbed my hand.

"Wait a minute! It just came to me. You said earlier that the Duke of Windsor didn't answer or acknowledge a letter asking about Millicent? And yet the Royals are supposed to have paid for the stone. Say, then, that the royal family does want Millicent's story to come out for various reasons. Who would want to prevent the truth being told? There can only be one person." She gazed at us.

"The Duchess of Windsor," she said. "The former Mrs. Wallis Simpson. Think about it. Isn't that the motive you've been looking for?"

Marion and I dropped in at home but Peter wasn't there. We drove to Toronto.

CHAPTER
NINETEEN

Peggy's theory about the motive made perfect sense.

It stood to reason that the Duchess would not want Millicent's story known. The marriage of Millicent and the Duke would not only dash the "love story of the century" to the ground, but there might even be legal ramifications resulting from an earlier marriage.

"The motive," Marion said at breakfast. "Now we have a motive and it explains everything— the break-ins, the thefts of the photos you had and the diary George McDrew left in Millicent's house. You led them to George McDrew and they flushed him out, tricked him. They may have thought he had other papers, documents. The same people could have contacted Owen, but Peter scared them off. It does make sense, rather, when you put it all together."

The buzzer went. We looked at each other. Peter, I thought– hoped– imagining he had decided to come to Toronto on the spur of the moment. I had expected him to call me after we got back to the condo, but he hadn't and I wasn't going to make the first move.

I pressed the intercom button, and a voice shot through it:

Sandy Trott's.

Sandy was not what I had expected: round-faced, chubby, dull blonde hair in a pony tail, wearing a track suit and a Hudson Bay parka. Thirty or forty, it was hard to tell.

"Charlie's disappeared." She didn't stop to remove her jacket or boots, but waltzed right in and collapsed on the sofa. She pulled a crumpled Kleenex out of her pocket, blew her nose noisily, and looked at me as if it was my fault.

"Disappeared," I said.

"After that man came to the door, we had a terrible fight. I told Charlie I was through with him, that I was going to my mother's and Charlie said, Fine, I could go, but not to come back. He was yelling and screaming and I went for a drive to cool off... I wanted to let him know he couldn't treat me that way!"

She wiped her nose with the balled-up Kleenex. Marion handed her new tissue. Sandy's boots were dripping water on the pearl carpet.

I should have been sympathetic, but she was so totally absorbed in her own misery in a strange, bossy sort of way.

"He was gone when I came home! He hasn't been at work and they're mad as hell. He was supposed to see customers in Kingston this week and he hasn't even called them. I don't know where he is!"

"What about the girlfriend?" I suggested. "Gloria."

More tears. She'd gone over there. Gloria started to slam the door, then Gloria's husband came on the scene and Gloria tried to tell him Sandy was the Avon lady, "...but I was so mad I told him what was going on! Charlie's going to kill me!"

"Why don't I make some tea," Marion murmured, going to the kitchen. I turned the television on. *Donahue*, a program about married transvestites.

"I know how you feel," I told Sandy when Marion brought the tea in. I snapped the TV off. "I went all to pieces after Charlie left me, but it was the best thing that ever happened to me. You're used to his abuse, the way I was."

"But what if he's dead?" she cried. "He could be dead. When we had our fight he said he was on to something really good. He said he'd be rich and famous and dump me. He said he wouldn't give me a penny."

We fixed her tea. I added sugar, Marion milk.

"He's probably just holed up somewhere. Maybe he went on a bender," I said.

"But he wouldn't miss work! He was unemployed last year. We had to live on what I made at the IGA. He'd show up for work, I know he would. I even called his mother, in case he went there, but she hasn't heard from him. Now I've got her to worry about, too."

"Oh, yes, Mrs. Trott." Sandy didn't even smile. "Good old Mrs. Trott. Do you know what this good stuff is that Charlie talked about?"

"Just something a guy at this tabloid told Charlie. Charlie called it a breakthrough. Some woman, Charlie said. That's all I know. Charlie was going to see her. That's what he was yelling when I walked out. He was going to see this woman and make a fortune."

She took a package of Export A from her purse, lit a cigarette, and blew the smoke out of her nose.

"It's supposed to be about royalty or something. He said it was dangerous. He told me you lied to me, that you were still involved in the story. It was supposed to be a secret, he said. That's why I came here. I thought maybe Charlie could be here. But I knew he wouldn't be, after I talked to your husband."

"Is that where you found out where I was?"

"I called your place. Your husband told me where to find you."

Did that mean Peter was washing his hands of the whole thing?

"I was already in Toronto. I couldn't just sit around in Orillia. I phoned in sick. There was no way I was going in to work today. I thought of calling the police but Charlie would kill me. So I came here to see if I could find the tabloid, but no one knew what I was talking about. I thought maybe you'd know where Charlie went. I mean, if you were still partners in this thing…"

"I can assure you we're not. We never were. That's just something Charlie dreamed up. But I do know the tabloid."

"How do you know that?" Her voice was suspicious. "Did Charlie tell you?"

"No, I heard about the tabloid from Owen Peterson, the man who turned up at your house," I lied. "It wasn't hard to find the name of the paper."

"I called every one. I didn't find it."

"Just a little imaginative digging," I told her.

Marion called Edgar Brighton, at *British Press*. He said he'd meet her at one-thirty at the Royal York for lunch.

The lobby of the Royal York Hotel is a good place to hang out. There are deep chairs and settees in the lounge area, and Sandy and I didn't look out of place among the visitors and businesspeople passing through. An accounting convention was meeting. Some of the men from the boonies had brought their wives, and like Sandy, they were dressed casually for a day of shopping in the big city. We settled in chairs and pretended to read newspapers, while Marion waited for Edgar Brighton, the *British Press* editor, twenty feet away.

Sandy was not pleased. She didn't see why she couldn't tackle Brighton herself. Charlie was her husband; she had a right to talk to Brighton. If anything had happened to Charlie, she had a right to know. She was Charlie's *wife*.

It was difficult to persuade her to go along with the status quo. "Marion's the one who contacted him," I told her. "Trust her. Just for now."

I think Sandy only agreed because she didn't know what else to do. She had come to Toronto by bus and she wasn't familiar with the subway system. She had lost the Grey Coach schedule and didn't know when the bus returned to Orillia.

"I doubt if Mr. Brighton would even talk to me," I told her. "We decided Marion should call him because she's English. If anyone can find out anything about Charlie, Marion can."

"I think I should at least be able to meet this Brighton," Sandy said.

"Don't worry. Marion will find out what she can."

"What happened to Charlie?"

She was still talking like this when Brighton appeared exactly on time, a tall man with a military bearing, dressed in a navy blazer and grey flannels, and carrying an overcoat over his arm.

Marion was perfect. She had put on a suit and looked like a tweedy English countrywoman in town for the day.

Luckily, Brighton suggested they talk at the restaurant in the Royal York, and we were able to follow them, although we had to sit across the room in the smoking section because of Sandy.

It was a long luncheon. Brighton seemed to enjoy the chance to discuss what was for him an absorbing and enthralling subject, the British monarchy. He was probably one of those fervent British expatriates who follow every move the Queen and her family make, I thought. He ordered another carafe of wine and leaned over to whisper confidentially, staring into Marion's eyes.

We couldn't have heard even if we'd been sitting right next to them. Sandy smoked one cigarette after another, hardly touched her egg sandwich, and nattered on about Charlie: he had threatened to change the beneficiary on his life insurance to his mother; he would take Sandy's name off their joint bank account; he would return to the States without her and file for divorce.

Finally, at quarter to three, Brighton and Marion rose. They were still talking as they left the restaurant and walked through the connecting doors to Union Station. We followed, Sandy still protesting.

Marion and Brighton parted at the newsstand, but Marion waited until he was swept up with commuters before telling us what he'd said.

Brighton had originally learned about the inscription on Millicent's stone in 1970 from a Dr. Frances Forward, who had been Millicent's physician long ago. In 1970, Forward lived near Peterborough.

Dr. Forward had been absolutely convinced of Millicent's claim and hoped someone would look into the story. This had led to Brighton's unanswered letter to the Duke.

After Charlie contacted him, Brighton had found Dr. Forward retired and living in Bushton, a small village near Peterborough.

She had agreed to meet Charlie.

"Brighton wasn't too impressed with Charlie and his talk of making millions," Marion said. "I told him a bit of the truth about Charlie and he wasn't surprised. He would have looked into Millicent's story himself, but his journal, as he calls it, takes all his time. And he doesn't have a car. He tried to interest one or two people, but no one believed it. That's when Charlie came along. If only we'd found Brighton sooner."

"But what about Charlie?" Sandy cried. "Did he see this woman or not? Didn't you find out if she saw him? He has customers in Peterborough he was going to see Monday but he didn't turn up there either. I should have talked to Brighton myself! Didn't you tell him about me?"

"All he knows is that Charlie was going to see Dr. Forward on Monday. The doctor can tell us if Charlie came by."

Sandy wanted to call the doctor herself.

"Look," I said, "you don't have a car. We just want to help you. Let's see if we can visit this doctor today. Then you can talk to her face to face. Wouldn't that be the best thing?"

"I just want to find Charlie."

"You will. I promise. We'll drive you there."

There are a few times when I've felt like a celebrity as a cookbook author, and calling Dr. Forward was one of those times.

She not only knew who I was, but she had all my cookbooks. A visit would be fine, she said; I could autograph the books!

She had seen Charlie at three o'clock on Monday.

She laughed when I said I had been married to him once. "Lucky for you, getting away," she said.

Sandy was reminding me loudly in the background about herself. "Let me talk to her! I want to talk to her!"

I handed Sandy the phone and she told Dr. Forward her story, repeating the details of the fight and Charlie's disappearance.

Finally she gave the phone back to me, saying the doctor wanted to talk to me again.

"I have just been talking to the present wife, I take it," the doctor said.

"It's going to be an interesting visit. I didn't tell her, but I've always had a feeling that someone would try to stop the story from getting out."

"It's all so complicated," I said.

"It is indeed. But come along. We'll talk when we meet. And we'll try to soothe your friend. Or should I call her your successor?"

The gently rolling countryside around Peterborough was blanketed with snow. It was almost five and overcast, growing dark, by the time we reached Bushton.

It was a small town of about 1,000, made friendly by the Christmas decorations. In the drugstore where we stopped so Sandy could buy cigarettes (she had been smoking constantly on the way; it was a good thing, I thought, that Max smoked too, or he might have complained later of the smell in the Mercedes), the entire front window had been transformed into a lit-up ceramic village scene.

Dr. Forward lived in the centre of the town, next to the library, in a white-framed cottage with green shutters. Loud dog barks rang out before we even knocked on the door, and I thought briefly of Beryl Sofer and Bunny and felt uneasy. Had someone broken into Beryl's son's place, and were we, by visiting here, endangering Dr. Forward? Was she already in danger because of Charlie's visit?

But the dogs dispelled these fears. They were two huge black labs whose frantic barking would have made the bravest gangster think twice. I wasn't too crazy about confronting them myself.

The doctor reassured us.

"They don't bite! Big friendly rascals, they're just glad to have company! Out of the way now, you two!"

The dogs didn't listen, but continued barking and wagging while she took our coats and I made introductions.

Dr. Forward was a tall, thin woman who had to be at least eighty years old, with grey hair cut into a square bob, and wearing, I was amused to see, Levi jeans.

It was a cosy place. A fire burned in the woodstove.

Books lined the wall. My cookbooks, ready for autographing, were piled on a round pine table.

The dogs covered any initial awkwardness. Chester and Gretchen trotted out their toys, rubber balls and old socks, for our inspection. They were younger than old Bunny, playful beasts who gravitated— another piece of luck— to Sandy, who was momentarily diverted.

Dr. Forward intuitively made a point of concentrating on Sandy's dilemma right away.

She said that Charlie had come by around three on the Monday afternoon. Charlie had spent half an hour with her, and as far as she knew, he'd planned to stay at a motel in Peterborough that night before going on to Kingston the next day.

Sandy repeated her story of the fight and so on. This time there were no tears. The dogs kept pestering her until she lit a cigarette and then they moved away from the smoke, woofing softly at the unaccustomed smell.

Dr. Forward suggested Sandy call local motels to see if Charlie had stayed in any of them.

"Use my study for privacy. The dogs won't bother you there. I'll get you a decent ash tray." Sandy had been dropping ashes into a potted plant. "I used to be a smoker myself, but don't tell anyone. I know you're a bundle of nerves right now."

"So you have come about Millicent," Dr. Forward said, when Sandy was behind the closed door of the study. "I couldn't tell what I knew, doctor-patient confidentiality you know, but I always thought someone would look into her story. And now you have come. And Charlie too. Two visits in a single week. That girl should call the police and report her husband as missing."

"You really think something's happened?"

"It's not impossible. Those abusive husbands usually don't leave their wives. They stick like glue. Poor girl. Manipulative bastard, isn't he? And you were married to him once," she said to me.

"Don't remind me," I said. "So you really think someone could have done something to Charlie."

"At risk of sounding melodramatic, I'd say it's possible. Charlie told me there had been interest in Millicent recently, and now that she's dead, I'd think there would be people interested in stopping the story from getting out."

"You believe her claim, obviously?" I asked.

The doctor sighed. "What can I tell you? I have to keep the doctor-patient information confidential. That's an absolute for me. I can't reveal what was in her medical file no matter how much I would like to. I told that fellow Charlie the same thing. Let's just say, I'm glad you're looking into her story. It deserves to be told."

"So you do believe it," I said, but I was disappointed. We'd come all this way with Sandy and the doctor wasn't going to tell us anything.

She must have read my thoughts. She folded her hands together and looked right at me. She was a small old woman but she wasn't a person to tangle with. The people working for the Duchess of Windsor wouldn't be able to frighten her, at least.

"I really do believe in patient-doctor confidentiality. It was drilled into me and I've stuck to it. It's not just the law. Call it a matter of principle.

"Don't forget I suggested to Mr. Brighton that Millicent's claim deserved looking into. That was after the inscription was on the stone, so I wasn't breaking a confidence. You can draw your own conclusions. I hope you don't think I'm being difficult. You mustn't."

"Newspapers were afraid of libel while the Duke was still alive."

"Yes, but after he died?"

"People thought— newspaper people— that Millicent was just an eccentric old woman with a fantasy," I said.

"I'm an eccentric old woman, too. You must wonder why I dragged you out here if I wasn't going to tell you anything, but I can tell you things that weren't in the medical file— anecdotal things, if you will. I used the same reasoning when I mentioned the stone to Mr. Brighton. I met him at a nudist colony, by the way. I've always been eccentric but I haven't always been old. Not that there aren't old people at nudist colonies, but I rather think I'd like to keep my old bones private."

She laughed and tapped her skinny knees.

"Mr. Brighton wrote to the Duke of Windsor and did not receive a reply," she said. "I suppose you know that?"

Marion said Brighton had told her that.

"We heard the royal family paid for the inscription," I said.

"Yes, Millicent said so. I don't think I'm betraying a confidence when I tell you that. We kept in touch by letter occasionally. At Christmas and so forth. What are your intentions regarding Millicent?" she asked me bluntly.

"To bring her story out. I knew her. She was a friend of mine."

We filled the doctor in on the background.

"That's what Charlie wanted to do, tell her story," the doctor said. "But I didn't trust him. All that talk of a bestseller in the works." She shrugged. "I didn't tell him anything, but he tried his darnedest to get something out of me. Offered me money, if you must know. After he left I wondered if I shouldn't have told him at least a bit, since he was the only one who ever turned up, but here you are now and I'm thanking my lucky stars I kept my mouth shut.

"You know, I have often wondered if the powers-that-be were sorry about Millicent when Edward abdicated. Someone from England wrote Millicent that Baldwin said, 'We should have allowed him to have his little Canadian miss.' 'Little Canadian miss!' Imagine that!

"It was a terrible time for Millicent when Wallis appeared on the scene. Millicent thought Edward still loved her, you see. She thought it was only parliament and the courtiers keeping them apart. He used to write her, but after Wallis, after 1934 or so, there was nothing. Not for a long time, at any rate. Did you know she taught up north for a bit?"

Marion answered that one. "Yes, near Meredith, where I live. It was quite the coincidence."

"She had her troubles in schools because of everything that happened," Dr. Forward said. "She taught for a while early in the thirties, but it was too much for her. I think it was having to keep everything to herself. I was glad when she had the inscription put on, but she didn't care any more by then. 'Now you can talk,' I wrote her, but they'd said she was to keep quiet even then. Everything I'm telling you now has nothing to do with the patient-doctor thing, by the way. I had stopped seeing her professionally by that time."

"She told a reporter she wasn't to say anything or sign anything," I said.

"It was a great pity the reporters didn't have more courage. If only her story could have been proven while she was still alive! I've always thought she didn't speak up because she didn't want to hurt Edward's feelings. After a while, long after he was married to Wallis, I think she convinced herself again that he still cared for her. He wrote, and they met once, when he came to Canada. He—"

Sandy was back. She had tried six motels, but Charlie hadn't stayed in any Monday night. He'd had a reservation at the Pine Hills Motel, but he hadn't shown up.

"Then you must try Kingston," Dr. Forward told her briskly. "He might have driven on to Kingston that afternoon."

Sandy wasn't easy to get rid of. Had Charlie mentioned her? she wanted to know. Had he been upset? How had he been? and so on.

Finally, we were alone again.

Dr. Forward shook her head. "I have a feeling she'll have to call the police and file a missing person report. I hope I am just being paranoid. Millicent used to say she had to be careful of *them*..."

"You were saying she saw the Duke of Windsor again."

"Yes, in 1950 or '51. I can tell you that. He and Wallis went to New Brunswick on a fishing holiday. Millicent went to New Brunswick. She wrote to tell me she was going. It was all very secretive. I don't know what happened. I didn't hear from her until Christmas, and she did mention she'd gone to New Brunswick, but that was all she said. I never questioned her. I assumed that the meeting had not gone well. I always wondered if she'd met Wallis."

A smile hovered on her lips.

"The famous Duchess of Windsor," she said. "Even I, I must admit, wanted to know about her. She might have been famous but she never stood a chance of being Queen, unlike Millicent, who could have become Queen. Millicent's story is a historical tragedy."

She called the dogs over and settled them beside her, stroking their ears.

"So long ago," she sighed. "I was a young doctor, just starting out in Toronto. Millicent didn't want to go to anyone in Guelph and so she came to me. A friend of hers would drive her."

"I think I know who that was. George McDrew. I told you about him."

"The man who hid the diary, who just died."

"Yes. I wish Millicent had married George instead of Edward."

"Oh, I doubt if Millicent would have married him. She was intent on her career, you see. She didn't want to marry, but Edward persuaded her. She felt desperately sorry for him and he wanted her so much. He offered to abdicate for her, she said, but she stopped him. And, as you know, they had the marriage dissolved. I've always thought it wasn't that Edward loved Wallis more, but that Wallis agreed to the abdication, and so he married her in a great flurry of publicity. He was king then, don't forget. Yes, I can see why people would want to keep the story from getting out."

"Not the British royal family," I said. "Not if they paid for the inscription. We think it's Wallis— people working for her— who want to hide the truth."

"Then it stands to reason that the Royals wanted reporters to investigate the claim, unlike the Duke of Windsor, who wanted to keep the truth hidden and Wallis content. Yes, it does make sense, Wallis' people being behind everything. I'd say you're on the right track there."

"I hope we haven't put you in any danger, coming here," I said.

"At my age? What does it matter? And don't forget Chester and Gretchen. They won't let anyone in, will you, you two?"

The dogs wagged their tails at the mention of their names. Chester woofed. "You should have these two for protection," she told me. "I wish I could tell you more, but I think everything else I know would be in the file."

"In the file," I said.

"Think of the information a medical file would have," she said.

"Something to do with a child," I said. "And a place, a place where the child was born. Even information on the child, where it was, what happened to it."

The doctor didn't answer. She looked wistful.

"You saw the child," I said.

"No, no."

"A place," I said. "You knew where she had a child, you knew her other doctor's name, the doctor who delivered her child."

"I wish I could tell you, I really do. Let's just say what I had was mostly second-hand information— information Millicent gave me. I'm afraid you'll have to be satisfied with that."

"I think Millicent had a child in western Canada," I said, as Sandy returned from the study.

Sandy hadn't found a trace of Charlie in Kingston.

"I'm going to call the police!" Sandy cried. "I know something's happened to him, I just know it!"

"Yes, perhaps you had better contact the police," the doctor agreed, "although I'm sure he'll be found safe."

"He said it was dangerous, and I never believed him," Sandy said. "I have to go to the police!"

Dr. Forward said the police station was just down the road, near the Esso station.

The doctor put on rubber boots and walked us to the car.

"Please be careful," I whispered.

It was only when we pulled up in front of the police station that I realized I hadn't autographed my cookbooks.

CHAPTER
TWENTY

Sandy insisted on going into the OPP station by herself, leaving us in the car while she filed a missing person report. Nor was she particularly forthcoming about what she had told the police. Returning to Toronto— it had started snowing again— she smoked moodily and would only say that the police were issuing a bulletin. Had she mentioned Millicent? "I told you I don't care about that! I just want to find Charlie!"

It was nine-thirty by the time we reached the Grey Coach terminal. The next bus left in ten minutes. Sandy bolted for the washroom.

"I'm going to end up driving her home on top of everything else," I told Marion. "She's going to miss her bus."

I really wanted to call Peter.

"Then she'll have to take the next one, won't she? The sooner we're rid of the wretched girl, the better. I almost feel sorry for Charlie. Perhaps he's run off."

"I'd better check on her."

I found Sandy crying in a cubicle. No, she didn't care if she missed the bus. I had an idea.

"But maybe Charlie's come home by now. Maybe he's there waiting for you."

She mumbled something I couldn't understand.

"You're going to miss your bus, Sandy. It'll be pulling out in a few minutes and who knows when the next one is?"

"I can't help it!" she wailed. "I don't care."

She missed her bus.

We drove the "wretched girl" to Orillia. The next bus wasn't for an hour and suddenly she seized on my brilliant idea that Charlie could be at home waiting for her. She just had to get home immediately; she couldn't wait for the bus; Charlie would be so annoyed if she wasn't there and so on. She'd just have to hitchhike. She couldn't wait a whole hour for the next bus.

Sandy had it all figured out: Charlie would be there waiting, and she could tell him that she had gone to Toronto to look for him at the tabloid press. We were to drive away and not let him see us. She'd say she took a taxi home from the bus terminal in Orillia. She knew Charlie would make fun of her for not driving to Toronto, but she'd say it had been his idea to buy the half-ton pick-up for a second car. She would tell him that if he'd bought a small Honda, say, she would have been able to drive in Toronto. And if he was mad about her taking a taxi when she could have called him, she'd tell him, "How was I supposed to know you were home?"

By the time we arrived on her street, her manic talk almost had me convinced that we'd see Charlie's car when we got there, but her semi-detached duplex was all in darkness with no car parked out front.

"I wish I was dead!" Sandy cried.

After she said that, we had to go inside with her, of course.

I had to help her with the lock, but Sandy herself snapped the light on inside the front door.

The place had been ransacked. The couch was pulled away from the wall, the coffee table overturned, and books and records had been pulled out of the "entertainment centre." An ugly orange sunset picture hung askew over the couch. It was a smallish room, just off the miniscule entryway, and the overall impression was of cheap, tasteless things tossed this way and that. The TV and stereo were still there.

"He said he'd trash the place if I ever left again! The bastard!"

In the kitchen a bag of flour had been dumped out and the cupboard doors stood open, with dishes piled on the table. An ivy plant sat in the sink, with half the soil spilled out beside it, as if thick fingers had burrowed in the pot.

Charlie could have done this, I thought, but why would Charlie look for something in his own house?

Sandy threw a dish against the wall and screamed.

"We should call her mother," Marion whispered to me.

"I'm going to kill him when I find him!" Sandy cried.

Marion quietly said that perhaps Charlie hadn't been here.

"You could have been robbed. You should—" she looked at me— "call the police."

"You don't think he did it? You don't believe me?" Sandy tugged a plaque reading "God Bless Our Home" from the wall and revealed a patched-up hole.

"That's why this goddamn thing's here! Take a look— he put his fist through the wall, and you don't think he'd mess up the place? I bet he's taken off to the States, just like he said he would! Down to live with his goddamn mother!"

"Why don't you call your mother?" I suggested, just as someone knocked at the door.

It was the next door neighbour, a man with a thin pointy face, wanting to know if anything was wrong.

"You might as well come in too, and see what that bastard Charlie did! Come on in, Jim, and see what the asshole I'm going to divorce did!"

"That's okay." Jim didn't want to be part of this, but he peered into the kitchen. He'd probably heard lots of fights through the thin separating wall. "As long as you're okay." He looked at me and I could see the disgust in his eyes. "I didn't want to call the police," he told Sandy.

"I'm getting a divorce this time," Sandy told him.

"I guess everything's under control," he said.

"Sandy was just upset, coming home to this," I said.

He rolled his eyes, shrugged and left, muttering he wouldn't mind getting some sleep some time.

Unbelievably, Sandy began tidying up as soon as he was gone. And unbelievably, we helped her. Marion kept telling Sandy she should call her mother or a friend to stay with her, but when we left (unbelievably, too), Sandy was actually polishing the coffee table.

We found a McDonald's and had our first meal in over ten hours.

We returned to Toronto the old way, through Newmarket and down Yonge Street into Willowdale, where I swung by Grace Greathurst's house. It was in darkness, although a light from the television showed in the front window next door. Marion, who'd been asleep, opened her eyes.

"Whatever are you stopping for?"

"I have no idea. Maybe I'll leave my card in her mailbox."

I left the headlights on so I could see. There was a streetlight at the corner, but Grace Greathurst's front yard and porch were in complete darkness. I couldn't locate the mailbox or even a slot, but I remembered where the doorbell was. There was no answer. I rattled the door knob, but of course the door was locked.

But— there was a movement in the window, by the curtain and it wasn't the cat. The curtains were apart in the middle, as if someone were holding the panels apart.

I gripped the iron hand rail and gingerly felt for the first step. I could not look at the curtains again. I could barely make out Marion's head; she seemed to have disappeared.

"Hey— what's going on over there?"

I dashed to the car, slipping down the steps. The porch light was on next door, and a man, naked to the waist, stood in the open door.

I gunned the Mercedes away.

Back at the condo, I fell asleep immediately.

When I awoke, the red light on the clock radio showed 5:02. I knew I had been dreaming again. I had been somewhere... dark. But... where? What was it?

What? That thing that was always eluding me, just beyond my reach and grasp? Somewhere in my sub-conscious was something vital and important and I did not know what it was.

Something— I closed my eyes and there was Charlie. It hadn't been Charlie in the dream, I knew, but in trying to recapture that vital something, I saw Charlie in an enclosed space, his fleshy face collapsed, tears rolling down his cheeks.

The schoolyard bully who has had his come-uppance.

I burrowed beneath the duvet and sought a cool place on the other side of the bed. No, Charlie hadn't been in the dream, but the clue I was missing had something to do with him. And something to do with me, too. Somewhere I had seen something, sensed something, something which would explain everything, but it was beyond me now.

CHAPTER
TWENTY-ONE

I awoke the next day, the day before Max's return, feeling homesick for Peter and wanting nothing more than to be back home in Guelph beginning my Christmas baking. I wasn't tired of Millicent's story, but suddenly Christmas and all the things that went with my new book coming out looked pretty attractive.

I called Peter at noon, catching him at home. We were both awkward.

"We dropped in after the service in Cambridge but you weren't there."

"I had to go out for coffee. We were all out."

"I miss you."

"Miss you too." Like a robot.

"We'll be home tomorrow. Max'll be back. We should be there in the afternoon."

"Research all done, I guess?"

"We're finished at the archives. And then Sandy turned up but I guess you know that because you told her where we were."

"Wasn't I supposed to?"

"We ended up driving her back to Orillia that night. Charlie's missing."

"That's what she told me."

We didn't say anything for a minute.

"Anyway, I'll be busy with the book and Christmas stuff. Baking and all that. So you won't have anything to worry about for a while."

"Worrying doesn't do any good anyway," Peter said.

I didn't call Sandy. We stayed in all day.

Marion insisted on doing the laundry before Max returned. The moose sweater was almost finished, with just the neck ribbing to be done.

So I drove to the airport alone to pick up Max. His plane was supposed to be in at ten-thirty but there was an early morning accident involving a semi on the Gardiner Expressway, which meant traffic was backed way up. I'd left in plenty of time, but by ten-fifteen I hadn't even reached Highway 427, and I still had to park when I got to the airport.

It was ten to eleven when I finally walked into Terminal 2 and Max was already waiting. I'd forgotten to empty Sandy's overflowing ashtrays in the back of his car. Marion had even reminded me.

I was profuse with the apologies, but he wasn't having any of it.

"My dear Carolyn! I know only too well the crazy traffic situation in this city. I am only thankful you are safely here!"

"Yes, if I'd crashed your car it would have been much worse," I said.

"Ah— what is a car? And it is only leased, after all."

If he noticed the ash trays or the mileage showing on the odometer, he didn't let on.

He had even bought us a present— frozen buffalo steaks.

"Perhaps I was being foolish," he said when he presented the cardboard box, double-wrapped in several layers of the *Calgary Herald*, to us. "It was rather a spur of the moment thing. I had business outside of the city and I could not resist. I have never eaten buffalo meat and I thought perhaps you have not also. So— here it is. Perhaps I should have brought chocolates instead."

Marion caught my eye: shouldn't we invite Max for dinner?

"You didn't have to bring a gift at all," she said. "Really Max, you've been more than generous."

"That's right, you are too generous," I added.

Marion gave me another look.

"You'll have to come for dinner then," I said. "The steak should be thawed out by this evening."

"But it is your gift. I cannot present you with a gift and expect to eat it myself."

"If you come to dinner," Marion said, "I can probably finish the sweater while we talk so you can get it in the mail to Germany."

We wrangled a bit, but in the end Max accepted the invitation. If we waited until he unpacked and made some necessary phone calls, we'd all drive to Guelph together.

Jake called just before we left to say that my book launch would be the first Wednesday in December at the Hendricks office. He'd arranged a book-signing at the Kitchener market for the next Saturday, followed by a talk at Seagram's Museum in Waterloo. Seagram's Museum is an old whiskey distillery, with a restaurant on the premises. Lots of sales there with Christmas in the air, Jake said. And *Winter Ovens* had been listed in the winter 1985 edition of *Books for Everybody*.

"And how's the new book coming?" he asked.

I said I wouldn't be able to work on it for a while because of Christmas and the cookbook coming out.

What amazed me about Max was that the man did not get tired. He read the newspaper while I called Peter at the store to let him know we were back and that Max was with us for dinner. He asked if Charlie had been found. I said I had no idea.

"There was a message on the machine at noon. A Mrs. Georgina Brown from Huntsville. She wants to talk to you about Millicent, said she saw the Meredith paper. But I guess you'll be too busy now."

"That's right," I said.

I had no sooner hung up, when the phone rang and a woman identified herself as Sandy's mother.

"There is something fishy going on," she said in a loud, decisive voice. "I've got Sandy over here. She didn't want me to call you, but I have to do something. I've called his mother too, down in the States. I don't know how high my phone bill's going to be. I've been on the phone to the police in Bushton and Kingston and Peterborough, but they can't tell me anything."

"I'm afraid I don't know what I can tell you either."

"That's no help at all. I never liked Charlie, but I've kept out of it. If I don't get some answers soon I'll go straight to the top. I'll call the Prime Minister if I have to."

"I wish I could help you, but—"

"What's this story Charlie was working on?"

"I don't know that much about it."

"Sandy says you're a writer and that you were working with Charlie." Her voice was accusing. "So how come you're saying you don't know anything about it?"

"I haven't been working with Charlie at all. He wanted people to believe that, but I had nothing to do with him."

"But you've seen him lately, haven't you?"

"He came to our store in Guelph. He was just passing through and dropped in when I was doing a reading."

"A what? A what?"

"A reading. I was giving a reading from a new book at our store. At my husband's store. Peter owns a bookstore."

"Wait a minute. I'm having problems here. If you have no contact with Charlie, what's he doing dropping in at your store? Can you tell me that? I've got one very upset daughter on my hands here and I want some answers and I want them now."

"I really can't help you. I'm sorry. I helped Sandy— we drove her to Bushton, she probably told you. I even drove her back home to Orillia after she missed her bus."

"That's another thing I find strange. Why would you go to so much trouble if you're not involved in this mess? I think you're covering up something and I'm going to get to the bottom of it. I've helped in campaigns. They'll listen to me at the Prime Minister's office."

"Look, I felt sorry for Sandy. I wish Charlie would turn up too."

"I'm sure you do! Then you wouldn't have to explain anything, would you?"

"Can you let me speak to Sandy?"

"Absolutely not. I finally got her to take some tranquillizers. I spent all morning at the doctor with her, running around. If you think this is a picnic, you can think again."

Getting rid of her wasn't easy. She went on like this for some time and finally slammed the phone down, saying she wasn't paying long distance charges just to hear a bunch of lies.

Marion had heard all of it, and when the phone rang again, almost at once, she took it, ready to do battle.

But it was Peggy.

The voice of sanity. She wasn't having a sale of her uncle's things at all. She was packing everything off to the Sally Ann and she was leaving on Monday.

And— she had found an envelope of photos behind the dresser. She was sure one of them was of Millicent.

I told Peggy I would see her the next day.

I was glad that Max, unlike a lot of Canadian men, did not join me in the kitchen while I finished getting dinner in between the phone calls.

He amused himself in the living room with a glass of wine, while Marion and I prepared the caesar salad. Peter hadn't been shopping except for coffee and milk, but I found half a red cabbage which I braised with apples, brown sugar and vinegar. I had rolls in the freezer and decided to make egg noodles with burnt butter sauce instead of potatoes. I finished defrosting the buffalo meat in the microwave and broiled it.

Peter came home promptly at five-thirty and kissed me, but I could feel his reserve. There was no time to talk anyway, because he had to be back at the store by seven. He left before dessert. In any case Max talked so much, going on about Alberta, the north which he hoped to visit one day, the food ("Superb! But absolutely superb! My nephew will never believe I have eaten buffalo meat!") and my book launch, which he would try to attend, or, failing that, one of the other events, that no one else had to make any effort at conversation.

Marion finished the sweater.

The phone remained obediently silent, and when Max left at nine-thirty, just as Peter was returning, there had not been another terrible phone call from Orillia.

Marion insisted on cleaning the dishes, giving Peter and me a chance to be alone. Peter was reading *The Spy Who Came in from the Cold* when I joined him in the living room. At least he had the book open— he re-reads LeCarré when he can't find anything else to read.

"I really meant what I said," I told Peter. "I'm dropping Millicent's story for now."

"I've heard that before." He kept the book open but he didn't look at it.

"But there's the book launch and then I'm doing a signing at the Kitchener market and giving a talk at that Seagram Museum place. There'll be interviews too. I just won't have the time."

"No time to visit this Georgina Brown when we drive Mom home on Sunday?"

"That's right. I promise. I'm seeing Peggy tomorrow but just to say good-bye. We can finish our Christmas shopping at Fairview Mall on the way. I know your mother still wants to pick a few things up. But that's it."

I didn't tell him about Peggy finding the pictures.

"I don't know whether to believe you or not." He put the book face down on his knee. "I can't believe you won't want to stop and see Georgina Brown on the way back. Doesn't it worry you that Charlie's gone missing?"

"He probably left his wife. She's quite a handful."

"Suddenly he's Sir Galahad?"

"I just mean they fight a lot. She showed me a hole he punched in the wall. She said Charlie came back and trashed the place. Everything was pulled out of the cupboards. She says Charlie did it."

"And you believe that?"

"No one's trashed our place."

"Yet. That'll be next. Just like the store. It gets worse and worse."

I told him about Dr. Forward. He didn't seem too interested.

"I just wish you'd sound a little tiny bit glad that I'm dropping this thing for now."

"What I wish is that you'd never gotten involved with it in the first place. Nothing's been the same since we went to Starleigh that night," Peter said.

Peggy looked tired and George McDrew's apartment was stripped. Pictures, ornaments and kitchen odds-and-ends were boxed, ready for the Sally Ann on Monday. She'd shipped the books and the dishes to the States. The photos, personal papers, and the cigarette case would go with her, on the plane.

"And there is nothing else," she said. "I went through all the magazines, all the books. I even thought of taking the mattress apart, but I can't see any cuts in it. There's no place he could have hidden anything. I checked the sofa too. I know he only bought it a few years ago because some of the neighbours remember seeing it delivered. A couple of them have actually asked me if they could take it off my hands. But everything's going to the Sally Ann."

But who had asked for the furniture? Peggy wouldn't know the people in the building. It seemed reasonable that one of *them*— the English half-brother, perhaps— could have posed as a resident in the building, I thought, but didn't ask.

Peggy read my mind.

"I checked the names. They're all listed on the mailboxes. People in the building wanted the car too, but I sold it. I could have driven it back to New York, but there'd be customs to worry about."

She took an envelope out of her shoulder bag on the floor and passed it to me.

I recognized Millicent's house in Starleigh. The garden was in bloom, roses cascaded over the trellis, marigolds grew in urns, and a large azalea bush bloomed beside the front path.

The young woman sitting on the steps had zinnias and daisies in her hands. She must have just cut them because they were held every which way, tumbling over her cotton skirt. Her long hair was swept carelessly back, as if she'd been working in the garden, but this style gave her a carefree, laissez-faire look. Her face was raised, as if she had been caught day-dreaming.

I knew those firm features, the line of that jaw and chin and brow, the direct, intelligent look around the eyes. She was handsome rather than pretty when she was older, but in this picture she was almost beautiful.

"That's Millicent," I said. "That's where she lived, her house in Starleigh. The garden's so pretty. It was getting rundown when I met her." I turned the snap over. There was no date or name on the back. "This must have been taken just about the time she went to Halifax, judging by the long skirt. She would have been in her late twenties, but she looks younger."

"I thought that was Millicent," Peggy said. "Why did she go to Halifax?"

"That's where she met Edward. Your uncle told me she went on a holiday to Nova Scotia because it was the nearest to Scotland she could get at the time. She went for a walk at night and Edward escaped his watchers. They met in a park."

I passed the photo to Marion.

"You told me so much," Peggy said. "Seeing the picture makes it all more real. I'm glad it's Millicent. She was much older when I met her. Look at the one of Uncle George and his car."

I would have recognized George McDrew anywhere. His face was almost boyish and a lock of blonde hair fell over his forehead, but the rest of his hair was so short that his ears seemed to stick out. The car, like the one Peggy had sold, was shiny and clean. George leaned an elbow on the rolled-down window.

The picture of Peggy showed a winsome and serious girl. She was sitting in a wicker chair in a garden— her aunt's in Cambridge?— and she looked tended, well-cared for, but too serious in her white ruffled dress.

Marion was still looking at Millicent's picture.

"She looks familiar. I'm not sure, but I wonder if I haven't seen her face in a book somewhere? I wish you had another copy," she told Peggy.

Peggy said she'd have a copy made and send it to us.

"I've got a friend who's a photographer. He'll do it while I wait. I'd hate to lose it since she was so important to George. Photo labs are always losing things."

"Of course," Marion said. "But she does look so familiar. You'd think there would have been more photos of her."

I thought of the bag George had been carrying the day he died. Had the envelope Peggy found slipped out of a larger one and fallen behind the dresser?

"And no thoughts have come to you here?" I asked her. "Being here in your uncle's apartment? You were saying there was something you just couldn't remember."

Peggy shook her head.

"I wish," she said. "I wish I could remember but I can't. If it comes to me I'll let you know."

She returned the photos to the envelope and put it back in her purse.

"Nothing. No happenings, no strange phone calls, no whispers in the night. Other than the people I expected to see— the lawyer and so on— the only people who've shown any curiosity have been from the building. I did see the detective, but that was only by accident in a restaurant. Actually, he recommended the car dealer, his brother-in-law as a matter of fact. But that was only because I asked him. McGuiggan Motors."

We talked for a while about Wallis' minions, and we left soon after that. Peggy thanked us and promised to write and to send a copy of Millicent's photo, but I was left with a feeling of something being unsaid, unfinished, and as we drove away I wondered if I should have told her about Charlie's disappearance. I hadn't wanted to worry her... but what if *they* thought she had found something in the apartment or knew something?

And what was it? What was I missing? When we said goodbye, I almost said to her, "You know, there's something I can't put my finger on. I want you to put your thinking cap on and see if you can come up with it," but her tired and sad face stopped me. There was a look of impatience, of wanting to be gone.

McGuiggan Motors was on our way out of Cambridge, along that awful strip of pizza take-outs, plazas and car dealers that you find in any city.

On impulse I stopped in and asked about George McDrew's car, saying I'd heard they'd taken it in and that I was interested in buying it.

The car had been snapped up as soon as the paperwork was done. "I could have sold ten cars like that," the bemused salesman said. "Everyone's been after it. You'd think I had the Queen's Rolls Royce here or something."

Peter and I drove Marion to Meredith the next day. It was dull and overcast and there was little traffic after we passed Toronto. Even Marion's house was dreary, musty. Hugh had the heat turned down and there was a big basket of unfolded laundry on the kitchen table. The African violets had been watered to death, but a croton was bone dry and near death. Hugh was testy.

While Marion bustled around getting lunch, I called Georgina Brown in Huntsville. She turned out to be the wife of the minister in Shaw River. She sounded disappointed when I said I wouldn't be able to see her until after Christmas.

CHAPTER
TWENTY-TWO

On Monday I baked the light fruit cake Peter likes, and Lebkuchen and Pfeffernusse, Pennsylvania Dutch recipes out of my first cookbook. Along with shortbread, rum balls, sugar cookies, and chocolate macaroons, I've made them for years. The annual Christmas bake-off, Santa's workshop in my very own kitchen.

Cass has been a recipient of my Christmas cookies. Marion and Allison get a batch. One year I even gave some to Molly and Jake. Jake said, "Alice B. Toklas' recipes I hope."

There was no mail. The telephone didn't ring.

Tuesday morning, I woke up at six after another dream— *what was it?*— and had a batch of Scotch shortbread in the oven by the time Peter sat down for breakfast. He'd been much happier since I'd bypassed the chance to interview Georgina Brown, as if he finally realized that I really meant to drop my involvement in Millicent's story until after Christmas. I know he hoped I'd drop it forever. He was talking about going south to one of the islands or to Mexico after Christmas. He was going to bring home some pamphlets from a travel agency, he said. Maybe if he hired someone to help Cass we could even get away for three weeks, he added.

"So the islands or Mexico?" he asked, as I took cookies out of the oven. "What do you think?"

I said Mexico but thought the Bahamas, where the Duke had lived.

I had another batch of cookies in the oven when the phone rang.

Sandy's mother. Charlie hadn't been found. We could expect a police bulletin on the news tonight, she told me. She had been advised by "higher-ups" not to talk to anyone, she said.

It was hard to get back to my cosy baking after that. I formed the rest of the shortbread dough into balls and flattened them with a fork.

The phone rang again. It was Owen.

"You're probably wondering why I haven't called. I did say I'd get back to you. I hope you weren't worried."

"Oh no. Not at all."

The sarcasm was lost on him. I knew the real purpose of his phone call was to prove to himself that All Was Not Lost.

"I've done some thinking on our friend from Willowdale," Owen said. "Doesn't it seem likely to you that she could have been investigating Millicent herself? That's why she gave me the wrong name, so I wouldn't catch on. I was down at the library just yesterday and it turns out there was a woman asking for that file they have on Millicent. Older woman, they said. Don't worry, I played it cool. Just mentioned that Millicent's story sure would make a good book and the librarian said someone else just said that not long ago and went over the file. You don't think someone could be getting the jump on you, do you? Like they say, you can't copyright an idea. The sooner you get going on this, the better. If two books come out on Millicent, it's not going to have the same effect.

"I thought I'd better warn you," he said when I didn't answer. "You hear from Charlie yet?"

"Charlie's still missing," I said. "His disappearance is supposed to be on the news tonight."

Owen said "they" would never allow it on the news. He thought Charlie was dead and that I should look out. I should buy bottled water, he said, in case they poisoned our water supply.

I let him blather on for a few minutes. He soon returned to the theme of his writing. He thanked me for my efforts on his behalf at Hendricks and said he'd acknowledge my help in the book of essays if they took it. He sent greetings to Marion. He reminded me to let him know about the writers' meeting I'd told him about.

As we spoke, I heard the familiar thud of mail being put through the front door slot and landing on the hall carpet.

I had a good excuse to cut him off: my cookies were burning. They were, too. Owen said "they" could have put arsenic in my flour.

Dr. Forward had written:

My dear Ms. Archer, (she was quite formal and the paper was thick, the handwriting in black ink).

It was a pleasure to meet you and also your mother-in-law, Mrs. Hall. Let us not forget, too, your young friend, Sandy.

I have recently had a visit from the police, who enquired about Charlie Trott's visit. I informed them that Charlie had visited me because he was interested in possibly writing a book about an early patient. I am glad to say the police did not express much interest in this book-writing business.

I must tell you that I am well-known locally and from time to time write small columns for the local newspaper on medical matters. Until last year I served on the school board. Therefore, I do not think the police were too surprised about someone visiting me for information. They did not say, but the impression I have after their visit is that they suspect Charlie met with foul play along the road, possibly with a hitchhiker.

I am indeed sorry I could not provide you with the exact information you wanted. After your visit, and considering Charlie's mysterious disappearance, I thought it better to place the file in my safety deposit box. I am confident my two four-legged protectors would keep away the most intrepid of intruders, but as they say, it's better to be safe than sorry. Do think about what I told you.

Also after your departure, I realized I had forgotten to tell you that Millicent called the Duke "Ted." She also called him "Daddy." At one time I did see a photograph of the two of them together. The photograph was taken in western Canada, to the best of my recollections. It was a casual photograph and there were others in the picture. This may be the same photo you saw.

I am going to write the Medical Ethics Board to see if I can dispense with the oath of confidentiality in this case. There! I have said it, and I assure you I will contact these people promptly.

I hope you were able to calm that troubled young woman.

It is difficult to express to you my pleasure in your interest in Millicent. Please do not give up your search. I cannot tell you how often I have thought of her over the years.

With fond regards,
Yours,
Frances Forward, M.D.

P.S. After your departure, I noticed you hadn't signed the cookbooks. If you are in this area, I would be pleased to meet again, and perhaps that time, we can take care of that little matter.

"Western Canada" was underlined.

Owen was wrong: the six o'clock news carried a short item on the regional news— just a thirty second blurb— that "salesman Charles Trott has been reported missing since last week. He is described as being 5'11" and weighs approximately 190 pounds. He is thirty-eight years old and has light brown hair and blue eyes. He was last seen in the Peterborough area. He drives a 1984 grey Cutlass. Anyone who has seen him or has any information about his whereabouts is asked to contact the nearest detachment of the Ontario Provincial Police."

They flashed a photo of a grinning Charlie receiving some kind of business award. It was the picture of a self-satisfied, over-fed man without a care in the world.

CHAPTER
TWENTY-THREE

There's a certain joy when an author holds a new book in her hands for the first time. I had been so involved with Millicent that thoughts of *Winter Ovens* had been more intrusive than anything else, and I hadn't experienced the keen anticipation I'd felt with the other books.

The thrill returned like a faithful friend when Purolator brought the box containing my ten free author's copies.

I liked what I saw: a cosy country kitchen, pots simmering on the wood stove, the table bedecked, a cat snoozing on a braided rug, and a young woman peering out of the window for the expected company.

Winter Ovens by Carolyn Archer.

"Bourgeois Art," Jake quipped when I called him. He was right, but if it was cutesy and kitschy, it was also warm and homey— safe— and I called Peter right away to tell him. He rushed right home with praise and congratulations and a bouquet of roses.

It was my day to receive gifts. The afternoon mail brought, finally, three replies to the ads: a dairy farmer in Georgetown had Millicent for a teacher in Grade VIII; a retired teacher from the same place taught with Millicent for a year; and a woman in Campbellville wrote that Millicent had boarded with her in-laws.

I phoned and made appointments for after Christmas. I didn't tell Peter about the replies.

Publication fever was in full swing: Jake had arranged a TV interview at our place, which meant I had to dash around and decorate for Christmas. We bought a spruce and I baked gingerbread men for decorations. I set up the nativity scene and hung wreaths on the shutters. In the middle of all this, a reporter from the Guelph newspaper telephoned for an interview. The TV interview was set for Thursday, Saturday I was to sign copies at The Bookworm, and I was going to do the same thing at a craft fair in Mississauga on Sunday.

By the time of the book launch at Hendricks, I had definitely put Millicent on the back burner. No one strange turned up to buy a book, and I knew— *I knew*— that no one would follow us when we drove to Mississauga.

Toronto meant a book signing at Coles in the Eaton Centre, two radio talk shows, and of course, the wine and cheese launch at Hendricks. Marion and Hugh had driven down, but Hugh was determined to make it back to Meredith the same night and Marion and I only had a few moments to chat in private. We had a whispered exchange about Dr. Forward's letter and then a hearty lawyer Jake had gone to school with swept me away.

There was a lull of two days between the launch and the talk at Seagram's Museum on Saturday. I used the time writing Christmas cards. Max phoned to apologize for missing the launch— he had been out of town— and to ask about the location of Saturday's talk. I wrote a short note to Peggy Lovely and said I would send her *Winter Ovens*.

Owen didn't phone. I didn't hear from the police, or from anyone else, about Charlie. I walked downtown, bought wool for a toque for Peter, and dropped into The Bookworm where my books were prominently displayed. I gave Cass an autographed copy. Peter and I went to the Bookshelf for coffee.

The thing about going to Seagram's in Waterloo was that I would have to drive there alone. There was no way Peter could take time off from the store on a Saturday in December.

I assured Peter I would be safe. I would only be gone a few hours and Max would be there. If any trouble came up, I'd ask him to follow me back to Guelph.

Peter was uneasy about my big solo trip.

"I never thought I'd say this, but I wish we had a car phone."

"Don't be silly. It's in the middle of the day. The place will be awash with merry Christmas shoppers. I'll be okay."

He insisted I place his old .22 in the back seat. "Just in case."

After signing books at the Kitchener Market without incident, I drove up King Street to the Seagram's Museum in Waterloo.

Usually book talks are held in an upper meeting room, but I guess the organizers expected *Winter Ovens* to draw more people than the usual poets and novelists did, and the talk was held in the large, cavernous main meeting room with whiskey barrels and distilling equipment forming the decor. The room was softened by Christmas trees with fairy lights, which caught the warm tones of the pyramid display of *Winter Ovens*. The air smelled of cinnamon and nutmeg from the restaurant.

It was early and people had time to look around the gift shop, but I went straight to the meeting room to get ready.

Owen Peterson was sitting in the front row, looking ridiculous in his bulky overcoat and a bright red scarf.

"Owen! What're you doing here?"

"Hendricks sent me an invitation," he said, and pushed his glasses up his nose.

Probably his name had been added to a mailing list automatically because of his "submission," I thought. Invite the rejects to local readings and they might be suckers enough to think if they attend and buy Hendricks books they'll have an in.

"I would have thought you wouldn't want to take a risk like this," I said, "considering the danger of poisoned water and so on."

The thought of Owen sitting right there, up in the front row, staring at me while I read and talked, wasn't pleasant.

I busied myself digging in my big carry-all for the notes for my talk, but just then several women came in. They had all brought old cookbooks to sign, and then who should enter but that jeweller Marion had met and his crippled wife.

I ignored Owen while I signed, but he made me nervous and my hand shook so visibly that an older woman said kindly, "There's no need to be nervous, dear. We're all your friends here, aren't we, girls?"

Old MacLeod saved the day.

"I see you have your husband with you."

"Oh no, my husband's not here."

"Oh. Then he's— " he pointed his head in Owen's direction— "isn't that the famous Peter Hall your books are dedicated to?"

He showed me the dedication in my second book. "To Peter Hall."

"No, that is definitely not Peter Hall!"

It broke my nervousness, and a few minutes later, when Max turned up and waved, my relaxation was complete.

Afterwards, there was coffee, tea, mulled cider and Christmas cookies. I sat beside a twinkling tree and autographed books. Sales were terrific. People milled around chatting and drinking. Max winked at me: he would wait until the others were through.

Owen, morose and looking hot in his overcoat, remained where he was. I had almost forgotten about him, but something nagged at me, something I wanted to ask him. Another book appeared before me. Finally Max was at the end of the line with three copies of my book and a cup of coffee for me.

"I thought you would not care for the sweet apple drink," he told me, "although the coffee is not very special in my opinion."

"But coffee all the same," I said. "My throat's so dry from talking."

"You were splendid, splendid. A virtuoso performance."

"Like an opera singer," I laughed.

Owen, unappetizing and seedy, appeared at my shoulder.

"I must talk to you," he interrupted brusquely.

"Later," I said, and looked meaningfully at Max.

"This can't wait," Owen said.

Max, like a courtier in a palace, took charge. He helped me gather my papers, and maneuvered me to the table of Christmas cookies. Owen returned to his seat.

"So you have your groupies," he said, "just like a rock star."

"You'd think my groupies would be little old ladies, wouldn't you?" I said.

"Does not one of your Canadian singers have a man following her? A farmer, I believe. I cannot think of the singer's name."

"Anne Murray," I said, and together we glanced back at Owen, sitting stolidly in his coat.

But Owen presented such an unlikely picture of a hopeless lover that Max dismissed him and told me about his recent trip to Quebec City. He would not be in Germany for Christmas, but he would be sending his sister and the wife of a colleague copies of *Winter Ovens*. Along with the splendid, wonderful sweater Marion had made, of course. I invited him for dinner over Christmas.

"I'd invite you for Christmas dinner but we're still not sure if we're going to Meredith or not."

"Ah, Meredith!" Max smiled. He was too polite to make it an insult, but his feelings were plain.

"I was thinking we could perhaps have lunch together today," he said. "If you are not too tired, that is. You are going back to Guelph?"

"Oh yes, home before dark. But I'd love a bite of lunch after this."

Owen was coming over. Max saw me looking.

"And lunch shall discourage this Romeo," he said, taking out his cigarettes. He extended the pack to me. They were German cigarettes, brought over by an associate in Kitchener. "Much superior to your Canadian brands, I must say. My throat likes them better."

I shook my head.

"Perhaps at lunch. My loyal fans would be shocked."

"At lunch, then. German cigarettes and excellent coffee. I know exactly the place. It is owned by a friend of mine..."

He lit up and drew the smoke in with pleasure. And expelled it in my direction.

"You will forgive me," he said, "but I am thinking you can use a little stimulation after your talk, vicarious though it might be."

And then I knew. Suddenly I had it.

I knew.

I kept my cool. I finished the coffee, and joined a group of women who were looking expectantly in my direction. One of them was from Maine and she wanted to know exactly where I had grown up (each book carries a small bio). MacLeod and wife were waiting also, to invite me for lunch at their place. I declined, saying I had another engagement later in Guelph, but MacLeod detained me with an interrogation about my progress in researching the teachers' book.

Max remained, smoking and drinking more coffee.

Owen hung around, glowering at me and not drinking coffee. I ignored him.

Finally, the last of my fans straggled out. I packed up the few remaining *Winter Ovens.*

"Just let me give Peter a call," I told Max. "I told him I'd be back by three and he'll worry if I'm late with the snowy roads and everything."

It was all I could think of. The phone rang and rang at The Bookworm until Peter, sounding harried, picked it up.

"I've figured it out," I told him. "I know who's behind everything."

But then Max was beside me, listening in a most uncavalier way.

"Okay then," I told Peter, "I'll tell Max that I can't have lunch. I'll be home right away. I'll see you in half an hour, forty-five minutes at the latest."

I hung up.

"Bad, bad luck," I told Max. "Someone from *The Globe and Mail* just happened to be visiting in Guelph and came to the store. You won't believe this, but Peter wangled an interview for me for this afternoon. I'd better get right back."

Max fell for it.

"Ah, bad luck for me not to have your company, but the most excellent luck for you, I must say."

"You do understand? It sounds so selfish and ambitious..."

"But my dear Carolyn! Of course I understand. We will postpone our lunch, that is all. I must be in Guelph next week. I shall call you, shall I?"

"Yes, of course. And I do want you to come for dinner over Christmas."

"It will be my pleasure. And next week— we shall go to the charming Bookshelf, perhaps? Or better yet— I shall pick you up on my way to Kitchener and take you to the restaurant of my friend, yes?"

"Yes," I said.

Max carried books to the Volvo for me and insisted on putting the carton in the back seat himself. I was afraid he'd move the blanket covering the gun on the floor, but he didn't even glance at it.

"Until next week," he said.

We shook hands. Regards to Peter. Greetings to Marion if you hear from her, and thank her again for the beautiful sweater of the moose.

He waved as I drove off. The Mercedes was parked nearby.

And then, Owen appeared, gesticulating wildly, but I drove away.

I didn't drive far, just down the street, where I pulled into the parking lot of a restaurant. Max would have to drive past there, I reasoned.

Unless he was making phone calls before leaving... Or, what if he went in the other direction?

I drove back to the Seagram's parking lot.

I could say that I had forgotten my scarf...

Max's Mercedes was still there.

I returned the Volvo to the street, pulling into the next side street where I would have a view of the lot, and waited.

It took fifteen minutes before Max drove by.

He was wearing dark glasses.

I had a feeling that he knew I was behind him, although I was careful to keep a distance between us. I followed him east along Erb Street, one of the main thoroughfares in Waterloo. There was enough Saturday traffic to serve as a shield, but then he turned onto the expressway. I kept Max's car just in sight. He was speeding, driving in an even more energetic, determined way than he had on the 401.

When he turned off at Victoria Street, I ended up right behind him, but soon he was several cars ahead in the late morning traffic. I never thought of stopping or turning around. I knew Max knew I was behind him, and any thoughts of stopping to call Peter evaporated. Soon Victoria Street turned into Highway 7 which led to Guelph. The thought occurred to me that Max would lead me to my own door to offer explanations— to tell the truth— but he kept going, turning north to Eden Mills.

He slowed down, as if he wanted to keep me with him. And now it was too late to call Peter.

I drove, keeping the tail end of the Mercedes just in sight.

I had a hunch where he was going: the hunting lodge near Meredith.

I was right. In Orangeville I stopped to get gas, but when I got on the road again I caught up with Max easily just before the turn-off to Highway 400. Any fear I felt was being replaced by exhilaration: now I would know. And if he was going to the hunting lodge, Meredith and Marion and Hugh would be close by...

Most of this trip remains a blur. Max gassed up outside of Huntsville, but soon he passed me on the open road. He was still wearing sunglasses and I thought of Millicent calling me a scaredy cat so long ago when the teenagers were loitering in the lobby of my apartment building.

And then— it was hours later, after four, but it didn't seem that long— I was following Max's car up the sleepy main street in Meredith. Hugh? Marion? We passed the Meredith Hotel, and beyond that the town library, where two woman came out, their arms filled with books. One had a child's toboggan, and at the Co-op a couple came out arguing. Past the liquor store, past the turn-off for Shaw River, past the Texaco, and we were in the country, turning off the pavement. I knew the road– Milton's Pass. I had been there with Peter once, visiting a school friend who had a cottage there.

But the place Max led me to was no cottage. Veering to the right, he turned down a side road– an old logging road which had obviously been widened, because the trees had been hacked away on both sides.

I followed the Mercedes through iron gates. Here the road was rougher and hilly and I had to put the Volvo into second. By the time I came to the lodge, the Mercedes was there, parked next to other foreign cars– one with New York plates– and a motor home from Florida. I didn't see Max.

The lodge was large, with a verandah running across the front. Firewood was piled to one side of the steps, and the curtains were pulled across the windows.

And then the double oak door opened and there stood Max.

I know he wasn't surprised, but his usual habit of camouflage asserted itself and he smiled. It was a practised smile, still hovering on the edge of civility.

I waited in the car with the ignition on and the driver's window open, my foot on the gas, ready to scoot away, while he came towards me. He was not carrying a gun.

"So. Carolyn. You did not drive home to Guelph as you had said you would."

"No, I followed you here. You knew I was behind you."

I could not read his eyes. The smile remained.

The front door of the house stood open.

"You even waited for me when I got gas in Orangeville."

I wanted him to know that someone might remember me, but he didn't react.

"Now you must come in and meet my friends," he said.

"I don't think so."

"I know why you are suspicious. It was the cigarette smoke, was it not? I should not have blown it so unthinkingly in your face."

"Yes, that's right. I recognized the smell of your cigarettes from the teacherage in Shaw River. It reminded me of American cigarettes. But it was German cigarettes. I recognized the smell today— I've smelled them before."

"The teacherage? Ah yes, the little log hut."

"You were there looking for something. You were at the lodge with Peter and Hugh when Hugh mentioned Millicent. It wouldn't have taken much to find out where she'd been."

"But you are wrong, my dear Carolyn. We knew before."

"From the library."

"From the library is correct, but we have many sources. And we know also that you stole the clipping."

"Then it was just a coincidence, Hugh mentioning Millicent and my new book."

"The book on teachers, yes. A fortunate coincidence. Your father-in-law is not very smart, or should I say he still does not know what you have been doing?"

"You bugged the condo, didn't you? You know everything we've done. But why? Why would you be interested in Millicent?"

"Yes, indeed. A provincial school teacher is not of interest to us. But it is cold out here. You must come inside and meet my friends."

"I don't think so," I said, but his strong hand reached into the car and gripped my wrist. Max took the keys from the ignition, and put them into his pocket.

When the hand came out of his pocket, it held a gun.

"And now I think you will meet my friends."

Six or seven German men sat on the two leather sofas placed before the large fieldstone fireplace. Deer and moose horns adorned the wall. A bearskin covered the space between the sofas.

A bottle of schnapps and several beer steins stood on a plywood coffee table.

Max took my coat before he introduced me.

"My good friend, the celebrated authoress, Carolyn Archer. The friend to Millicent."

There were murmurings in German. Someone laughed. There were two old faces there, but the others were middle-aged, except for one young man (who had gone to the Mennonite farm near the Kissing Bridge?). It was this young man who laughed, and one of the older men reproved him, and said to Max: "But we are all friends here. Please put the gun away, Max."

His German accent was hardly noticeable.

Max answered in German and sat beside me on the sofa. Max poured himself a schnapps.

"You must excuse Max," the older man said. "He is the most cautious of us all, you see. It is always a worry for him that we will be intercepted, but he does not know we have many good friends. I hope that you shall be our friend also."

My first reaction had been to not talk at all, but now all I could think of was to play along, to play for time. I wanted to get out of here alive. I knew, then, that they had killed Charlie. At least I had mentioned Max's name to Peter.

"I don't have anything against you," I said. "I just want to find out why Max has been following us."

"And why do you think Max has been following you?" the same man asked.

I explained about the smell of the German cigarettes.

The man said something to Max in German. Berating him for being so careless, perhaps. But then, to me: "You must forgive me. I forget you do not speak German. It is natural for us when we assemble, you see. I myself have been in Canada many years, but it is always a pleasure to speak the language of one's homeland. You must excuse our lapses."

"I don't know what you want from me."

"But you are mistaken. You want something from us. You have come to us, have you not?"

"I only wanted to know why Max— and some of you— have been trying to find out what we know. I don't know why you'd be interested in Millicent, even if she did marry the Duke of Windsor."

Faces changed when I said the Duke's name.

"Surely there is nothing strange about a fascination with history," the man said. "History is the most fascinating subject in the world. You in your own way are also a student of history, are you not? Perhaps it is the history of the garden and the kitchen, but it is history just the same. And now you have stumbled on much more fascinating history, I think."

"Millicent was my friend, that's all." The man— the leader, he had to be the leader— reminded me of Ewan MacLeod. Could Ewan be part of this group?

"But not a good enough friend to know all about her, or you would not now be investigating her life, I think? Am I correct? I think I am correct. So let us say she did not tell you everything. At the same time, you were her best friend at the end of her life, were you not?"

"I like to think so," I said, and thought of George McDrew, who had really been her best friend, even if Millicent hadn't realized it. And yet, and yet— what if she had distanced herself from him for his own protection? What if she had not told me everything for the same reason? I tried to think logically. She had met the Duke in Canada again, according to Dr. Forward...

"We too are interested in her story." The faces around the room were bland. "Perhaps, however, for different reasons. But it is all to the same purpose. We all want to know the truth. The truth is important. We discover the truth and then we tell the world."

"Tell the world, what?"

"The truth. Only the truth."

"The truth is that Millicent was married to the Duke, but you already know that."

"Yes, that is a fact. Tell me, are you married?"

"You know I am." I glanced at Max. His face remained impassive.

"And there are few secrets between husbands and wives."

"In most cases, yes."

"That is it, then."

"But I don't know what secrets Millicent shared with the Duke. Believe me, I would tell you if I knew."

"But you do know, my dear."

"Charlie told you I knew something, didn't he?"

Like the mention of the Duke's name, saying Charlie's brought a reaction. *He told you before you killed him. You tortured him.*

"But I don't know anything other than what you know from bugging Max's condo. I would tell you if I knew something. Why should I keep it a secret if it's the truth? And—" I turned to Max— "all you had to do was ask, instead of scaring us to death. We could have talked like civilized people."

Only, this group had to remain secret, I knew.

"The Duke was a great man!" the young man said. No one corrected him or told him to shut up. "His abdication had nothing to do with marrying Mrs. Simpson."

"He wanted peace between Germany and England," I said. I recalled Marion prattling on in the condo about the plan the Nazis were supposed to have had to put the Duke back on the British throne. They wanted to kidnap him to keep him from going to the Bahamas. I knew the Duke visited Hitler, but I hadn't paid much attention to this part of the Duke's life because it hadn't related to Millicent. It came after Edward was involved with Mrs. Simpson.

"It is natural. We all want peace and harmony in the world. The last world war only came about because of international intrigue."

He looked at me and did not continue. He didn't have to say the rest. It was that old line about Jews and Communists causing the war. I knew there had been something in the paper in 1984, and this year too, about neo-Nazis and their denial of the Holocaust. Did these people belong to the same group?

But— what did they want with anything I knew about Millicent?

"If you would only tell me what you are looking for! But you're talking in riddles. How can I help you if I don't know what you're looking for? You people broke in at our house and at my publisher's, didn't you? Can't you simply tell me what you're looking for? Wouldn't that be easier?"

No one answered. Finally the leader spoke to Max in German. There were no apologies for the shift to German this time.

Max turned to me.

"I would like a word in private with you, Carolyn. Let us go outside."

His hand went inside his pocket, but it was the younger man who took out a gun. He followed at a distance as Max led me outside. Suddenly the forest quiet was broken by loud dog barking coming from the direction of a smaller log house, set near the edge of the woods.

I tried for levity.

"This is a fine thing. I thought we were friends. What's going on? If this keeps up, I'm going to take back my invitation for dinner."

This fell flat. I felt Max's hand on my elbow.

"This way."

"No, not this way!" I shook his hand off. "What're you doing? Taking me to the dogs? How are you going to find out what I know if you kill me?"

"Do not be melodramatic." He sounded impatient.

"You killed Charlie, didn't you? Maybe not you, but someone connected to you. How could you turn on me this way?"

"You worry about your little life very much. But what is one life in the face of larger causes?"

"Bullshit," I said. I stopped walking. "Can't we just talk like two normal human beings? Tell me what it is you want and I'll give it to you if I have it."

I was trying to remain calm, but my voice was shrill. Max was unperturbed. He gripped my arm and began pulling me toward the little house. The barking grew more frantic.

"If you think you'll get me in there, you're crazy! I'll run for it. You'll have to shoot me down outside. That's how Charlie died, isn't it? Mauled by the dogs? You thought you'd frighten him into telling you what he knew, but he didn't know anything. He just had a big mouth and liked to brag. He thought he'd make a million bucks with Millicent's story, but he didn't know one single thing. Maybe he told you that I knew, but I don't have what you want, either. I don't know anything about it. Let go of my arm."

Max did.

"So what didn't Charlie know? What didn't he have? You are keeping something back, are you not?"

"Why should I tell you? You have to kill me anyway, now that I've found out about this group of– Nazis. That's what you are, isn't it?"

"It would be better if you told," Max said.

"But I don't know what you're looking for."

"You must know," Max said.

We faced each other. I'd like to think Max showed some regret, some shame, but he didn't. He was cold and disciplined.

"Give me a clue," I said.

"Millicent gave you something. We have received confirmation. Official confirmation. It has been documented."

"*What* has been documented? I bet this official documentation is something Charlie told you!"

He grabbed my arm again and pulled me roughly.

"You will tell me! Tell me what Millicent gave you!"

His rough treatment brought a shout of encouragement from the young fellow. I turned my head to where he stood, near my Volvo, and saw him drop to the ground.

Owen Peterson emerged from my car. He held a gun with a silencer on it.

CHAPTER
TWENTY-FOUR

Max grabbed me and I felt the cold, hard nuzzle of his gun against my neck.

"I'll kill her."

Max didn't yell. His voice was as cold as the gun against my skin.

"Drop your weapon," Max ordered Owen in the same cold voice.

"Fine with me," Owen said, and dropped the gun. "You have about five seconds to live. I've got you covered from the back. You don't think I'd come here alone, do you? Don't move."

He lifted my old quilted bag, which I'd left behind in the box that held the remaining copies of *Winter Ovens*. The bag I'd had in Toronto with me. The bag I'd never cleaned out.

"Shoot me and my man will get you in the back," Owen said. "You're not very smart. You only had to look in the purse. I just discovered what you've been looking for. You never thought she'd carry it around with her, did you? Only she didn't know what she had. I think I'm going to burn the evidence, as it were."

"Drop the bag!" Max ordered. His voice was excited now and I could feel his hand trembling. But the gun pressed harder against my throat. "I warn you! Do not try anything. I will shoot her. Your man can shoot me, but she will be dead, too."

There was a click against my neck as the hammer was cocked.

"I think you risk her life quite happily," Max said, "as I risk my life for a larger cause, but you will die as well. Don't forget that, old man."

"You're mistaken," Owen said, and through the panic and fear I recognized dimly that his voice was different: almost cocky, and definitely English. *Do you think a person can mask an accent?* I remembered asking Marion, but this memory fled. Peter! I screamed in my head.

Owen was taking something out of my purse.

The little address book Millicent had given me years ago. I hadn't used the address book in ages. Most of the addresses were outdated and some of the pages had fallen out.

"No!" I screamed, jumping forward, and Max grabbed my throat with his large hand. This time the barrel of the gun was at my forehead.

No, don't make a move! was what I meant.

Owen didn't pay any attention.

"I think I may give this to you if you want it that much. But first you must let the girl go."

"I will kill her first," Max said.

"You don't want it, then? Don't you want to live a little longer? You are not so brave after all. I only have to give a signal to the man behind me and you'll be dead. Let the girl go and you'll live. I'll even give you what you're willing to die for."

"No!"

Max screamed. I couldn't see the front door of the house from where we were, but I saw Owen looking that way.

Max followed Owen's eyes and the gun came away from my head, at the exact minute as Owen slit open the address book, lit it with his lighter, and threw it in the snow.

"A little strip of negative, and now it's gone," Owen said.

"You– !" Max raised his gun to Owen.

And dropped at my feet, a hole between his eyes and a surprised, horrible look on his face.

"Get in the car," Owen said to me quite calmly. "Don't mind Joe in the back. He's not going to bite."

Owen removed my car keys from Max's pocket.

A man, dressed entirely in white, huddled on the back seat of my car.

Owen backed the Volvo down the road, just as someone came to the door of the house. Shots rang after us, and a bullet zinged against the back window frame, but by that time we were on the road, heading for Milton's Pass.

The man in white– "Joe"– spoke into a microphone. It sounded like "down," but I was too panic-stricken to understand.

Too– astonished, surprised, shocked? There is no word for what I felt. And Owen...

More shots rang out and I knew one of their cars was behind us, but Owen gunned the motor and then we were past the gates and on Milton's Pass with the trees whizzing past.

Owen didn't slow down but rammed the car over the unpaved road until we came to a clearing near the highway where– a helicopter waited.

We were at a farmhouse somewhere on a back road east of Kitchener. Translate "safe house." We had landed at the Breslau airport, where a dusty black car awaited us. ("We'll look after your car," Owen said, as if I cared about that. The next day, the Volvo was parked in our driveway).

Joe had disappeared. One minute he was there, the next he wasn't.

"But how do I know they won't still be after me? After us?" I asked Owen.

"Because I burned the little address book. Let me get you some brandy."

Owen's speech was different. He looked different. Gone was that gawky stupidity, that beseeching, "woe is me" air I had found so irritating. He was still "Owen Peterson," but I was sure that wasn't his real name. Who was he? Who did he work for? The Duchess of Windsor? But it was hard to focus on these questions. I was still in a daze: almost killed, but rescued by *Owen Peterson* who wasn't Owen Peterson at all, but *working under cover*. It was all— fantastic, unreal.

"Drink this," Owen said. "We'll talk later."

"I have to call Peter."

"I'll look after that. Don't worry. It's over. You'll be all right now."

I took the glass and Owen went to sit on the other side of the fireplace. It was a well-kept, modernized farmhouse that looked as if the owners were away. I remember few details and although I've driven around the area since, I haven't been able to find the house.

I didn't drink the brandy.

"Who are you?" I asked.

"Owen Peterson," Owen said.

"You're an agent."

"If you like. Why don't you have a little sleep and I'll call Peter."

"I called him from the museum in Kitchener and told him Max was behind everything. He's probably out of his mind with worry."

"We'll get you home, don't worry." Owen smiled, but it was a take-charge smile. A man in control. The hopeful writer had been a cover. I took a cautious sip of the brandy.

"Do you work for the Duchess of Windsor?" I asked. "We thought the Duchess had hired someone to cover up her husband's earlier marriage."

"No, I don't, although the premise makes sense, I suppose, if you forget the Duchess' incredible egoism. Do you really think she felt her place in the sun threatened by a Miss Millicent Mulvey?"

"Who do you work for, then?"

Owen shook his head. Was I warm enough? The heating had been kept low, but he'd adjusted the thermostat.

"I think you owe me an explanation."

"Let's just say I've kept my eye on you. Watching the watched as it were."

Something occurred to me. "When I was signing books and a woman asked about Peter today, I knew something was wrong but I couldn't put my finger on it. Now I know. You'd seen my books and you knew I was married to Peter, because after the first one, all the books were dedicated to him. I should have caught on sooner."

"A mistake on my part. I'm glad you didn't catch on."

"What if I had?"

"I would have said I didn't notice the dedication, I suppose. If there'd been a real problem, my place would have been taken by someone else."

"Were you really called to a meeting at the Holiday Inn in Kitchener?"

"What do you think? Would I have broadcast a meeting far and wide if there really had been a meeting? I'm just surprised that only Peter turned up to relieve me of my briefcase. I mentioned it at the library, at the newspaper, and of course I told Charlie."

"Peter took a bus downtown and photocopied the valuable documents."

"I know that. Quite hilarious, really, but I wasn't expecting to see Peter there. I thought Charlie would tell someone else."

"Who?"

"There's no purpose in telling you that."

"One of his customers around here?"

"Instead he came to Guelph to tell us," I said when Owen didn't answer. "His wife didn't say that Charlie had missed a business appointment in Kitchener, too."

"The man he planned to see could have been out," Owen said.

"Out following Charlie," I said. "I imagine Charlie flaunted it far and wide that he was onto something big, something that would make him millions and get him out of the rat race. You work for the royal family, don't you?"

"I don't work for the Royals, but let's say there's a connection. I do wish you'd drink your brandy."

"You've put something in it. You want me to sleep. But you owe me more."

But did he? He'd saved my life.

"Why the journalist act?" I asked.

"It lets me poke around, ask questions, make a nuisance of myself. People see me coming and think, There's that jerk, Owen Peterson, who wants to see his name in print. I was just preposterous enough that no one took me seriously."

"And now you'll leave. Become someone else."

He shrugged.

"I still want to know who you work for."

"It's not in your interest to know, Carolyn."

"Then what did you burn? What did those— those Nazis— want that they would have killed for?"

"Think of Edward VIII. Read the histories. What record has never been recovered? Something dangerous for him to retain."

Owen wasn't smiling. He wanted me to figure it out. I had the sudden suspicion that even here we were being watched. Listened to. Maybe the room was bugged. Maybe Owen had orders not to tell me.

"You were the fictional half-brother in the hospital, weren't you? And you came to the bookstore asking Cass about Millicent."

"I've been everywhere," Owen said.

"Whose house is this? Can you tell me that?"

"It belongs to friends. They've gone away for the winter."

"Maybe it's your house, for another role."

"I wish it were. It's rather better than the grubby apartment, isn't it? I must admit the role of Owen Peterson has been tiresome at times."

"What about Charlie?"

"He's dead. I have no proof, but I'm certain he's dead. The police won't follow it up. The police won't contact you again."

"And George McDrew?"

"He was frightened to death."

"They took papers he had, pictures."

"Yes, but they didn't find anything. They weren't really interested in Millicent, only in what she had. And I found that. I think I should telephone your husband, don't you? Let him know why you're late getting home."

"But if the phone is bugged?"

"That little matter's been looked after."

"You'll be gone and safe, but we'll still be in danger."

"Oh, I don't think so. We'll take— precautions. And they know I've destroyed what they wanted to have."

"But I've seen their faces."

"Let me put it this way. With one exception, they won't be around tomorrow. They'll be too busy running for cover, I should think."

"They're from somewhere else," I said, and when Owen didn't answer, I took his silence as assent. I remembered the Florida license plate.

But this precise memory triggered another memory: Marion talking about the Duke of Windsor's wartime activities.

"The record of the talk between Hitler and the Duke of Windsor was never found! Everything else was there, but not that."

I thought Owen wasn't going to respond, but he did, after a moment's hesitation.

"That's part of it."

"And he gave it to Millicent for safekeeping. He knew he could absolutely trust her. She was the one person in the world he could trust. Did he give it to her on a trip to Canada? Dr. Forward— " I started to explain to Owen about Dr. Forward, but I could tell he knew all about her— "said Millicent met him in Canada in 1950 or '51, I think. He must have given it to her then. But he would have known she'd be in danger. Max said they'd had it confirmed. Edward must have told someone. My God, Edward was ready to sacrifice Millicent! He didn't care for her at all any more. Did the royal family know about this? If they did, they put her life in danger by having the inscription put on the stone!"

"Unless they didn't know," Owen said. "And why do you think the Duke *gave* her the record in 1951? Perhaps he wanted it back. Did you ever think of that? Why couldn't he have sent her something for safekeeping during the war? Who could he trust more than anyone else in the world? Her loyalty to him had been proven. Say that little item was later lost, or misplaced..."

I asked again who he worked for.

This was his answer:

"Let's say I'm with people who worry about the spread of fascism. The re-birth of Nazism."

He let that sink in, and then he added: "You'll never be able to write about this, you know. No one will believe you and— it could be dangerous."

I think it was a caution, not a threat. I want to think of it that way.

"You are here to monitor these people," I said.

"They're very dangerous," he said.

"And the people today were— the leaders? From all over?"

"If you like, but it's not good for you to know these things, Carolyn."

"You could have warned me."

"I did, many times."

"Yes, about poisoned drinking water!"

"Completely in character for Owen Peterson," Owen said.

"But if you had told me the truth!"

"But I didn't know what you had. If you had anything. I thought you did, but I wasn't sure."

"You broke into our house."

"Not so you'd notice."

"What about the mess in the store?"

"Leave that to the goons, the underlings. Not my underlings, by the way."

"You didn't know what I had until you looked in my purse."

"No. I thought it would be hidden— elsewhere. In a box of some sort, if you must know."

"Millicent never gave me a box. And if she'd known what was in the address book, she wouldn't have given me that. She wouldn't have put my life in danger!"

Owen didn't answer, but he went to call Peter.

I fell asleep and when I came to, a taxi was pulling up in front of our house in Guelph.

I never saw Owen again.

Some mysteries can never be completely solved. I am sure, for instance, that Millicent would never have given me the little book if she knew what it contained. She *could* have lost the book, found it years later, and given it to me. Perhaps the Duke had been angry that she'd lost it and giving it to me made that bad memory go away. At the same time she couldn't bring herself to destroy something *Ted* had given to her.

Dr. Forward said that Millicent had been reticent about the 1951 visit. It made sense to me that she had been unable to return what he asked for. Marion believes Millicent received the box and book in 1942, when the Duke received a telegram in the Bahamas signed, *All my love, Mary R.* Mary was one of Millicent's names, and R for— Renfrew: a name used by the Duke at times.

Marion thinks she has solved more of the mystery: the date, the early forties, is significant. It was after Rudolf Hess had flown to Scotland. There has been suspicion that the Duke was involved with Hess, and she thinks the record Owen destroyed was also about Hess and his supporters.

This makes sense. *That is part of it*, Owen said. The Duke (and the Duchess; I keep not mentioning her) visited Hitler in 1937. But many Englishmen were pro-Hitler then, and for appeasement. Would this conversation between the Duke and Hitler have been so shocking, so startling...?

And would people have killed for it? Risked their lives? There had to be more. It is my opinion these people wanted to reveal the truth about the Duke, and therefore rehabilitate Hitler, perhaps prepare the way for a new Hitler.

Fantastic, fantastic, fantastic. Almost unbelievable. The story behind the story. The real mystery. I will never know for sure.

I have even thought that there was really nothing in the address book, that Owen removed something else from Millicent's house before I got there.

Other mysteries: Charlie's death was never solved. His body wasn't found. Marion thinks Sandy was quietly compensated. But every once in a while, I wonder if someday I will turn on the television and see Charlie's mother requesting information about his disappearance on *Unsolved Mysteries*.

I am sorry Charlie had to die. He occasionally haunts my dreams. Sometimes Sandy is in the dreams too, blaming me or asking if I know where Charlie is. But I've heard nothing from Sandy and I have not contacted her.

True to Owen Peterson's word, we haven't been troubled with any more break-ins or tailings.

I never wrote the teachers' book which Jake said would be so boring, but I did, finally, after Christmas, and after cancelling the first appointments, visit the three people who had answered my ad. The dairy farmer and the retired school teacher said Millicent had been a good teacher, but strict. They spoke about her eccentricities— her love of the Scots and occasional put-downs of the English; her poetry-quoting; her sometimes finicky manners.

The woman in Campbellville was more forthcoming: Millicent had told her mother-in-law about the Duke back in the late thirties.

The mother-in-law was gratified when the inscription went on the stone.

I did, finally, reach Mrs. Greathurst. I had forgotten to ask Owen about her. She told me that she "wasn't sharing research," but then she cryptically went on to hint that Millicent was really not Millicent, but a Romanov princess! Mrs. Greathurst was a nutcase, who had simply been cagey with Owen.

Georgina Brown, the minister's widow, told me that Millicent was a typical old maid and she couldn't imagine her having had any kind of love life. Millicent had, however, spoken to her about visiting "the farm" belonging to friends in Alberta one summer.

I left the interviews at that. Months later I heard from someone else, but he had been taught by a different Miss Mulvey.

Peggy Lovely did not answer my Christmas card. I never tried to contact her again. It wasn't just hurt pride or disappointment, but I kept thinking of Owen— when he was still "Owen Peterson"— saying, *Think of the opposite of what I've put down.* If west is east, then cannot "son" be "daughter"? Did Peggy find something, or remember something, to suggest or confirm this? It seems better, for her own safety, not to pursue this, but I think of her often and I wonder if the reason George McDrew's sister was unkind to the little girl was because Peggy wasn't a relative at all.

After Peter's relief that I was unhurt, I expected us to recover our happiness, but it took a while. In February, we went to Mexico, where Peter had his wallet stolen. This incident revived the tension between us. That summer, I went alone to Maine for a month, and wrote Peter a letter suggesting a trial separation. I never mailed the letter, and when he arrived without warning on a foggy day in August, I knew we still had a future.

Two years later, I published another cookbook, *Keeping the Harvest*, about home canning. In 1988, I wrote a book about farm wives, and the beginning of the nineties saw the publication of my first mystery, *Trouble in the Kitchen*.

When Hugh first learned the truth about Millicent and the goings-on at the lodge, he was more upset by the fact that, as Police Chief, he hadn't been advised of local danger, than by Marion's secrecy. He wrote a letter to the British Embassy. Whatever reply he received stilled his grumblings.

Hugh retired two years ago. After a trip to England to visit relatives, Marion and Hugh opened a bed and breakfast. Their relationship was strained for a while. Marion spent a month in Guelph, but she never seriously thought about divorce or separation.

The Duchess of Windsor died in 1986.

So I'm left with Millicent. I know she married the Duke and that she loved him all her life.

As to whether the Duke continued caring about her— who knows? Who can prove if one person loves another? When the snow melted, I visited Dr. Forward again to autograph my books for her, and she said, "But the important thing is that she loved him, isn't it? Isn't it better to love and have feelings even if the love isn't returned?"

She did not receive legal permission to open her files.

I believe the Royals paid for the inscription on the stone and I don't think they knew Millicent had the secret document. I like to think that, anyway, and why not? The Duke had ceased confiding in his family because they did not like his beloved Duchess.

Here is what the reply from the royal archives at Windsor said in response to my letter asking not if Millicent's claim were true, but only if they had information: "Our files do not have any information about Miss Millicent Mulvey, *but it is of course impossible to disprove this story.*"

They didn't have to add that "but"; it is almost as if they wanted someone to look into the claim and tell the story of the royal Prince and a Canadian school teacher.

And memoirs by Sir Alan Lascelles, one of the Duke's aides, mentioned meeting a *Miss Mulvey* in Canada in the twenties.

A love story is how I think of Millicent's story now, although I often wonder if Owen Peterson (Where is he now? Who is he pretending to be? Did he work for the British, for the Israelis?) really destroyed the secret document.

A love story, yes.

Love can be a complicated and dangerous business.

AFTERWORD

Good fiction suspends belief. While I hope this novel has achieved this aim, the curious reader will ask, "Could this story have happened?"

All the characters in this book, including the invented Millicent, are fictional. However, any student of history who is interested in Edward VIII will recognize historical facts and dates.

There is a tombstone in a Cambridge cemetery with an inscription by a woman claiming she was married to Edward VIII, Duke of Windsor. A local resident went on record saying he had seen a marriage certificate and photographs. A reporter wrote to the Duke of Windsor in 1971 regarding the inscription. There was no reply.